SHORT STORY ANTHOLOGY
VOLUME TWO:

What I'd Say To
EINSTEIN
If I Met Him
ON THE DANCE FLOOR

Frank Talaber

Photo By SueB Photography

Digital ISBNs
EPUB: 978-1-7775269-8-6

Print ISBN: 978-1-7775269-9-3
Amazon Print ISBN

Copyright 2021 by Frank Talaber
Cover art by: Miblart

Frank Talaber, Writer by Soul.

A natural storyteller, whose compelling thoughts are freed from the depths of the heart and the subconscious before being poured onto the page.

Literature written beyond the realms of genre he is known to grab readers; kicking, screaming, laughing or crying and drag them into his novels.

Or as he has often said: Write like your soul is on fire and the pencil is your voice screaming.

You don't have to be mad to be a writer, but it sure helps.

Canada's Foremost Off-Beat Author

Enter the literary worlds of Frank Talaber

OTHER NOVELS

Urban Fantasy Genre

Stillwater Runs Deep Series

Book One:	Raven's Lament
Book Two:	The Lure
Book Three:	The Awakening

Urban Fantasy/Crime/Mystery/Paranormal

The Ainsworth Chronicles

Book One:	The Joining
Book Two:	The Mystery of Ms. Teak

Short Story Anthology Series

Volume One:	What I'd Say To Buddha If I Met Him In The Pub
Volume Two:	What I'd Say To Einstein If I Met Him On The Dance Floor
Volume Three:	What I'd Say To Agatha Christie If I Met Her Around A Campfire *(soon to be released)*

Spiritual/ Science Fiction Genre

Seeds Of Ascension

Book One:	Spirits Awakening
Book Two:	(tentatively titled) I'll Bet Skywalker Never Had Days Like This!

Table of Contents

NOVEL TEASERS

Foreword

For those of you who are new to my books, welcome! What kept you? No, seriously, thank you for buying, or obtaining somehow, my latest muse. I hope you enjoy meeting these characters and stories as much as I did writing them. Some are old friends of mine you've met before, but some are brand new. But for now, let's get this new party started, shall we?

"So how do you know you're an author?" The question has been asked of me many times.

"In my soul," is always my answer.

But no one has yet asked "When did you know you were an author?"

To answer the question that no one has yet asked I would say "I guess in Grade Three". The project that day was to write about a recent field trip. I won't go into detail but my memoires had everyone in stitches laughing; a couple of my classmates said later that they'd never laughed so hard.

Somewhere inside of me that little muse grinned from ear-to-ear and very quietly began to poke away at my sanity. Muses do that, you know. That, and make you remember important things, like never run from a hungry grizzly. Well except when he's on TV, then you can run, poke your tongue out at him and tell him funny jokes. Although bears never get funny jokes, I've discovered. In fact the only thing they really understand is "Hey there's a few rotting salmon in the next stream. Way better on your preference ladder for a snack than my scrawny body."

Later, in High School, is when my muse woke up. She hasn't shut up ever since. The first day of a creative writing course our assignment was to write half-an-hour non-stop on anything and everything. Staring at the blank, lined, pages I could only ask "I have to write for half-an-hour non-stop? About what????"

The teacher replied, "About anything and everything."

So used to being told what to do in school in those days, the idea that I could just do something on my own and be let loose, seemed beyond bizarre.

"I'll give you a zero if you don't fill the page," was his response.

Incentive, then. The muse wrung her hands in mirthful glee.

I simply stared in bewilderment at the blank page and wondered what kind of easy five-credit course did I think I had signed up for in a moment of insanity?

My hand shook as I held the pencil to the paper and very thoughtfully put down, 'the walls are beige; the girl in front of me is a blonde; I wonder how old the gum stuck under my desk is; and I am so frigging bored. (I thought if I can put anything down, then the odd cuss word should be acceptable).

But at some point, after about a week, the muse lost patience and snapped. She (I know it's a woman), whacked me upside the head and took over, controlling bitch. The flow began, just as the teacher had said it would. By the end of the day I'd filled four to six pages, my pencil a blur trying to keep up with the whirling dervish inside my subconscious. She hasn't shut up since, and I don't intend to have her stop either. You'll probably find me on my deathbed, pencil in hand, a hundred and three years old, and there will be a long jagged line scribbling down the page, stating...

...To Be Continued. Because some stories never end.

A Witch
After My Own Heart

Mist crosses the far side of the valley like a lover that caresses, ever so slowly and deliciously, the aroused flesh of its mate with long sensuous fingers that probe down between the naked tree trunks.

The soulful cry of a loon, floats over the still waters. So hauntingly familiar like the voice of a long-lost brother. Is it waiting for the same as me as I wait on the shore?

The leisurely flow of approaching mist over the waters reminds of a woman sensuously crossing her legs, soft flesh gliding on soft flesh.

I'm crazy to be here on the shore, waiting, while back at the campsite my friends sleep safe and sound.

I wait here in the chill of the dark.

The moon forges a cleft in the mountains and hangs there like a distant voyeur in the cloudless sky. If it had lips would it lick them in nervous excitement like me? Does it also wait for her?

My teeth chatter in the late autumn chill. Leaves, discarded like old clothes, litter the ground in a tapestry of colors. Fear clings to my brow like tree sap, will she really show up like she did for my father?

I will always remember his dying words as he spoke of the rapture and passion only the love of a witch could possess.

Will she come? One part of me trembles and prays not. But the other part grins an insidious leer and prays to all the unholy gods to bring her here tonight.

I laughed then, I laugh no more.

Fog shrouds the far side of the lake and with methodical movement begins to arrest everything behind its cloak as it sweeps towards me.

The lone loon begins another haunting cry. Mist swirls forward and wraps itself around the graceful bird. Enveloped in vapors its song cut short.

CRACK!

A splash draws my attention.

The lifeless body of the loon floats before the fog.

She is here.

I shiver in fear and turn to run. I fear I've made a grave mistake in coming and hope it's not too late to leave. From behind me her voice whispers my name like the heavens shining through a cathedral's stained glass windows. In those mewling murmurs that speak of all the hushed desires a woman can have for a man.

I shake in mortal anticipation recalling the stories my father told me as he lay dying, of Ximena, the beautiful witch that seduced men with her body and mystical call. A native siren that only called to those who could answer. How she took from her lovers every ounce of passion, of intensity and if she disapproved, of life. He told me of the indescribable pleasures that I couldn't even begin to comprehend. I knew my father as a man of great passions. He said that Ximena could unlock the doors to your soul. It did to his.

Instead of running I hesitate, wanting those pleasures that had driven him mad with desire. I want to understand. Why did he come here and why did he return to allow her to drive him to the brink of madness? But most of all I wanted to make love to this creature of carnal lusts. To be enslaved to the same passions as he had endured. Heaven help me, or the more appropriate word is Hell, I wanted Ximena, the witch.

Mist advances to a foot from the shore. And stops.

My breath comes in wispy gasps as she slides aside the veil of fog as a lover sheds clothes and stands before me.

I gasp, she is utterly beautiful. My desire surges as a feel the familiar throb from my loins.

Raven hair hangs loosely about her face covering the luscious curve of her breasts. She wears a skirt of translucent material that resembles stars in the night, twinkling. As she saunters towards me the gown shimmers with the radiance of aurora borealis.

She lifts one hand to her mouth and watching my reaction, I watch each finger slowly, oh so slowly, enter that sensuous red mouth as her tongue ever so quietly licks and probes at every fold of her fingers licking the blood and feathers of the loon from her fingers. God, help me, I want that tongue to be licking at me.

I am extremely aroused. With a wave of her hand, my clothes fall away like silk sheets slipping from the bed. My hardness juts out. She smiles.

She stands before me now, her breath like rose petals in the morning, tickles my nose. With one hand she reaches behind her back and lets fall the shimmering cloak covering her body.

It melts away into the reflections of the still waters. Large brown nipples stand erect jutting amongst her dark tresses of her hair. Her hand caresses the surface of my chest and stops at my own aroused nipples. A tweak from razor sharp nails draws the smallest bead of blood. I twinge in pain, she smiles again.

Down my trembling abdomen her hand trails and everywhere her nails rake, a thin trail of fresh blood is released. I gasp only when her hand, unabashedly, reaches between my legs and caresses me.

She cackles a cackle I sense older that the arrival of whites to these shores. For a brief second I shake my head trying to release myself from the spell she is casting.

I shouldn't be with her. How old is she? Unknown, for even in the First Nations legends she was ancient and beautiful for the fortunate few that lived to tell.

Her hand on my shoulder forces me to my knees. "Smell my desire," she commands with sensual, deep husky authority. I breathe in the heady musky fragrance of her body. It is too late, I am lost. I run my hands up the outside of her soft legs. I want to taste her. I feel every hair as it raises in shivered delight under my fingers. A moan escapes her mouth as she bends over and rakes her nails down my back. So lost in her charms I don't feel the kiss of the night on my newly exposed flesh and cuts. With both hands she forces my face into her and shudders.

Blood pools at my feet, I lick her.

The spell begins.

A dizzying lightness overcomes me. I look around. Gone is that triangle of pleasure I had swam in. Feathers spring free from every cut made. My arms grow in strength and litheness. Feathers sprout. A stray breeze sings to each feather, calling to their purpose.

Feathers adorn me, my lips elongate to form a beak and my feet now talons meant to rip and tear. I have been transformed, for the most part into some sort of eagle.

A savage cry rigs the air as Ximena flies upward, she the same as myself. I test the vigor of my own wings and let out a shriek of passion. She will be mine.

As twin birds of prey we circle, on the hunt and our prey is each other. A vicious dance of passion ensues. Who desires whom the most?

Razor edged talons reach out in tender caresses. Beaks meant for the rending of flesh cross in a tender kiss. We swoop upward in ever tighter circles, higher and higher. Our cries shriek the night air.

Seeing an opening I lunge forward and grab her. We plummet to the earth. My talons encircle her waist and pull her against me. The softness of her breasts crush against my chest, insighting my arousal. I want, no need this to be quick. Locked in our tight embrace we begin to plunge to the ground, the air whistling by as our loins begin a rhythmic slap. Our hungers racing to beat the arrival of the ground rushing up from below.

Wind sucks out every breath I take. She cries out her pleasure as we explode in orchestrated delight. I open my eyes and only see the earth welcoming us into its solid embrace.

Darkness reigns.

My body is gliding through water swimming lazily enjoying the delightful feel of the rivers current as the soothing gurgle of water enters my gills. Content I merely relax and swim knowing from my father that Ximena is far from being satisfied.

Above me the iridescent glitter of scales reflects. It is her. The waters coolness can't contain the burning hunger inside. I want her again. With a flick of my fins I reach her. She is still enjoying the leisurely currents. Slowly swept along, our fins rasp against each other. Shivers through my body, and while she is being very submissive I seize the moment and wrap my body around hers, instinctively knowing how fish mate.

She reacts, begins to do the same to me. Surprised by her speed and strength I realize she is only toying with me. Faster and faster we spin through the water. I try to keep up to her maddening pace. Shredded scales flash and sparkle bedazzling the senses. My fish-like appendage melts away allowing my maleness to enter her. We fight on, twisting like great white sharks in heat. I catch the wide-eyed look in her eyes, I've aroused her, she is very hungry for me. I explode as does she, a shower of her eggs and my sperm litter the water. Succumbing to my exertions, I merely watch the eggs and sperm settling onto the sandy bottom of the lake as my eyes close. She is gone.

I wake. Cold earth welcomes the pad of my four feet. The moon overhead is silent, yet as the wind bristles the thick fur on my back

I am overcome by the desire to serenade my love to it. A single, long desolate howl escapes my jowls. Cold mist escapes my nostrils and I begin a cacophony of howls, until my breath is spent.

In the distance I hear another calling. My sharp ears grasp the direction and off I speed. As I run, the wind combs through my fur and only the thudding of my paws answers the gasps from my throat. My tongue lolls out in hunger and impatience. I know the cries are for me, on I run.

There on a rocky outcrop she squats, heavy breasts heaving, head back, ears erect and throat open, her breath splays upwards as she sings her desire to the moon.

I stop and reply. She faces my direction, the harsh redness in her eyes catches a voracious hunger inside. While my own desires have already begun to be satiated, hers have only begun to be awoken. I know I can't back down now, it would mean my death. I must prove myself to the appetite of this witch in order to keep my life. My nostrils sniff the musk of her arousal. She is very excited and leaps from the rock disappearing into the underbrush.

I yelp in panic and distress, unable to find her. Ximena bursts from the brush and we collapse in a fury of snarls, fighting for dominance, snapping at each other. This time I surrender to her as with mouths, not of our own, we bite at each other locked in a macabre sixty-nine position.

Our snarls of rage and dominance begin to change pitch, becoming howls of pleasure and submission to our passions. Her spit dribbles from her face soaking into my fur as I explode and all goes black once again.

On and on the madness continues through the night in a symphony of pleasure and tortured desire. How many times tonight? I've lost count until swollen and sore I lie panting on the beach.

Ximena stands naked above me and reaches for my tortured member. Her tongue licks her lips and wants more. I wince in pain unable to find the strength to respond. I know I must and yet can't get hard anymore. She glares down and smiles knowing she's exhausted every iota of desire within me. She throws her head back and cackles in an ancient voice. Have I satisfied her enough to live?

Bending over me she cuts the flesh over my forehead and pulls from her lips a feather from the loon killed at the beginning of this evening. I watch the sway of her breasts, ever the temptress, unable to respond, yet wanting to nibble on those engorged nipples some more.

She smiles knowing I still want her and places the feather along the seeping fresh blood oozing down my face. Ever the witch, she cackles once again revealing teeth crooked beyond belief and I shiver spent beyond reason.

Radiant and aroused, maybe she'll look for another lover tonight. I struggle to get up, and heaven help me, I still want her. "I know," she whispers into my ear. That is the answer that saves my life as she rises and shakes her dark tresses.

The shimmering robe rises from the waters and covers her body again. Have I satisfied her? Not even a 'thank you' escapes her lips as she walks back into the envelope of mists. I live and perhaps that is knowledge enough.

The night's final spell begins as my body transforms into the black and mottled line of the loon killed earlier. I know come morning the others will find me naked and bleeding on the shore. What will I tell them? I don't really care. For now I'll glide these waters singing my mournful cry, knowing there will be a next year.

Full Moon Madness

Drumbeats, hearts melting. Your memory haunts the corridors of my sequestered dreams, where silhouettes of mountains fill the horizon and tinkles of orchestrated mewlings shatter the chill of a full moon night in northern British Columbia. A land I swore I'd never caress again, especially on All Hallows Eve, the only night these mystical doorways can be traversed. A dimension where nothing is real and everything revolves around dreamtime perception. The realm of the witch called Ximena.

I shiver in anticipation and fall to your arms as I have fallen in eternity. Stars skim by with dizzying velocity as cackles of entrapment seduce me and pull me in. You are there, everywhere and nowhere. Your voice, a breath like spirit things that steals across abandoned graveyards at the stroke of midnight, races along the ends of my hairs. Clouds pulse with vibrancy, and even the dirt stirs beneath each tentative step I take, unsettling me with the undulation of something sentient as I walk. Where does it begin? Where does it end and where are you?

A kiss from sanities edges rests suddenly, on my lips. I wait. A thrumming like chants of Arcadian monks breaks the silence. Razor-edged talons sing across my back, stealing at my soul. Sweat pierces my skin and your finger, born of unearthly matter, appears to whisk blood and perspiration away to your lips. I fall to my knees, the breath of my eagerness mingling with the night air as skitters like ten thousand crabs on echoing porcelain are tugging at the void. Where are you? I question the foggy veils.

Your face parts the clouds with the same ease as the moon that slides behind them. Dawn's light will banish me from this place and return me to my reality, but only if — I pause in whispered prayer — if I live through this night. The twisted reality of loving a witch.

Melodic laughter, I look up, you are sauntering across the glade wrapped only in layers of diaphanous silk, full breasts swaying with each step, awaiting the taste of my lips. Air incensed with the cloying enticements of sandalwood swirls at your approach and I remind myself that this was my idea to open the doorway back into this region of sybaritic pleasures. A domain so arcane and bizarre, I can only weep in sorrow at your plight and feed you even more, an environment where the hiss of a breath bears more actuality than sun-sustained vitality, where my fear fuels your sustenance and my sweat feeds your soul's growth in ways I'll not comprehend. Nor care to, when the taste of your lips is sweeter than honey drizzled down my throat from ten thousand bees fed the purest of nectar and just as intoxicating.

You stand before me now, naked, wonderfully naked beneath the silk, a smile spreads across your face and draws me in with the entrapment of a spider's web. Will my plan succeed?

"You return." Disembodied whispers lick at me with the severity of an icicle thrust against my neck as light races from your eyes into enveloping pools of darkness sucking me in. Seduction unparalleled. I'd forgotten the exquisite carnality you wreck as the sheer lust of my response becomes a throbbing, aching hunger, to have you, to be possessed by you.

"Help," I cry to the fraying threads of rationality binding my barely clinging sanity. Sanity's stolid gaze answers back. *This is what you truly crave. This will be your reward.* Reassuring arms vanish, threads snap and instead of anchoring me from this lunacy, my sub consciousness kicks me from the cliffs of reason. I scream in the delirium and fling myself instead into the depths of your passions.

It began as my father lay on his deathbed. He told me of the unbearable ecstasy of loving you, and died making me swear I'd never visit you. I agreed, but I think he feared otherwise.

Rapturous insanity begins as appendages melt away and rough scales begin to cover my body. Warm rocks scrape beneath me and my tongue slithers between unhinged jaws. Tasting the air, sensing for you. A rattler's warning disturbs the hush and you uncoil from the darkness. I slide towards you, rattles buzzing in excitement as you lunge and wrap around me. We twist, tumbling between the rocks, reveling in the flexibility as scales scrape where hands once used to. Touching, fondling, arousing, each seeking to twine about the other, lost in the power of long muscles coiling and uncoiling in a macabre hypnotic waltz.

Who are you? This past year I've studied my father's papers trying to decipher or understand your existence, and more importantly, how to stop you. Dad was a professor of anthropology and native studies at UBC, how he discovered you I'll never know, but he paid a heavy price for loving a witch. I know you'll return every year to bleed away at my life essence like you did his. Last year's encounter left me in hospital for months, hovering between life and derangement. I have other designs on my fate this time and press a shaman's soul catcher underneath my tongue, praying it will work.

I grasp you tight and squeeze. Your skin splits and feathers sprout, wings burst free, a phoenix reborn. Your new body shakes free from the snake's shell and flies away, cackling that age-old cackle that creaks like ancient bones on sacred rocks. Splitting this form I take flight, relishing the strength of this avian species, comfortable with each beat of my raptor's wings.

Two warriors, predators on the hunt as we dip and soar in Valhalla's pillowed canyons. Until I lose you in veils of Cumulus vapor, I panic.

A screech. Claws scour my back and in the blink of a hawk's eye you're gone. Reminding me this is your world and your territory. I know I cannot play this game long and hope to survive. Blood flows free from jagged wounds. My life force, your meal, leaves me in a red spray as I plummet, feigning death. You cleave through the clouds again, talons extended, that killer's stare centered in the core of those yellow predator's eyes. At the last possible moment, I twist and let you hurtle by.

Darkness again. I blink my eyes open and hear the crunch of snow beneath my ursine paws. The moribund whiteness of the Arctic ice cap spreads as far as I can see. You've taken control again.

A glance. Snow, mountains of bluish white and jagged ridges of ice everywhere. Thick padded paws thump down. Ursine breath grates in the thin air as I lumber over snow and ice blending into the moribund hell of the northern wasteland. Breath condenses in the chilly arctic air, with only the brittle crunch of ice dried of any moisture, ringing in my ears. I sniff, knowing in this form my vision is useless, but I can smell a rotting carcass ten kilometers away.

I sniff again and begin to pick up my pace. The hunt is on, she's near, the musk of her hunger gives her away and this time it will be me that takes her.

I roar, clearing a mound of snow. Ximena turns, not expecting me. She closes her eyes as I lung for her throat and all goes black once again.

On it goes through the evening, becoming creature after creature. Changing, reveling in the sensual pleasures of the myriad forms, but finally the night nears to a tiring end and it is time for my plan.

Feline eyes wink from the shadows and you spring on a cougar's padded paws. Snarling, I fling aside passivity's covers and leap first, my jaws sinking into your throat's softness, enough to hold you and not crush your windpipe. You resist in rage, spitting, snarling.

Fear sinks into your eyes and as you struggle to escape. I have you, this time. We shift into a madness of forms: eagle, lizard, orca, grizzly bear, lion, and finally back to our true forms, but never does my grasp let you go.

"How dare you! This is my game." Your voice pounds inside my head. My grip doesn't relinquish. The soul catcher has done its job. *You are mine.*

The witch, the mistress, caught at her own game.

The fevered contact of your body, its sinewy suppleness sends cravings to my loins, resonating desires as old as creation. I thrust forward, not caring if you're ready, because I know you are: you're always ready. You cry out as I enter and for a moment become lost in ecstasies throes, flinging yourself towards freedom from the damning ache inside. The same ache I suffer for you.

As we make love, shudders ripple the surface of this land. The dawn, the harbinger of the night's end, is here. I've timed this precisely. Desperation mirrors in your gaze as you struggle with renewed effort. The need to release from within wanes beneath the more basic need of survival. The one who thrilled to the adrenalin of the hunt, and lived off the fear in the eyes of the helpless knows she must now escape with the coming collapse of her world. Our forms blur, the landscape a maelstrom, driving you on, your eyes noiselessly screaming for mercy as you sense your demise.

Everything wavers as cracks streak the sky, revealing another view behind the one plane we stand on. Reality for some, the other side of the magical looking glass, for others. A spidery multitude of ever-smaller splinters of realism fissures this realm until all that's left is the vision of me still clenching your throat, fragmented over a million slivers of silver. "How can you do this?" You plead in terror. "I loved you."

You're lying, I know it. You have to be. I must press on.

But I cannot doubt myself now; this has to end. I couldn't survive another year. *As did I*, I tell myself and that is why I must continue this to the very end. *As did I.*

Everything falls away like a background blanket pulled from a painting, uncovering my reality. You attempt to melt away but can't, this is my world now. I pull the shaman's soul catcher from my mouth and fling it into the ice waters of a mountain stream. You wail like a dozen gypsies burning at the stake at the realization of what I've done, but it is too late. Whatever remains of your world is sucked into a cavernous void. Drained beyond belief, I sink into blackness, knowing I've won.

I cling to the boughs of life, fading in and out of consciousness. Haunting my every moment she is constantly there, pulling at those spirit threads of love and desire that I've tried to sever. So hard to believe these are mere dreams, I fight to wean myself from the cradle of her arms, the voracity of her lips. Finally I stare out at the snow fluttering over the Northern BC terrain and sit up in my hospital bed. A nurse enters.

"How's it going?" she asks. "I see you've finally decided to join us."

"Where am I and how long have I been here?"

"Prince George Hospital and today is the twenty-fifth of November."

I've been out nearly a month.

"The doctors, as you can imagine, have a few questions to ask you. Especially why you'd get lost in the woods a second time."

"Who said I got lost in the woods?" I hadn't told anyone.

"Your wife. She found you. Apparently you'd been wandering in the wilderness for a couple of weeks."

"My wife? I don't have a –"

With the flowing grace of a loon gliding over serene midnight waters, a native woman enters the room. Cascading moonlight dances from her soul in the flood of raven-colored hair down her back. Elegant, yet fierce lines radiate her earthy face that I've never seen her before, yet I've known her forever.

"Hi, darling," she purrs with a familiar feline growl. Around her neck, dangling on a leather necklace, rests the soul catcher. *How?* "I'm glad you're feeling better. I was so worried about you."

Her touch is electric. I already know the feel of her softness pressed naked up against me, and the throb of my want calls from deep within.

An eerie question haunts my realization as my head falls back into the security of the pillow. Who caught who?

Often on full moon nights I catch the soul catcher nestled between her full breasts, glowing with an ethereal brilliance and smile knowing I've brought home the witch of my heart.

Polaroid's Cellular Walls

Black stiletto leather boots rose above the knees of the black and white photo of a young woman leaning against a Harley in the Polaroid I pulled from a box of my dad's college papers. A look of carnal aliveness resided in her eyes. Her skirt was lifted to eye-opening heights. Long black curly hair flowed recklessly over the unbuttoned lace top, exposing a delicious profile of her nearly naked breasts, with the edge of erect brown nipples threatening to be exposed. It was hard to tell but it looked like a tattoo of a flower adorned her left breast. As if daring a gust of wind to reveal the hidden curves of my fantasies.

I'd agreed to clean out some of dad's stuff after he passed away. Only what would dad be doing with such a picture?

I read the faded inscription on the back.

> To Janice.
> The most passionate lover a man or woman could ever have.
> I'm yours body and soul.
> Love C.

Frowning, I held the photograph up to the scrutiny of the sun.

The dust of old, unanswered ghosts danced in lewd rock ballads as the photograph fell from my bloodless fingers and catatonia slammed rationality from my mind. I knew those eyes and that smile, underneath the makeup and the luscious scarlet lips was someone I'd known my whole life.

Impossible.

Mom?

My dad's faithful, loving sedate and quiet companion for the last forty years.

If she'd had desires other than looking after dad's needs and raising us kids, I never knew about them.

Dust specks, highlighted on a ray of sunshine that stole through the window, drifted by as denial dug its acrid claws into my throat.

I had to ask.

In the nursing home, Mom sat sipping at her strawberry tea. She wore her long grey hair in a bun. Her blouse buttoned to her throat, her skirt reached to well below her knees and her lips unadorned. Mother as I always knew her. The epitome of gentility: cultured, conservative, confined.

The strawberry tea failed to sweeten my mood. Sweat clung to my palms as the picture burned in my pocket and pulled at the corners of my mouth to speak.

"Did you clean out your father's stuff?" Mom asked.

"Yes, I did, I—" I didn't know how to begin. "I—ah—came across some of his journals. I didn't know dad kept any of his college stuff." I fell silent, trying to ground myself and work up the courage.

Mom sipped at her tea. Her eyes bore that stare mothers always possess when they're seeking the truth from their kids.

My lip quivered.

I couldn't do this.

"Then you found the picture," she said seeing my nervousness.

I nodded, stunned. The teacup rattled as I set it down. I reached into my pocket and I gave her the picture.

She sighed and ran her hand, lovingly, over the surface. "I could lie to you, but I won't.

This picture was your dad's way of keeping me his all these years."

She stopped and sat up straighter. I saw a look on her face that I'd never seen before, a haunting aliveness. The girl in the picture. "I met Janice in high school. We had nothing in common, but we became friends. In college we moved in together. She joined a bike gang and we tried everything imaginable; booze, drugs, sex."

"We got stoned one night and next thing I knew we were making love. One of those experiments you try when you're young and willing to take risks. Being a rebel I suppose. Before I met Janice I'd never even fantasized about sex with a woman, but I enjoyed being with her more than I ever thought possible. The thrill of living life on the edge, I suppose. Things you experiment with as you try to find out who you are as an adult."

I opened my mouth to speak, only nothing came out. A lifetime of set images came crashing down like a china cabinet full of elegant dinnerware. "What happened to her? To Janice?" I finally managed.

"She died in a horrific motorcycle accident and large parts of me died with her. I met your dad in college shortly after. He was everything Janice wasn't; rich, secure and very confined. For whatever reason, he chose me to be someone worth saving."

Those last words hung with bitterness. "I made the mistake of telling him about my past, although most he knew already. Somehow he found this picture I got back from Janice' parents after she died. They told me they didn't approve but I was the one person that brought life into her life. Life that was stolen from my heart."

She paused, tears streaking a face that I'd never seen cry. "He kept it as his insurance that I would never leave. After Janice died that part of me in the pic died as well and I didn't have the courage to escape. So I gave up. Eventually, I grew to enjoy the confines of his cage and convinced myself it had kept me alive, sane and became the prim mother you know."

I still couldn't match the woman sitting before me, the mother I'd always known, with the woman in the photograph. How much of her personality, her true self, had she lost in that transformation? Dad was always strict with us kids and mom. Now I understood why.

If this happened today I would have saved the photo to my cellphone and, I paused as realization hit me, conversely this woman wouldn't have been my mother and nor would I have been born. Perhaps mom would have lived a life of happiness with Janice.

She wiped at tears unbuttoning her blouse and pushed the edge of her bra aside.

The rose tattoo in the picture. So delicate, so beautiful, yet so foreign to the person bearing it. I remembered mom rubbing at that spot whenever a moment of anger occurred with us kids or with dad.

"Janice and I couldn't get married in those days so we cemented our love by both having a rose tattooed on our breasts. Your dad hated this tattoo and resented the fact that it gave me the strength to continue living the way he wanted. I refused to remove it, swearing it would disfigure me."

Her look of aliveness left like an unfamiliar stranger on silent footsteps. We only talked for a few more moments, mom was quite weak. I left learning more about my mother than I'd ever known.

Mom passed away the next week. Before she died we talked much about her past and I really got to know this person called Caroline, my mother. At her funeral I slipped the picture beside her, next to her rose tattoo. As the casket slowly entered the cold earth, I heard the throaty throb of a Harley in the distance.

Hitchhiking,
West Coast Style

Ovoid eyes and hooked beaks stared down at me from the totems in Stanley Park. I shouldn't have come here. I'd been going mad for two days. Each minute ticking by, not knowing whether they were alive or ...

No, I couldn't go there. That's why I came here, to get out of the house. To be where Denise and I first met. Where I proposed to her. Where the sacred memory of us would always remain, alive. A sigh escaped my lips as I notice a native elder standing out among the throng of tourists.

A battered Montreal Expos baseball cap studded with various pins adorned his head. Twin braids of white-fired hair trailed down a dirty denim jacket. He leaned heavily on an ornate cane, the handle embellished with an orca. At first glance you'd take him for a hobo, yet his demeanor spoke of something unexplainable. Mysterious, like mist oozing across moon-fallen waters shrouding calling loons.

My cell phone rang.

"Doug Thornton from Search and Rescue. We've located the airplane."

"Thank God!"

"It went down in rugged territory south of Bella Bella on Hunter Island. We've dropped a man there ahead of the S and R team."

"Have you found …?"

"Sorry. No trace of them. Only found the body of the pilot."

A chance, then?

"We'll do an area search as soon as we can get men in there. They may have walked off or been thrown from the plane as it went down."

No. They were alive, I knew it.

"The area's very remote, no trails or logging roads even close."

Hunter Island? I grew up there and knew the terrain well, often accompanying my dad on fishing trips along the coast. I remember his paranoia about the cougar population, wouldn't let me out of his sight. "Okay. I guess all I can do now is wait."

The whish of bus brakes signaled the arrival of even more bantering tourists. I shouldn't be here among the teenagers hugging in front of cameras, kids screaming, running rampant, but this was all I had of Denise right now. How could this be happening? I was to join them at our summer home in Bella Bella after my business meeting. Nothing mattered now. I'd give it all away in a heartbeat if only I could have my wife and daughter back.

The elderly native caught my eye again. I turned away. Conflict I couldn't handle right now. Totems, with eyes that shone only bleakness, glared back.

"The top one is Raven. The Trickster, we call him."

I jumped.

"Yeah, sure," I replied in noddy-dog mode. Only aware that time was quickly running out for my family.

"Time has never been kind to Raven."

"What!" *Had he read my thoughts?*

He smiled, "Charlie Stillwaters. Native ska-ga."

"Ska- what?"

"Oh my! Can't you whites ever get it right? Just try shaman."

"Shaman." Great, my wife and eleven-year-old daughter were either dead or close to it and I was standing in Stanley Park talking to a native witch doctor who'd not bathed in the last ten years. "Eric Lawson. You must know lots about these totems then."

"Yup, carved a few, traveled some."

"Traveled some?"

"Yeah. In my journeys to 'over there.'" He smiled and pointed to the sky. "And over there." He pointed to the trees. "And under here." He thumped the ground.

Wonderful. I was conversing with a lunatic. "Right, shamans. You, like, astral travel or something?"

He chuckled. "Well, most of my traveling is usually courtesy of Greyhound or BC Ferries."

Despite myself, I smiled at him. "What?"

"Usually I stay in my cabin and watch baseball games. Love the Expos, you know," he said, avoiding the question. "Just visiting relatives on the mainland. Thought I'd see what the cheap tourist crap totems look like."

"Cheap tourist crap?"

"Yeah. For example, take the one with the mortuary box on top. Boxes were important to us, and that box would have held the bones of our chief. Only the real thing would have been a bentwood cedar box, made from one piece of wood, heated and bent into shape. Pretty clever, my ancestors."

"Oh," I said not really listening.

"Care to see a shaman's totem? Follow me."

Why, I don't know, but I followed him. I caught hints of wood smoke, sagebrush and age emanating from him as we walked. Smells that reminded me of my childhood on the BC coast. I envisioned Charlie sitting before a fireplace in some beat-up cabin in the woods. When I was young the native kids told us of shamans and their weird powers, never thought I'd actually run into one, especially now.

He half shuffled with his cane. What if he had a gang waiting to beat me up and rob me?

"I always have a million questions running through my mind when I walk through the woods myself."

He did it again. The unknown quotient. He knew things I couldn't comprehend.

"There it is."

I stared up at the massive cedar, one of the few spared the first kiss of the white man's axe settling Vancouver. "It's a tree."

"Not just any old tree. Trees with a single stem and twin trunks we call portal trees. They're sacred. We believe as you pass through the center you can walk through dimensions."

I blinked several times. My wife and child were dead or dying and I was standing with a native fruitcake before an old tree.

"If you disbelieve me, go ahead. Walk through it."

I'd had enough. I must have been completely mental to listen to him at all. I began to walk away. "Sorry, this is stupid. I really shouldn't be here."

"It's at those times of our lives when everything we hold dear is in danger of being taken away that people often turn to new beliefs." He whipped his cane up at me. "If you have nothing to lose," he smiled, "you have nothing to lose."

We stared. Spirits walked through the hollows of his eyes like mist that curls up mountain slopes.

A raven cawed ominously, daring me.

"This is silly, really." I scrambled up to the tree and took a deep breath. Suddenly nervous, I touched the cool strands of cedar bark. Raven cawed again.

I stepped into ...

... darkness.

Pulling at me, tearing. Black yanked at my sight like the pitch of coal tar shimmering on moonless nights. Tumbling, twisting, turning into insubstantial blackness as ethereal winds howled past, through unending canyons of ebony. The cry of harps strung taut sang to blackness, the serenade of a lone coyote to its lover the moon. Finally, like bones baked to dust under a sun's brutal gaze, I crumbled. Fingers of breeze tore at each sundered section and stole away again. Scattered, flung into the sea of nothingness.

A hawk's cry died on the stillness.

Until only rumbles shook the inky quiet. Peels of soft dribbles, raindrops, first one, two, then hundreds of an approaching thunderstorm. Unending haunting sounds, with no place to land, whisked by.

I reached out, dizzying voices spun around me. Something cool, wet, solid. I grabbed at it. Anchoring myself to roots, and the decay of thousands of years. The earth, holding me, securing me. A connection to all that once was and all that now is and in the end to all that will be.

I held as bits, pieces, here, there, floated by.

Whispers; hushed voices.

My fingers, dozens of them, reached down through the muck, finding purchase, a place. I became the root.

Still the voices swam by, singing. Flowing?

A river of consciousness.

Was there a way to find my family?

When you have nothing to lose you have nothing to lose, he said.

I let go flowing down through my roots into the enigmatic river of non-corporeal substance.

Hard tendrils swam by. Roots of other trees. I grabbed one and allowed myself to flow into it. Up the stem and into tens of thousands of leaves, staring out at the ocean from along the BC coast.

That's it. The way to find them, kinda like hitchhiking a portal highway, west-coast style.

Only how to locate them?

Boxes! He said something about important boxes. A memory stirred, from the fishing trips along the coast with my dad, near where the plane had gone down. I'd often bring along a little plastic box. In it I would place things like a notepad, pencil, dice, modeling clay, mini rain-hat. And what else?

A whistle. Yes! And a smiley-face badge. How could I forget?

Three summers ago, on a picnic, I'd shown Amber the box I'd concealed inside the hollow tree. It had still been there, after all this time. I told her it was my safe place, my secret, now hers.

He knew, Charlie. Important things in boxes. The cunning shaman had somehow known.

The box had kept me from getting scared. God, what crazy things kids do. Where had I lost all that wonder? I beamed inside, gone was the cool business executive, gone was the dour financial wrangler that had succeeded in the paper world of human affairs. I laughed and let go again, letting the child inside full of wonder lust, of swashbuckling on stars imagining great worlds to explore, in again, after all these years and went skateboarding down into the sea of voices.

Find my box and I knew I'd find my family. Amber would remember. The S and R man said the plane went down on Hunter Island. Where my box was. I concentrated, telling the whispers to guide me, take me there, to my box, my family.

Where I spent summers with my dad. And …

As I flowed through the earth, spikes of fear cut into me.

Danger.

Amber calling, screaming through the void. So close.

A cougar's growl rent the air.

I surfaced, staring at the scene below. Denise's blonde hair was matted with blood, her body unmoving, and Amber clutching my plastic box. Her clothes were torn, her skin covered in cuts and scratches. Brave girl, she'd led her mom here. Another scream as the cougar advanced, spurred by the smell of blood.

Helplessness paralyzed me. All I could do was watch. Or was it?

I'd come this far, I wasn't about to lose them now.

The cougar stood underneath a massive Douglas fir. I flowed up into it and slammed myself into a large branch. Again and again, shaking it. At first nothing, then a small crack resonated. Screaming inwardly I tore at myself with everything I had. A snap rang through the air as the branch finally sheared away and a part of me fell earthward. The cougar looked up, too late. A thud echoed and red rain carpeted the forest.

"See Mommy, Daddy said this was a safe place. I told you." Amber clutched the happy-face button and held the whistle to her lips.

Denise stirred, blood trickling down her face. "Blow darling, just keep blowing. The rescue men are nearby."

The tree she leaned against bore two trunks emanating from its main stem.

So *that's* how Charlie knew.

I heard someone yelling and saw the flashes of bright orange approaching.

Satisfied, I transferred myself back to the portal tree and fell to the ground in Stanley Park.

Wetness on my forehead, I reached up and felt blood oozing out. I was back in my body again.

Charlie had vanished. Had I dreamt all of this? Had he whacked me in the head? I was beginning to wonder if I'd just had some sort of bizarre dream when my cell phone rang.

"We've located your wife and daughter. They're pretty banged up but safe. Lucky though, nearby we discovered a cougar, crushed under a fallen branch."

Tears of thanks flooded earthward. Childhood memories, of the mystical shaman, flooded in. Stories I stopped believing in, until now.

I turned and touched the portal tree.

"Thanks Charlie." Somewhere a raven cawed and I knew I'd never look at another tree in quite the same way.

Postcards

'**I** stared into your eyes as we camped on the grassy mountainsides of Mt. Kilamanjaro. In the distance, across the hot languid savanna, lions roared as they lay with each other, bellowing a hungry lust. At night the distant thunder of tribal drums pounding a compelling, sensual beat. Under the full moon natives danced around huge fires, releasing ancient passions. While we danced naked to our own ancient rhythms.'

...read the back of the postcard from Tsavo Kenya. The front bore two lions rolling in the dust of Africa. It was addressed to Eleanor from D. I filed the postcard into Box 38 and kept on with processing the day's mail. Such was my life, such was my mundane existence as a postal clerk in Smithers BC.

I'm Silvia Henderson, 29, single, unfortunately unattached and employed by the post office for the last eight years. I spent my days filing other people's mail, reading other peoples lives. Oh yeah, I'm not suppose to, its a small town and we don't get cable what can I say?

Who was this exotic lady traveler? Who would go to Africa and make love under the stars? A week later another postcard:

'We are in Cairo, lounging outside the pyramids. Hot sands burn at the touch. As does my sun burnt skin. Your lips cool, wet and hungry devours the parched terrain of my flesh. Setting brushfires wherever they *light. Starting primitive hungers and consuming fires in my soul. Hungers for you. To Eleanor from D.'*

On the front, the pyramids of Giza, and a camel rider staring up at the manmade mountains.

Actually I should be a little more precise here, I've worked for the post office for the last eight years and was just recently transferred here from the Boston Bar office. So I have no idea who Eleanor is. Her name rolls off my tongue elegantly and exquisitely, as I'm sure this lady must be.

A week later another, on the front the Colossi of Rome:

'We walk the corridors where once gladiators fought. Ancient sweat, ancient blood soaks these sands. Battles arranged here, fought to the death, long ago. Nights filled with cries of mercy or patient waiting knowing the morrow could bring freedom to a slave or death. Your hand trembles as it touches my face. I stand behind you, mine touches your sides, your legs. You turn around as my heart cries out for more and on bended knee I pleasure you as if this night were my last.'

God, where does one find love like that, surely not in this small town?

That afternoon a simple voice rents the air. "Box 38 please."

I look up from the back of the room and see you for the first time. But the face is not right. You can't be Eleanor, not the statuesque beauty who drinks a mans passion and leaves him limp, then hungers for more. No, the woman I see is too ordinary, too much like me. She bears glasses, horribly outdated, hair that hangs limp from lack of washing and certainly no exotic makeup. You're barely 5'4" and plain, so drearily plain. I want to introduce myself, say hi, yet that would be a rape of your privacy. Grounds for my immediate termination. Instead I watch as you sort your mail, throwing the ads out into the open garbage box for junk mail. You stop and read the postcard from Rome. I watch as your cheeks flush slightly and your fingers caress the inside edge of your blouse. I know, you are her.

You smile slightly, a lewd hungry smile. I should know that smile but don't. I should be wearing that wanton smile, but don't. Then incredibly you turn to leave and pitch the postcard into the mailbox trash and walk out.

My mouth falls and rolls into the dust lining the corners of this office.

You who have lived so passionately, so vividly real have thrown it away. Discarded trash. Horrified I wait a few moments and when no one is present I search the open trash and pull your postcard from the bin. It's folded and stuffed into my pocket quicker then a kid stealing candy.

For the first time in my life, my sterile existence I hear the words "that bitch" enter my head willingly. She's thrown away things until now I've not even had the courage to dream of, or even fantasize about at night. How could she?

At lunch I hear a voice, mine distant and quivering, of someone I've never known. "Yes Advantage travel, book me one for Kenya, yes Africa." I shake from fear and excitement, realizing that no longer will I dream of being under an African moon, hanging bloated in the humid air, and dance naked with natives, while drums pound an ancestral beat.

Stanley Park

Propped up against an ancient cedar, older then I can trace my ancestry back in time, I sit in Stanley Park, Vancouver, BC. It had rained yesterday, the midday air still retains slight traces of that freshness, although quickly vanishing in mists heated by the summer's searing rays. Birds chitter freely in the background. The ever present buzz of traffic is strangely non-existent here. The pace, the flow of life is here as it always was before man came along and transformed the area outside of Stanley Park into a bustling city.

Perhaps this is not the usual thing to do for a twenty-seven year old woman. I should be out living life, not reading about it from my mother's past. Dreaming of what she went through. But today marked the first anniversary of my mother's death due to cancer. That disease took her early, too damn early. Mom was my best friend, my dad I never knew, never met, not even in pictures.

This park, and this tree, is where when she was my age, she used to hang out. It was also where she eventually fell in love with her soul's mate. It is where she lost him too. She relayed parts of this astonishing story to me, most of the time I never believed her. At least I didn't truly believe her until I came across her journal with its fading inked pages. Fading like my memory of her.

It's mid-July, just like in mom's book. The sun begins to mercilessly beat down as I sit. I pull the brim of my baseball cap even lower to shelter my eyes. Sweat has beaded my forehead. My long blonde hair is tucked under my cap. I've often been told I've the same figure and looks as mom. Did I have her passion and zest for life? Or did that intense, all consuming kind of romance she got sucked into, die sometime in the past. Guys just didn't do the sort of thing mom experienced anymore. At least none of the ones I ever met.

July 09, 1971

He was older than me by twelve years. That in itself made his existence undeniable to my parents. I decided to begin this journal since our chance meeting two weeks ago. Too much has happened too fast, too crazily.

He, being Jake O'Hara, was dressed in black dress pants, white ruffled shirt and vest. His hair was slicked back, although quite disheveled, but it was of the darkest black I'd ever seen and longer then acceptable. He always had a curl of bad boy locks that hung down, especially after we made love, that I wanted to sweep back in place. He'd grab my hands, without any warning, and pull me into him to steal another kiss from my lips. It was like being shoved face first into a raging thunderstorm, the sheer exhilaration, the passion and the fury, especially that exquisite fury. It lurked behind the steel blue of his eyes. But that was then, this is now.

He'd been part of a wedding ceremony the night before, one of the best men. Jake had gotten drunk and passed out on the bench just across from me. I'll never forget the blood red of his eyes and the slightly sour hint of alcohol on his breath, the first time I saw him. I'll never forget the hunger in those eyes, the hunger he had for me. The image of a gaunt gray wolf came to mind. A wolf on the prowl, mysterious, deadly and wonderfully unpredictable.

I'd been laying against this large cedar tree in Stanley Park for awhile reading a book. Which one didn't matter it was just a diversion while I relaxed and worked on my tan.

I'm twenty-nine and just finished med school and ready to go on in life as a doctor. I had already accepted a rural position in Prince George for two years as my first assignment. It was the only thing available for a woman doctor at the time. I didn't care to work in a small center, but I was too eager to get on with saving people, maybe that's what attracted him into my life? Yes, I had everything set up ready to go, on schedule. My life set. Then Jake O'Hara entered.

Irish rascal and lover of life. Tormentor of my soul. That first day he said few words, while his eyes did all his talking. They stared at me, held me captive and ravished me all in the same glare. I knew what he wanted of me the first time he saw me. I had been the apple of many men's eyes, but never the fire for their soul. Nor the hunger for their existence.

I remember looking up as a shadow fell across my body. "Excuse me, but you're blocking out the sun, I'm trying to get a tan." I said rudely to him, my first words. A simple request, how complex my life was soon to become.

"Do you come here often?"

"Why would I tell a complete stranger? Especially one who looks like they just woke up after a good drunk."

"Because if you did, I'd be more presentable next time I met you. I realize I'm in no shape to be talking to the most beautiful girl I've ever seen."

"Excuse me, but that's a horrible pickup line if I ever heard one."

"That it is and I can only offer this in apology." He pulled his white and pink carnation from his lapel and handed it to me. It was half crushed and a little limp from too much partying, a lot like he was that day.

Yet there was something beautiful about both of them, even when they were at their worst. "For you."

As I reached for the carnation I knew I shouldn't have. That simple act would forever change my life and begin me down unknown paths where I never imagined I'd ever tread.

As I took the flower he reached forward, took my hand in his and placed the carnation in the center of my palm. His lips brushed across the edges of my fingertips. Without a word he rose and left. His eyes, intense maelstroms seared their gaze into my heart. Melting it and at the same time creating that want of hunger for him. God, I don't know how he could do that, but he did.

His lips, so soft, so warm, so hungry. A shiver rent its way across my skin. A shiver of heat, even warmer then the sun that beat down. Or was it not his passion but mine that I felt on the taste of his lips? "I'll be here tomorrow, same time." I yelled as he walked away. Already smitten by, this handsome rogue of a fellow.

I watched him walk away with a cool, reserved, almost dignified stride. A garter half stuck out of his back pocket as he receded from view. Yes Jake O'Hara was a scoundrel, as well as a gentleman.

He told me later that he'd put that garter on my leg someday when we married. I told him that was some real blarney.

I closed mom's book and settled back for a moment before rising. How does one find that kind of romance today? Not from any of the men I'd run across. Their idea of romance was to take me out on a date to a hockey game and supply the beer. I rose and began walking back to my car.

I passed an elderly man. He walked with a dignified walk. One I'd expect from a high cultured individual. He clutched something in his hands, a small box of some sort. His eyes bore a dark, cold stare from their steely depths. I turned to study the old man for a moment, something about him was oddly familiar. That was my undoing. Who these days studies the old as they walk.

Books, car keys, everything went flying as something slammed me into the ground. I hit the grass with a thud and for a moment everything went blank.

As I came to I heard a deep resounding male voice. "Look, I'm so sorry, are you all right?" He kept saying.

"What happened?" I asked regaining consciousness and staggering to my feet.

I stared up into the face of a very handsome Vancouver bike cop and handsome wasn't very flattering. I could see the true concern radiating from his eyes, eyes of dark brown mystery. Delicious mystery. He had a solid square cut face, that spoke of honesty and of principle. A man that would jump on his steed and ride to rescue the damsel in distress. Judging by the strength of his arms as he effortlessly lifted me up, I'd no doubt he could fight his fair share of dragons.

"My apology, there's been a suspicious character lurking about and I thought I spotted him a moment ago. I came around the bend in the trail and unfortunately there you were."

I bent over and picked up my car keys and books, noticing the solid cords of his legs that jutted out from his police uniform shorts.

"I usually don't go bowling over beautiful ladies. I'm sorry." He lifted my left hand to his lips and placed a gently kiss on the back of my hand. Was this how mom felt as shivers of aroused delight surged through me, I thought when Jake O'Hara kissed her hand. I felt my legs begin to buckle, turning to ice cream on a hot July sidewalk.

"Ah that's okay, anytime. It's not every day I get bowled over by a good-looking bike cop."

He blushed a little. "Well if you're okay, I must continue on my way. Do you hang out here often?"

"Yes I'll be coming here every other day or so depending on the weather. I have some reading to catch up on."

"Good, I'll keep an eye out for you."

"I'll be reading by the cedar tree." I pointed to the tree in question and noticed something white on the ground in front of it.

He drove away, I didn't even catch his name. But I had a feeling I'd be seeing him again.

Curious, I walked back to the base of the tree and saw what the object was.

It was a pink and white carnation, placed with the greatest of care. I picked it up. It was damp as if sprayed with water to preserve its freshness or as if someone had shed tears over it. Glancing around I see other crumpled dried out remains of flowers, even in their death I know they were once carnations. I stroke the petals that seem as soft as cashmere. Looking up I search the area, but couldn't see the figure of my mom's broken heart, or of the man I'd never seen, only had stories told about, my father Jake O'Hara.

Real Thirst Quencher

His smile held the sweet softness of a wolf's leer. The shadows, hidden in the blue of his eyes, bore places my soul feared to tread. Places of dark whispered passions, of hungers under the guile of fervent dreams borne on sweaty summer nights. Or glimpsed in those moments of stark awakenings and cold, sober realizations before reality filters in to dispel the memories of a night's dreams.

As he talked his fingers thrummed on the counter, each thump begging, pleading at my heart, tearing at the veils of womanhood inside. His lone earring glinted in the neon lights.

"I can't." I stated with a quiver in my voice.

"You can't or won't." His words swooped on me like a bird of prey, a circling eagle on a helpless field mouse.

My blood pulsed. *Never*, I whispered lying under my breath. To give into the likes of him would be to lose all of my dignity. Yet, he was the sort that didn't take no for an answer. Could I ever look myself in the mirror if I let him get his way, just this once? I was a woman of honor, of valor.

So, I always thought. He would use me for just one thing.

A waft of his cologne, woodsy, enticing, pulled at my civilized wrappings of discrepancies. Help me, I wanted him, the quivers inside threatened to cave in my resolve. His lips red and full, begging of soft promise surrounded by a forest of bristles. Seduction in the midst of rugged hardness. That was it, wasn't it? He was dark, mysterious, unknown. A rogue. The handsome rogue kind that my mother warned me to stay away from. The kind that wore safety like a paper umbrella. Mere ornamentation flung aside at his slightest whim. I smiled, there were times when that didn't seem so bad.

I stole a glance into his eyes, into the steely blueness of his soul and shivered. A wolf's hunger is never truly concealed. And when it was over I'm sure he'd discard me as he did countless others. In his eyes I only functioned for the moment as the focus of his hunger's needs. Would I be woman enough to make him forget all others, to commit only to me? I snickered, oh to have such lofty and idealistic thoughts. Still, to be the focus of such incendiary cravings.

No, I had the final say. I could resist, if I wanted to and I needed to. "No," again I said it. "No," mustering up my resolve.

"Damn, do you know what this means to me, how much this entire night depends on you."

Did I? My insides trembled in harmony to the quakes sending shivers of electricity ranging across my skin. To go out with someone like him, just once. A mere date, that's all. Women sitting behind a thousand visages of gentility would squirm in consternation at the notion and what would they do given the opportunity with a man of his rugged physique? Would they take the chance? To be with someone like him. Someone uncontrollable, someone unconfined by society's restrictions of appropriateness or perhaps I had what it took to tame his savage bestial nature, to leash him to me, to make him desire only I above all others. Or just let him ravish me?

"Damn." His confidence cracked. His feigned bravado, his sheer masculine grace, like a lion impassioned in the heat of battle. Terrifying to behold, mystifying to dream about, tantalizing to fantasize over. If I let my resolve dissolve from me just this once, to let him ravish me with his ways. To give in and be his. Just once. No, I held my position very seriously, I was in a place of trust, and I could not disappoint those who put me there. This was my first time, my first full time job; sure it was at night, but it was work. I couldn't chance it. I was starting university in the fall and needed this summer job to pay for the tuition.

"NO ID, NO BOOZE." I stared unbending under the fearsome passion of his gaze. A flush inside burned cinders down to those places only my darkest passion lay.

"Damn. Sure you're old enough to work here." He turned and stormed out in frustrated disgust.

Just barely, I wanted to say.

One of his friends met him at the door "So, no go?"

"No, we'll have to buy drinks at the club, damn." He looked up at me for a moment before disappearing into the darkness of the night. "Yes, I guess Moxies it is." He said just a little too loud, for me to hear. A glint stole across his eyes as he turned and looked quickly in my direction, his eyes eating up my body. A true male, always on the prowl.

I watched him as he walked away, one eye on him the hard contours of his rear in his jeans a size too small, too confining. Nice.

The other eye on the clock. It was nearly 11:00. Good, my shift would be over in an hour. A glance around the liqueur store told me there was no one else here. I was alone. I picked up the case of beer he had hoped to buy. I still had a couple of hours to party, if I wanted.

No, I just wanted him.

I stared at the box of bottled beer. Waiting. Just like he would be at the club. I paid with my tips.

Flipping open the cardboard top I pulled a long-necked beer from its place. Glass clinked on glass. I spun the cap off and took a long guzzle.

"Damn, he was good." I said tossing the remains into the garbage.

"Cold, refreshing and satisfying."

A Clear-Cut Case
Of Madness

"Portal trees, a double trunk growing from a single trunk."
The Vancouver Parks guide added, "They believed that by walking through the center you could travel between dimensions. Anyone care to try?"

Several in the group laughed. Someone commented, "Stupid things people believe in." But I noticed no one accepted the challenge.

Earlier in our tour of Stanley Park the guide had taken us to the totems. Something about the carvings, eerie ovoid eyes and hooked beaks, pulled at my soul. Then, to the famous hollow cedar; nearby, this unique tree.

"No takers?"

I stared apprehensively at the space between the trunks. A raven cawed ominously, daring me. "Go ahead. I'll catch up," I told my wife.

Once alone, I scampered up to the tree. "Silly, really." I took a deep breath, raven cawed again.

I stepped into ...

... darkness.

Tumbling, twisting, turning, into insubstantial blackness. Ethereal winds howled past, through unending canyons of ebony, reminiscent of eagles' chants. Darkness pulled at my sight like the pitch of coal tar shimmering on moonless nights.

Pulling at me, tearing. Finally, like bones baked to dust under a sun's brutal gaze, I crumbled. Fingers of breeze tore at each sundered section and stole away again. Scattered, flung into the sea of nothingness.

Rumbles of an approaching thunderstorm shook the inky stillness. The cry of harps strung taut sang to blackness. Peels of soft dribbles, raindrops, first one, two, then hundreds, disturbed the quiet. Unending haunting sounds, with no place to land, whisked by.

Bits, pieces, here, there, floating by.

Whispers; hushed voices.

Reaching out, I felt something cool, wet. I grabbed at it ... something concrete. Anchoring me. The decay of thousands of years surrounding me. This was the earth, holding me, securing me. My fingers, dozens of them, reached down through the muck, finding purchase, a place.

I was the roots of the tree, on the edge of a clear-cut. Chainsaws like angry hornets buzzed, spraying a rain of chips like a perverse snowfall. The stink of bark, like blood thick.

I tried to turn, to smell, but couldn't. These senses no longer existed.

Others did, one of connection to a river of consciousness. Awareness of others, millions like myself. I flowed into my roots and joined them, basking in the earth's energy until I came upon a zone the others avoided. Curious, I entered the realm of stillness.

I didn't understand, until I looked up into the source of the unearthly quiet. Everywhere I ventured, the same. Frozen screams of terror from roots that bore no trunks, no souls, only death and everywhere the stink of mechanical entities cutting away.

I shuddered as the chainsaw bit into me. The silent cry of my brethren reverberated as we crashed to the earth.

I screamed and pushed back, breaking contact with the trunks. A raven cawed, lost in the dense greenery.

I stood up, brushed myself clean and knew I'd never look at another forest in quite the same way.

The Bridges
of Picasso's Heart

O n the coldest day in mid January in Vancouver, clouds hang like thick ragged graying blankets over everything and bitter cold rattles the outside panes on the whim of the wind, like ghosts begging to get in scurrying in the darkness from window to window. As all spirits do in the dark seeking entrance, only this isn't a ghost story. Just one that haunts me still.

While white caps crown the oceans waves like spirit horses and rain thrums a relentless memory of the summer's heat, shimmering passions and ... you.

To fading memories that stink away in this heart. Festering like a raven in an overcoat, dressed in black on black walking in stilettos sharp as razors through my heart.

Of you.

So much, so little realized, so too late to do anything now.

Of you.

Only in the scheme of life, young, naïve, not knowing what it is like to fall in love and to crash in despair when that love is shattered. It is never ordained when the special one enters your life. Some know, intimately. A sense. Knowing. This is her/him. Some years later, others never twig, that in the bump of shoulders along a street corridor, someone, perhaps while on the cellphone, just walked past. Searching for the one, as you focus on the minute screen before you. Gone into the background mist, drifting away.

Others remember a face in dreams, at weddings, school photos. Twigs of belonging, phantom echoes, reaching out from the recesses of your mind, of another past. Calling to each other still. Perhaps in this lifetime. Some the lucky.

Most waiting for the next and the next. Forever hoping, this is it.

A Romeo that seeks a Juliet.

A tune, a date, a touch, a smell calls it back again, awakening memories that won't stay shut away.

* * * *

I had met you in previous meetings. Caught off guard, neither of us were ready for each other.

Somewhere a lesson had to be learned or a past overcome in this lifetime. Or perhaps a great love like everything else has to have its place to germinate.

Or perhaps a combination of many things, some unknown and maybe earlier in time we hadn't the clarity to appreciate or understand the depths of endless love.

In some way I sense I've met you before. In another time, another life. I've always known you. And in this life I've searched long and hard to find you.

Perhaps it is the journey of two hearts and souls. A journey wrought with sadness, control and an undying need. A need to seek one's soulmate. A need that gnaws one's soul that out there on this planet sleeps the other half of this soul. We had much to overcome and a great deal of growing to do.

Was all this pain and learning was necessary in order to discover each other? In order to understand each other. In order to love each other. Unknowingly we have been moving to each other like spring moves to summer.

As the waves roll to the beach, as the sun moves to caress the horizon, as the moon rises in the night sky to dwell amongst the stars. As previous lifetimes have prepared us for this love.

Nothing in life is co-incidence, neither is the gravitating of me to you and you to me.

For in my soul you've always been there and in my heart you've always resided and always will.

April 28th

In the distance over the telephone I hear you. You put out a plea for help. As everyone around me falls away I focus on the resonance of your voice. In some small way I respond. Hate how your voice on the phone sends tremors through my heart. With no intentional thought I ask you to meet. I only know I'd like to get to know that face and voice that awakens the stirring of twinkling particles of an interest long forgotten. I must see you up close, personal.

May 2 Sherlock Holmes Pub

The others in my group speak. I wait nervously for you. Will she show? She is late.

Disappointment washes away as I see you walking up the stairs. As you approach the words of the others grow to whispers and flutter away on silent breezes. Only your face and voice matters.

What is it that draws me to you? You to me? I must find out.

"Wendy, I presume."

"You must be Frank."

Our first words together.

The others no longer mattered. I only wanted to talk to you. Enchanted by the beauty of those eyes and touched by the gentleness of your soul I talk, we talk. It doesn't matter. I want to get to know you and inside I sense I've always known you.

We continue our conversation downstairs. As we talk the realizations begin to filter through. We have much in common. I don't want to leave, I could have talked to you all night long.

That night I fell asleep, your face floating before me in my dreams, haunting me in its mysteries. I only know I must meet again, any time, any place.

I dream of kissing you, of holding you in my arms as the stars swirl overhead. As the earth cools and the moon rises. While in the distance a hungry wolf cries its anguish.

To hold you in these hands that ache to touch you. Hands that tremble in the fear of what passions would be stirred in that first caress. I sound crazy, obsessed, is this what it is like to fall in love?

I sleep but not well as my soul begins its dance of life and love. Of passion and caring. It is out there playing with the twinkle of stars. My fantasies speak of seeing you again.

May 6

It is agreed. We will meet for supper at your place. I arrive, nervous, I enter. Your face and smile wash away my insecurities. Supper is light, the wine leaves me heady. Your voice trails across the air like sweet magnolias shifting in the breeze. In our conversation you talk of wonderful books. I mention "Bridges of Madison County" We both agree it was fabulous. Your dog is a shih-Tzu. I used to own one too. Strings of common ground begin to weave as we talk. Nothing like this meeting is co-incidence.

After Supper we sit on the coach. Your nearness fuels my passions. Your face stirs my desires. Your eyes. Our stares lock. I begin to fall within the endless pits of your eyes. My eyes melt into the soul mirrored inside. The fingers of my soul begin a dance as they walk along the hillside of your being. So drawn in, so comfortable, so unexpected.

I pull back for a moment, "I am afraid to touch you," I whisper in the trembles of my heart. Am I ready for this? I know if I move to kiss you that I will not stop. I know that the floodgates of my passions and desires will be thrown asunder and racing down the corridors of my heart all will be washed before its path.

Our hands touch. The electricity has already begun to fuel the fires raging inside for release.

Is this too soon? I throw caution to the stars and the celestial winds of heaven.

May 25

I come over. The lights are dim. The music is enchanting. You draw me downstairs. A massage table waits. The touch of your hands, gentle firm and reassuring. This is a gift of touch. After a week of hard work all dissolves to the gentle flow of time unceasing. Only the stroke of your hands. My body is thankful, my soul at peace. A gift of touch, a gift of love and caring. No more beautiful a gift could one bestow on me. My skin will never forget the caress of your hands and the whisper of your lips.

In one of our earlier meetings you bring me a chocolate bar, A Mr. Goodbar. I graciously accept and eat it. It was a test. I passed. We saunter the aisles of the bookstore. Hoping that we could be alone. To shed the ritual of clothing. To enjoy each other as much as our eyes drink in the lust from our souls.

May 27

Nights of beauty and loving are so rare they have to be written about. Just like great wine has to be capped, to savor. Tonight we slip away from the routine of life to catch a sneak preview. The movie about the book that gave us commonality. "The Bridges of Madison County."

So sad is the final scene. Clint standing there in the rain, oblivious to it falling on him. His attention, his focus on one thing only. The sight of his true love. His heart sheds more tears than the rain flowing in the gutters. His eyes beg, implore for her to come join him. He stands silent, unwilling to break his word of oath not to interfere in her world.

She must find that courage, that strength to break the bonds she has set and go after that which she desires the most. Her hands grip the trucks inner door handle of the man she choose as her husband.

The man she cares for, but knows she doesn't love. The deepest, truest love of her life sits waiting just ten feet in front of her. The man that took her to places that she didn't know existed. Too late, the moment, the strength are gone. The self-doubts begin to shoulder their way in again. She'll return to her world not knowing how incredible their love could have been. Should have been.

How sad I think to throw one's beliefs in front of themselves and stop from going after the one that your heart begs, go to. The one that my heart says is the one to grow old with. The one that my heart knows is true.

May 28

The sound of the shower fills our ears. Lights dim, candles flicker. Expectant breaths hang in desire. The silk of soap slides over skin. My tongue licks beads of moisture from your warm flesh. You turn into the exposed core of your desires. Silent moans escape us.

So began our night. A night of pleasures sated, of fantasies aroused. A night of gentleness after. Of hearts held together, the world spins by and we fall asleep in each other's arms.

An earlier night is remembered. I had invited you over. Supper was made. Wine chilled and passions heated. I turn from you in the bedroom. You fall to bended knee. The air kisses my exposed flesh, soon joined by the wetness of your lips.

The next morning awake in each others arms. A slow dance of awakening passion begins. A kiss becomes an exploration of sensuality. The mood is lazy, the love is slow, long and drawn out.

Each second is lost, each minute surrendered. Time has no bearing on a lovers pace. Time measured in moans, and sighs of dark released yearnings.

June 1

You leave for a week long business trip. The next day I call and something in your voice has changed. You tell me you've met someone there and don't want me over after you get back. That we are done. Being true to your feelings and not mine, I comply. As suddenly as it has started, we are finished. The ominous click on the phone confirms this and I listen to the static on the line for long moments before the operator tells me to hang up.

Stunned, my heart crumbles and like Clint in the movie my hand falls from the door handle and I watch you drive away forever.

Later in the movie she sees her necklace around his neck many years later. He never married, he'd found the beauty and soul in the photographs that he yearned for. And like in the movie I am left with the memory of what if, what could have been.

On occasion I drive by the Sherlock Holmes pub and memories I wish I could stop flood in. A tear springs, I see the hand clutching the door from the scene in the movie and wished I'd gone after you.

Only in the end I'm an aging man clutching a Picasso in my mind...

Of you.

One at a Time

"**D**rop it, old man."

Walden O'Grady stared at the two street kids who appeared from the shadows of the alley just off Hastings Street. Scruffles, his Yorkshire terrier, growled. Walden tightened his grip on the leash. "See, I told you Scruff that going for a walk after dark in this Vancouver neighborhood wouldn't be a wise thing."

Snick, snick. Two switchblades glittered in the neon of the streetlights.

"Drop your wallet. Right fucking now!"

The second kid, blond-haired under his dirty bandana, edged forward. "Geriatric old bastard, let me cut him open."

Walden studied the two youths, the shake of their hands, the bloodshot sheen in their eyes, the callous hunger in their words, a haunting familiar site. Carbon copies of Bobby, his grandson, the last time he saw him alive. Scruffles growled louder.

The two youths advanced, Walden stood his ground. The old man knew what was driving the pair. He knew too well their drug-numbed senses were allowing them to only see only one thing, their next fix. Nothing else mattered, certainly not some old gray-haired man and his cute lapdog.

"Stupid old man," the first said, with the devil dancing in macabre delight in the drugged haze of the child's eyes. "I ain't asking again."

The second kid hesitated slightly.

Walden saw something familiar reflected in the eyes of that one. He had seen it before, in the face of his dead grandson, Bobby.

The first punk lunged at Walden. His knife sliced only air as the old man's open fist punched upward. The knife went flying, landing with a clatter somewhere in the darkness. Walden drove his knee into the kid's groin.

"What the fu-" was all the kid managed to get out before the air escaped his lungs. He collapsed to his knees, retching up the contents of his stomach.

"Derek!" The second one yelled and advanced towards Walden, switchblade held out menacingly. "Too bad you had to be a hero, old man."

Walden turned sideways, letting the blond kid stumble by. His elbow slammed into the back of the youth's neck and he crumpled rag doll-like to the ground. The kid's knife skittered along the sidewalk, stopping just before Derek, who was done heaving his guts.

"Now you die, old timer," Derek said as he reached for the knife.

Walden nailed Derek in the back of the neck with his foot. He joined his blond friend in dreamland with concrete pillows.

"Which one, Scruffles?"

Scruffles, who had sat patiently until now, padded over to the blond kid, sniffed and whimpered.

"Yes, I know. I'd have picked him too. He does look like Bobby, doesn't he? I think we can reach him yet. The other is too far gone." Walden picked up the kid and slung him over his shoulder. "Getting too bloody old for this Scruff, too old."

"Untie me, you old bastard," Howard shouted as he came to. His hands were tied behind his back and one foot lashed to each leg of a metal chair. How long had he been tied up? The dull ache from cramped muscles and sunlight streaming in through curtained windows answered his question. His nerves cried for something to fill the scratchy ache crawling through his veins, like ants with electric needles for feet.

Howard looked around. Where the hell was he? The room was small, and old. But all the buildings in this area of Vancouver were old. He could be anywhere. Yet this room appeared more lived in, quaint. Vague memories of being in his grand parents home, when he was very young surfaced. Things were too clean here, not like the scummy drug houses he frequented filled with the smell of urine and feces.

"Good morning. I see you're finally awake."

Last night's events flooded back into his throbbing head as he recognized the old man he tried to rob. "Fuck you."

"Such vile words for someone who should be a little kinder considering the current situation they're in. However, you might as well get the anger out of your system now, as we've lots to do. Care for some breakfast?"

The sizzle of eggs and bacon frying assailed Howard's nose and ears.

"Screw you, I ain't hungry." Howard only wanted to get out of here and satisfy the other hunger burning inside of him, the one that food would do nothing to quench. "What the hell is going on? Are you some kind of sick old pervert?"

"I guess by some peoples' standards you might say that. But really, who gives someone the right to judge what others do as abnormal? Ever think about that?"

Howard shuddered. The old guy's words were a blur. He needed to get some more crack into his system, although at this point any sort of drug would do. Saliva ran down his lips as the hole in his guts continued to grow and burn. "What are you going to do to me? Beat me up, whip me, you some kind of sicko. Going to make me suck your dick or some sick thing like that."

The old guy frowned. "Son, you must lead a brutal lifestyle out there on the streets. No, let's just say I believe in the old ways of doing things. I've a crueler fate planned for you."

"Crueler fate? Shit." Visions of horrors haunted his mind. "Jesus, you're going to rape me, cut me up and stuff me into the freezer, just like that serial killer in the States, aren't yeah?" Howard struggled at his bonds; horrors worse than lack of drugs fired his instincts, yet the corded knots weren't budging. He stopped as the pressure, the hunger, the terrible want pounding in his head, took over. Now, more than ever, he needed a fix. This was becoming too real. "Let me loose or I'll scream, you old bastard."

"Go ahead. There's no one around for miles and the name is Walden. Just in case you were wondering." He walked over to the window and opened the curtains.

Howard focused outside for a moment. Greenery everywhere as brilliant sunshine filled the room. They weren't in Vancouver at all, but in what looked like some sort of cabin in the woods. He shrank back in his chair. His world, his confidence, evaporated like the wind stirring fallen leaves in a gutter. The overwhelming grip of fear, of real helplessness, sunk home. He'd never been in the woods before, let alone seen more than a couple of trees in any one spot and those were usually marked by graffiti. Concrete and steel was home, not the shades of alien greenness waving gently outside on the wind, with tree branches clawing their way at the window, trying to get in and devour him.

He turned away and noticed the dozens of pictures lining the mantel. Kids, many like him, all smiling, all except the faces in two faded black and white prints. Then the driving need from within buckled him over.

"Fuck you, old man," Howard screamed from between gritted teeth as cokes hunger ate at him with merciless teeth. *He was some kind of sick perverted fuck.*

"Well, since your vocabulary is rather limited and my cooking is unappreciated, I think its better that you spend a little time with yourself." Scruffles barked twice as Walden disappeared behind Howard. "Well, except for some. I guess you just got a bigger share of breakfast, old buddy." He said to the dog.

Howard craned his neck to see what the crazy old coot was up to. He heard the creak of a door before he felt himself being dragged backwards.

"Hey, what the-"

"I'll check on you every few hours. Don't want you doing something like choking on your own spit or anything."

"Go to Hell," he started to scream as the old man closed the door.

"Sure you wouldn't like a bite to eat, after all."

"Fuck you." Howard growled.

"First, normally around here you have to say one of two magic words before I get you anything and neither of those are correct. Second, you'll obviously need to dry out before I can have an intelligent conversation with you."

"Eat shit, old man." Howard screamed again as the horror of his situation hit him.

"Close but no winner on that lottery ticket, in case you've forgotten, the two magic words are please and thank you." Walden closed the door and put on some loud classical music. "Ah, a little something soothing to enjoy my breakfast with."

Howard's rage took control and he screamed mercilessly until his voice was hoarse and he had nothing left inside. Bled dry of any emotions, only one thing remained; the cravings. Reaching down into his soul, possessing him, and eating him alive, again and again. Then for the first time in many years, great sobbing tears wracked his body as he cried.

The next few days were a blur. There was a toilet, bed with a fresh pillow and sheets every morning. Walden kept him strapped either to the chair or by a metal leash to his bed. At least until Howard trashed the bed, which Walden then removed.

"If you're not going to look after what I give you then you don't get to have it, rule number three." Howard's response was of his usual four-lettered variety. That night he slept huddled in the corner with only the metal leash chained to the wall, cold around his neck keep him warm. He'd ripped most of his clothes from himself, either because of the puke he'd spewed up on more than one occasion or in the screaming agony he suffered as the drugs began to leave his body. Time, days, became meaningless.

The door opened to his one room cell. So much of his life seemed to have become focused on that door. Walden poked his head around the corner. "Care to try some food now?"

Tears streamed down Howard's face, he'd cried most of the night again as he curled himself into a ball trying to keep warm. The shakes had left him yesterday and now he could feel his body's craving for food. "Yes."

Walden stood there with the tray in his hands, tapping his foot. "Please." He said weakly.

Walden sat a tray down on the floor and pushed it towards him.

Howard stared at the plastic plates. "What is this crap, haven't you got anything like Twinkies or hot dogs and potato chips and coke?"

"This is a healthy meal. Salad, cooked carrots and peas, plain spaghetti, I was going to add some sauce but I didn't think your stomach would take anything spicy. A glass of non-Lactaid milk and for desert, Jell-O. Of course if you don't want it I'll take it away."

"No, please don't. I'll eat it."

"You're looking better. I see the drugs have finally left. I think I can begin to see a real kid inside there." Walden said as he looked down at the boy. Scruffles padded in, gave the boy's arm a lick and sat there quietly whining.

"Let me guess the stupid dog probably feels sorry for me too."

"He might, although what he really wants is your spaghetti. Loves the stuff. Come on Scruffles, let's go."

Howard's weak voice spoke as he and the dog reached the door. "Could I have my bed back, please?"

"Are you going to kick the shit out of this one too?"

"No."

"Sure."

A nearly inaudible "Thank you," broke the stillness.

"If I can find any clothes to fit you, I'll bring you some later." Walden closed the door behind him.

After Walden brought him his bed and some clothes, Howard cried again. He began to realize what Walden was doing was coming from a place of kindness, but it had been a long time since someone had been nice to him and not beat the crap out of him or made him to sexual favors for a fix.

Howard remembered when he'd lost his new running shoes in grade one and the stink of alcohol on his old man's breathe as he beat him. He hit Howard even harder when he started to cry. "Be a man and not a baby, I'm doing this for your own good. It's a tough world out there, pussy's won't last ten minutes," he hit him over and over. That night Howard cried himself to sleep. He never cried after that.

Walden squatted in front of him. "Did the food stay down last night?"

"Yes."

"Okay, time for the next step. Let's go for a drive."

Walden untied Howard's leash, although he retied his hands behind his back and shoved him into his car. Scruffles leaped into the back seat with him.

"Now what the hell is going on here?"

Walden remained stone-faced as he started the car and pulled out onto the road. Howard squinted, unused to the sunlight.

"Are you letting me go?" Silence prevailed. "Obviously not."

As they drove, Walden maintained the silence between them. Howard glanced down and realized even if he got his hands untied the inside passenger door handle had been removed. The only way out was through the old man. "So tell me, who's the two kids in the black and whites?"

"My grandchildren. The only two I had. Lost them both to drugs."

"Then all of those others are ones like me, aren't they?" He knew the answer before he'd even asked.

"Only the ones I could help. There were a few I couldn't reach. But after I let old Scruffles pick them, my odds have increased greatly."

"You picked me to save, because of a dog?" Howard was stunned. Scruffles wagged his tail and barked twice as he ran back and forth on the back seat. "My savior, eight inches high and full of fleas. Great, just great, I'm supposed to feel honored."

"The same smart ass attitude my grandson had, and most of the kids have, before he did himself in. I often wonder where that bravado comes from, I think it's from fear."

"Fear, I ain't afraid of nothing."

"That's just it though. When you live in a continuous that state of fear, you can't see it. You're afraid of everything, Howard. I see it in your eyes: of these woods, of the drugs, of your next fix, of me molesting you, of life itself." Scruffles barked, as if to back up his master. "Most of all, of letting in your true feelings and emotions."

Silence prevailed for a few long moments. Howard swallowed hard, the old man was right. "My old man beat it out of me, usually with a bottle in his hand."

Howard watched the cold stare on Walden's face droop, and for the first time he noticed a glimmer of emotion cross the old man's face. "How long you been doing this?" Howard said, wanting to change the subject.

"Too long. Let's just say I lost my grandkids in the sixties. Free drugs, free love and all that stuff. Only I found out that nothing in life is free and being on a permanent high comes with a high price tag, one that enslaves you and takes away everything that you hold dear and love."

"Yeah, right. What if I like being high? I like escaping from my life. All I got to go home to is a drunk old man who beats his wife and kids because he's pissed at life and takes it out on us. My older sister is fifteen and hooks for a living. Been doing it for a couple of years."

"Christ, you've got it rough all right, kid."

"No shit, Exlax. At least on drugs I can escape."

"So you decided to give yourself a death sentence and gave up on life."

"What, by doing drugs?"

"No, by giving up on yourself. That is a death sentence. Yours is just a slower form of suicide. You're slowly becoming a carbon-ungrateful-hating-life-copy of your dad."

Those words dug hard into his heart. "What! I hate my dad."

"Hate's a strong word. He's just the way he is because of the circumstances in his life as he grew up. Ask him someday and if you say you've got a home, how come you're homeless?"

"I'm not homeless."

"You are in your heart."

"Piss off." But the old man was right. Howard fumed, his dad had told him about all the times his own father came home drunk and beat his wife and him. *So, will I someday become like him? Is that what Howard is saying?*

Silence reigned as they finally arrived at their destination. Howard had no idea where they were, only that they'd been driving for a couple of hours ever deeper into a place he'd never journeyed. There were no street signs, like in the city, only trees that seemed to get thicker, higher and tighter. The only thing he was sure about was that the old man wouldn't harm him. He could have done that long ago, when he was high on the drugs. Howard hesitated, that last sentence, it felt odd somehow to put drugs into a past tense. Scary, but good.

Finally Walden stopped the car and pulled over in front of a thin, well-worn trail that disappeared into the thick brush. Howard swallowed twice as the old man helped him up and untied his hands. There was only this road and miles of unending forest. Obviously no need for bonds. "That's our destination, that dirt trail?"

"No, up there." Walden pointed to a cliff that jutted out of the mountainside above them. Walden pulled a backpack from the trunk and placed Scruffles into one of the pouches. "Four k's, so let's hurry we'll need to get back before dark."

"No problem old man, I'll leave you in the dust." Howard spun around and took off down the trail.

"Okay, hotshot. I'll give ya a couple of minutes head start. Just keep an eye out for bears and as we get near the top, mountain lions."

"Yeah, right, the old fucker is just trying to scare me." Howard slowed down. He spied a good stick and picked it up. "Just in case." He'd never seen a bear or a mountain lion, except for on TV.

A river of sweat drenched his clothes as they stopped for a break about half way up. Howard bent over trying to gasp in enough air into his lungs, while Walden looked like he barely broke a sweat, as he stood there waiting for him. "Okay, so you're in better shape than me."

Scruffles gave a little bark, as if laughing at Howard. "Hey, how come the mongrel gets to hitch a ride?"

"In dog years he's eighty-three, which gives him ten years on me, and anyone that old knows Moses on a first name basis rates a ride in my books."

"You're seventy something? Holy! How'd you get in such shape?"

"The same place I learned to do hand to hand combat, in the army in the Second World War. Where many of my friends died.

Died, to give kids like you the freedom to poison your lives. I do this trail two or three times a week. Okay, let's go."

Walden reached the top first, unslung the backpack and pulled Scruffles from the pouch he was happily snuggled into. The dog scampered around, looking happy to stretch his legs as Howard put his hands on his knees, struggling to keep from throwing up.

Walden walked over to the edge of the cliff.

"Inspiring. I never get tired of being up here. That's a lush, old growth cedar valley below, uncut. Some of them trees were young when Columbus first introduced lung cancer to the Europeans."

"Okay, cool view." Howard gasped. "When do we eat and head back?"

"After some meditation."

"Medi-what?"

"Med-i-ta-tion. Something you probably have never done in your life."

"What kind of crap is this? I've done enough sitting and thinking in that hell you call a cabin."

Walden didn't answer. He'd already composed himself and sat cross-legged, eyes closed. He took in several deep breaths. Scruffles calmly walked over to the old man and plunked himself down, looking like he'd done it a million times before. Howard eyed the backpack and the old man. *He was so close to the edge of the cliff, it would be so easy to-*

"If you're thinking of pushing me over, the car keys are in my pocket and it's over a hundred kilometers to the nearest town in any direction."

"Damn dog," Howard muttered. "He'd probably bark if I got within five feet of the old man, anyway." He strolled over to the edge and sat down beside Walden.

"Take several deep breaths, deep from your diaphragm, like this. Whenever a thought enters your head, push it away. Think of nothing and allow yourself to open up."

"Sounds like you've been watching too much Star Trek." Howard smirked. He was in a good mood. It had been a long time, years ago, before he was hooked on drugs, since he'd been happy. The comment the old man had made earlier entered his head. *What was it? Being homeless in his heart.*

Even though Howard pushed the thought aside, something remained behind, clinging like a hook to the one place he tried to deny existed anymore.

Howard sat down and tried crossing his legs, but couldn't. "He must be double-jointed," he muttered and took a couple of deep breaths. It was harder than he thought to not think, but eventually every time a thought entered, he pushed it away until no more thoughts came. Until only a calm emptiness remained, a peace he'd never felt before and then he began to feel it.

He felt it first coming up from the valley: the chirp of birds, the rustle of leaves, from somewhere below, the sigh of running water, his own measured breath and finally nothing. Only the peace of the forest prevailed and the sound of his own existence as the serenity of the universe settled inside of him. How long he remained like that he had no idea. Time had become a non-issue. It was the most amazing sensation he'd ever felt, a high no drug could ever duplicate. Tears began to stream down his face.

Howard was quiet as he buckled himself into the car; they hadn't said a word on the way down. It just didn't seem right to be talking. Instead he caught himself watching the sun setting and the long shadows cast on the trees, things he hadn't noticed before. There were a dozen questions he wanted to ask Walden. For now, Howard was content to relish the sensations of peace. Afraid if he said anything it'd wreck this feeling of quiet contentment, of finding a place called home. Scruffles licked his hand and for the first time he scratched his head.

In fact he didn't even realize that he drove all the way back to the cabin with no cuffs on and even more surprising was that Walden let him sleep with no chain and the door unlocked to his room. "I think you earned that much trust," Walden remarked as he headed off to bed. For the first time in many years he dreamed. Dreamt of peaceful meadows, of watching billowy clouds roll by, of playing tag with his sister when she was younger and of chasing Scruffles, of all things, in the wildflowers.

The next day they got in the car again, Howard thought they were going to go back on the trail, but they headed off in a different direction. "Where are we going?"

"Taking you home."

He gripped the doors handgrip. "But... what if I don't want to go back? What if I'm not ready?"

"I can't keep you. That's kidnapping. Besides, who is ever ready? All I can do is show you another side of life and trust you'll find your path and your purpose. A life hopefully cleaned off the drugs."

Howard fell silent as they continued driving. Shivers of fear and abandonment sent wildfires racing along his veins, threatening to torch this place he'd discovered inside of him, a place that had just started to blossom from the depths of hell.

"I know you're afraid, and that's okay. I'd be scared shitless myself. Why don't you try closing your eyes and do the meditation thing."

He closed his eyes; only instead of meditating he fell asleep, unable to keep the thoughts from streaming in. His dad with a bottle beating wildflowers into a pulp, while drug-dealers leered from behind dark clouds.

Walden woke him as the car came to a stop. They were at the same place where they had first met. He sat, at first unwilling to leave the security of the car as Walden walked around and opened the door for him.

"Trust me," Walden said to him, "this won't be easy, trust yourself, and you'll know your answers. Listen to that still voice you found on the mountain top."

As Howard got out, Walden pulled a camera from his pocket. "Smile."

Two flashes blinded the kid as he stood on the harsh concrete of the sidewalk.

"Here, take one of these pictures to remind you of our time together. Take this card and fifty bucks. Can get you a bus ride or a decent meal. There's a bunch of phone numbers on the card for places that can help you."

"Is yours in here?"

"No. What I do is not judged legal by many and I never cared to look out from the inside of a jail cell."

"Why do you do it then?"

"I never helped my two grandkids. But do know this, Howard. I pray every night for them and you. Good luck." Walden walked around the car and got inside.

Howard looked down and saw Scruffles staring up at him from his seat in the car, his head cocked as if to say goodbye. Just before Walden closed the door Howard said in sincerity, for the first time in many years. "Thank you."

Howard stared at the picture; he looked so content, happy. He stuffed the items into his pocket as the car drove off and looked around. His neighborhood, yet everything felt strange. No trees here. Dirty and hostile. Foreign, he took a step forward and his foot kicked something lying on the sidewalk. A needle, perhaps one he'd used in the past. The instant desire, old habits of wants, hungers erupted. It'd be so easy to do it, get back in the groove. Wipe out reasoning, life itself. Drown in the self-contained worlds the drugs created, knowing only one thing, how to get the next fix.

"Fuck," he yelled as he crushed the needle beneath his heal. Where was the serenity of the forest, the peace of the mountain when he needed it?

The old man was right. This was a crueler fate. He no longer fitted in, nor did he want to and that was the problem.

He just wanted to go home and crawl under the security of his bed covers. Home? His old man. Oh God, he didn't want to have to deal with his old man. Howard sat down on one of the graffiti scrawled benches and rested. He stared long and hard at the picture of himself. As the odd car cruised by he closed his eyes and tried to do the meditating thing. Staying awake, this time, erasing thoughts and after a while he felt it, the overwhelming calmness of being on the mountain. Howard smiled as he rose and headed home.

Scruffles whimpered softly as Walden drove down the dark streets.

"It,s okay, Scruf. He'll find his way if that's how it's meant to be."

A few blocks later Walden sat waiting for the light to change. In a doorway a drunk had slumped over. He watched two kids on the street corner exchanging packages. Scruffles barked twice.

"Yeah, I think you're right. It's time for another walk."

Scruffles barked again in agreement.

"I know, there's a lot of them out there. It's too bad we can handle only one at a time."

If You Play This Story Backwards, You Won't Get Your Horse Back

The most bizarre experience of my life started as I was travelling late one night to **Sin City**. All of a sudden my car began to vibrate. The lights started to fade out and the wipers quit. In the rain I knew trying to drive this **Highway** was going **To** be **Hell**. Not wanting to drive all the way **Back in Black** I pulled over. The radio began to cut out and I switched from the country station I usually have on to another station that came in clearer. It was a rock station, they were having a AC/DC weekend. After listening to several great tunes I looked up and noticed the **Heat Seeking** it's way out from under the hood of the car.

I carefully popped open the hood to my car and found the source of my problem. The alternator was red hot and not kicking out any **High Voltage**. I knew that if I didn't do anything to lubricate it, the alternator would probably **Shake Me All Night Long** or seize up leaving me stranded.

With a **Flick Of The Switch** I opened my power trunk and searched until I found an old can of engine oil. "**I'll Cover You in Oil**," I said and went to do the **Dirty Deed**. Only the lid to the can was **Done Dirt Cheap**; it was stripped. "**Let There Be a Rock** around here that I can use to bash open this lid," I cursed looking around in the pitch blackness of the night. But, I must add as **Those of us About To** use a **Rock** in the Dark know, this is no easy feat. What I would have given to have a stick of **TNT** to blow up my car right about then. After awhile I gave up. The rock didn't work, it wasn't sharp enough. Searching around I found a discarded bottle that used to contain **Whiskey** and smashed it **On The Rocks**. I used the broken end of the bottle on the can to open it.

It seemed like hours but finally I was done. Before climbing back into my car I decided to take a leak right beside the car. After all I was in the middle of nowhere.

Suddenly my dog, who'd been asleep through this whole ordeal, started going crazy in the back seat. Just as I was about to **Hail Caesar** to settle down, we were flooded by lights coming from high in the sky. Everything went dark as I realized me, Caesar and the car were being sucked up into an alien spaceship. Talk about being **Caught With Your Pants Down**.

When I woke up I was aboard the spaceship and I knew a **Jailbreak** would be impossible as all the aliens had **Big Guns** strapped to their sides.

"Well, we could **Shoot** you **To Thrill** us, but instead of **Firing Our Guns** we'll give you a chance." One of the aliens said. Only they spoke no words, it was like the thought was planted in my head. I knew if they could do that they could probably read my mind and if **That's The Way I Wanna Rock** with these bad boys then I'd have to **Roll** with the flow.

A card table appeared from nowhere. "Ever play **Ballbreaker** poker? It's all the rage out in the Galactic Federation," another said.

"Not a **Whole Lotta**," I told the **Rosie**-faced alien.

"**Are You Ready**? The game consists of three hands. Win two out of three and we'll set you free." The alien sat down across from me. Well, I knew the alien was a female when I dropped a card under the table and as I **Chased The Ace** I dropped, I saw under her skirt that she had no **Big Balls**.

She won the first round easily and I barely won the second. Just when I was beginning to feel confident, she dealt the cards one last time and said, "We'll see **Who Made Who** now and know this." She stared straight into my eyes, "I've never lost a game on fifty-eight different solar systems."

Well, I kept a **Stiff Upper Lip** and thought hard. I still had AC/DC tunes playing in my head and wondered what Angus, Brian, Phil, Cliff or Malcom would have done? Then as I prayed for insight it hit me as **Hard As A Rock**. Bon's immortal words whispered in my head, like an electric ghost from the past, and I knew I had her. Counting the cards played, I knew she had to have **The Jack**. "So you alien **Girls** think you **Got Rhythm**?" I said coolly. "Well **Hell's Bells**, If **Money Talks** and If **You Want** my **Blood**, then I'll walk **The Razor's Edge** and **Sink The Pink** King." I threw down my cards.

She was absolutely **Thunderstruck**. The aliens were **Shot Down In Flames** at losing their first ever poker game and let me go. Not only did AC/DC save my life that night, but I swore off country music forever and changed to listen only to good old rock. As a side note to this story, I boogied all the way into town that night, and still ended up seeing **Bonny**, my **Mistress** in time **For Christmas**.

A Horse Without
A Cause

I've met a few horses (and maybe you have as well) that give you that look of excitement in their eyes, teetering on the brink of insanity. As if the intelligence trapped within that equine body wanted to whisper something profound, something mad. But dared not, scared to break some unholy law of nature.

I'd gone on a three-day backpacking trip behind Harrison Lake in BC. The first two days was great just me, greenery and cedar trees bearing several hundred years of relaxed growth.

But the horse, well, he was different he gave me that unusual glare when I met him chewing on grass on a high plain in the Stein Valley. He had a sleek jet-black coat adorned with dozens of scratches, a modern day stand in for Black Beauty from the TV series. His other outstanding feature, was his rakish mane; with one tousle of hair between his ears that gave him that James Dean look of mischief and trouble. It suited him.

"You'd make better time on four legs than two," he had no qualms about snorting to me. I must have looked as flabbergasted as a Jackal stuck in a pen of lions. A native elder told me later it was sacred First Nations land we were on. The shamans would come here to meditate and find their spirit animals. Had I just found mine?

I sat around my campfire that night, the horse preferred standing, which wasn't a surprise. "You ain't catching me sleeping with cockroaches and worms crawling all around. Probably get one up your backside. Damn two-leggers, strange uncivilized, unsanitary bunch." He made no effort to disguise his glib tongue.

I wolfed down beans and wild Jack Pine mushrooms over the campfire. He munched only fresh grass, different nutrients, same results. After a while I couldn't tell which one of us smelled worse. I think it was the horse. Although I'm thinking there was maybe a few mushrooms of the more out-back-talking-to-little-animals kind in that bunch if you know what I mean.

He told me his name, but I couldn't bray it back in English. I hadn't, at least up to this point in my life, like most of us, bumped into too many talking horses, so I just called him Horse.

Giving a smug toss of his mane, he told me how his ancestors. Pure breed stock that came over with the conquistadors.

Of course, you're probably wondering right about now the same thing as I was when he opened his mouth. Why other horses don't talk.

"You two-leggers think you're the horse's hooves, using your two front legs for things like wiping your rear ends and holding that thing between your legs you call a stallion's pride. Bah, I'd say there's a few nervous female mosquitoes around every time you whip it out." He snorted almost falling over. "Most of us can talk except the penners."

Penners was his expression for horses in captivity.

"Could never figure out your breed. Walk around miserably slow on two hooves and then make slaves out of us to get you around faster. You're a bewildering lot. Most penners can't even think for themselves, ain't got the brains. Slavery, I call it and I'll have none of it.

On the other hand the female penners are soft and smell great. There's something very sexy about a mare with a clean, brushed coat that brings out the stallion in me." He brayed kicking his front legs in the air. "Yup, a night or two with old Horse here and they forget which end of the straw is up."

He'd snorted loudly about some of his adventures. Maybe that's why he chose to talk to me, that old rebel-at-heart thing. I imagined his parents raising their hoofs and saying don't go off talking to the humans; it'll get you into trouble. He didn't care, besides how could I prove it out here miles from anywhere?

Being a writer I always carry a tape recorder, but only got a lot of snorting from him on the tape. Perhaps those mushrooms I ate were really magic ones and this was just a bad delusional dream.

In the end I bade him farewell. He had good sense, for a horse, but be careful the next time a horse looks you that wide-eyed flicker. He might be sizing you up for a few words when there's no one about to prove it.

Making Snow Angels

ellow streaked the unending whiteness. Wind howled from the hollows of its dry throat over the frozen wasteland that had never in millions of years bore any greenery or life.

I shivered as a moan of desiccated air pierced the chill of −30 Celsius. Low in timbre, unsettling, like the brittle creak of bone under a sarcophagus lid.

This was probably one of the stupider things I'd done in my life. "Climb Mt. Everest. The greatest high in life. Are you chicken?" My best friend John said to me.

I finished peeing and with a shiver zipped myself up, feeling my testicles clamp themselves tight against my body for warmth. Right about now, I'd wished I'd learned more humility and less testosterone poisoning in my upbringing. I didn't feel too macho right about now sitting on the side of a mountain with nothing but white and more white for a view.

Frost crunches with a gritty glasslike sound as I walk. The moon, viewed so close from 22,000 feet above sea level, dances behind fleeting clouds. Moving in and out of focus.

My breath billows away in the intense cold. Mere minutes earlier I'd been tucked away, safe in the fragile warmth of our tents. We'd hiked to the second base camp and everyone was exhausted including myself. I listened in the darkness as the voice of winter calling woke me up. Only I realized what I was listening to wasn't the sound of snow rustling over ice nor frost cracking under its own growing weight. I clicked on my battery light and realized Yanqui, my Tibetan guide was wide awake. I knew he heard it too, he'd been up Everest many times. "What is that, Yanqui?"

"Go to sleep. There are things even rich Americans shouldn't know anything about." He spoke in his broken English and closed his eyes. Prayers seeped from his lips, I watched his fingers rubbing a set of Tibetan prayer beads.

"What is that?" I ask again, louder. I wasn't about to take no from some hired guide. My Caucasian inbred cockiness taking control.

He rolled over and closed his eyes. "Lay still and it will pass."

"Yanqui. You'll not sleep until you answer me."

He sighed as he turned his head and opened his eyes. I could see the fear scrambling reason, pitching nightmares into his darkness as freely as candies picked out at the five and dime store by children.

He whispered one word in my direction and sent several utterances of prayers to the heavens. "Yeti."

"What?" Had I heard correct? He rolled back over and pulled the covers tight around himself. I'll get nothing else out of him tonight. I dressed, pulled my camera free and stuffed it inside my vest, thinking if there is such a thing then a picture would be worth a fortune. Maybe even pay for the trip. Or better yet publish a book. Fame, fortune and women, I smiled. I could see it now. The handgun, I brought from the states as a last minute thought, I stuffed into another pocket.

I unzip the tent, ice's breath steals mine away with its frigid caress. "I've got to take a piss. Be right back." Call me a disbeliever, call me stupid.

"Yeti, my ass." I said loud enough for him to here. I know his eyes were on me. Watching, praying to whatever Buddha gods he took stock in. I stepped outside, gasping as the wind's breath of ice catches mine again. Probably just some old trekker's tales meant to scare the foreigners, I laugh to myself.

Right then and there I'd wished I'd hired a Caucasian guide, preferably a yank, but I'd heard the best Sherpas were all from Nepal. He'd been up these slopes several times. I was the one treading in new territory and unknown zones. I'd never stopped at caution before, nor would I now.

I thought about one of my last winter experiences as I whip it out to empty my bladder. Smirking, I decide to carve a snow angel into the ice with my stream on Mt Everest.

I'd worked in an oil rig camp up in the far north of Alaska. I was one of the guards that night when a polar bear broke in and stole one of the sled dogs from the natives that we had to hire in order to run the camp. The bears were always a nuisance and feared little else besides our guns. I was in its zone then, only I didn't realize I was intruder into its home and not the other way around. I chased the bear for miles over the broken landscape of snow and tundra before losing it on a Skidoo. The sight of a seven hundred-pound polar bear eating the sled dog as it ran fascinated me, in a moribund way, and stayed with me for a long time.

As I was returning to camp my skidoo ran out of fuel. In the excitement, I'd forgotten to check the tank. I walked back clutching the rifle nearly a mile in the middle of the night, walking over or around the heaves of ice and snow. It took a couple of hours. I remember clutching the gun tight feeling like I was being watched. When I got back to the camp I'd found out the polar bear had returned ahead of me and taken another of the dogs. I discovered the fresh tracks the next morning. Somewhere in that journey home it had passed within mere feet of me. Probably watched me and judged whether I was worth the effort.

"Pretty good Angel, if I say so myself." I muttered as I finish streaking the snow with my urine and look up. Again that low eerie call of winter's voice, crying over frozen desolation. Only now I see what called and it had nothing to do with wind nor snow. I watched a wall of whiteness separate from whiteness and blink at me.

Something had stood there the whole time, watching me.

I wasn't scared then, with that polar bear. Too stupid to be scared.

I was now. Something to be said for laughing at stories of the unexplained and the unknown. Until you bump up against it and realize that it might, just possibly exist.

I had no idea what a Yeti was supposed to look like, but this thing was huge. Seven, maybe eight feet tall. Shaggy fur hung in dirty white knots. I caught a whiff of something rank as its breath drifted over area in a dense fog. Its hands hung down to its knees. The nose and ears were nearly hidden under the dense fur needed to protect the creatures at these extreme temperatures. The only thing I could really make out were the eyes, staring at me, and as it let out another long unsettling cry, teeth. Long, white teeth. Longer and sharper then were needed to chew roots and vegetables, I stared stunned. Those were carnivore's teeth.

From behind me came echoes of that low whispering cry. The creature turned slightly, listening.

My bladder threatened to unload again and I felt the last of the urine seep down my leg as I realized that new sound was no echo. There was another one nearby. A mate perhaps.

It took another step forward. Wind whistled through its white fur. It was studying me as much as I was studying it.

I could rush back to the safety of my tent. Safety? What good would layers of nylon be against this beast?

I felt for the gun snuggled in my pocket. Security? Disdain colored its eyes. I knew in that moment, that if it chose to, the gun would be useless. A bazooka would have a hard time taking down something that size.

I meant nothing to it. I was merely an annoyance, like a pesky insect. Perhaps simply a meal. Those eyes bore into my soul as moonlight glinted off their dark depths and wind gasped its chilled breath between us.

Incense, in that breeze I smelled pungent incense. Overwhelming my mind, pulling at me.

It wasn't possible, not at these altitudes. The voice of my reason spoke. Reasoning, the world I usually dwelled in, the world of my upbringing. The world I was now leaving as an echo began reverberating up from the valleys below.

OM. Repeated over and over, until the O chilled my blood and the M vibrated into bone marrow. **OM**.

Endless chanting by Tibetan monks. A mere word used to reach nirvana, to talk to God.

Orange clad monks, I turned and found myself in a room full of them. What the hell? I ran my hand over my head. I was as shaven as them. This was crazy, I was one of them. **OM**.

Reaching nirvana to them, madness, crazy madness to me. **OM**.

The relentless sound drove deeper into my soul. Peeling away surface layers, past the veneer of childhood. Past the ways of technology and science. Coring its way down into the depths of my being. I screamed, only nothing came out except: **OM**.

I wanted to scream louder, but didn't, afraid of what would come out. Resistance I knew was futile.

Sparkles of light danced around me. Sprites, fairies, and angels, real angels. Spirits, all cavorting gaily on my sanity's dance floor. Foreign smells, somehow I knew so well, filled the air. Jasmine and Sandalwood. A harp strummed its melodic chords.

I was helpless in the grasp of whatever was happening, whatever wanted into my soul. Connection, was inevitable as the light seeped in pulling back the walls of my knowing like peeling onions and shedding tears.

Layers fell away, shedding the heaviness of my world, enlightening me from their burden until I stood with nothing but the sheer essence of what I was. Into that poured the sun, stars and the dark firmament that held everything in its place. A universe was being poured in until I thought I'd explode. I saw strands of my DNA doubling and doubling again as I expanded to hold it all. Touching, merging and depositing seeds of light everywhere inside of me. Connecting.

I was no longer, what I came here as. My earlier brashness and arrogance melted away in the mixing of awareness and knowing. Change was sometimes a slow evolution, for some. For others, a mind-blowing roller coaster ride. A constant in life never set on an even keel.

My hand touched gunmetal. The hardness of steel shocking me back to the frozen slopes of Mt Everest where I stood. I could I-

Realization sprung its forbidden one-way trap. I couldn't.

To kill it would be to kill myself. Connection, everything was connected, just as I died with each plant crushed underfoot. Reborn with each bud springing anew at the dawn's bursting of life. Awareness was knowledge, I'd been told.

Knowledge was freedom and at the same time; shackles. The greater the freedom, the tighter the binding of the chains. In that moment as I looked over the unending whiteness I was more scared then I'd ever been. Ice crystals stung my hand as it fell away and the gun skittered off the crust of the snow disappearing into the night. I blinked and realized I was alone in the darkness of that mountainside. The yeti and its mate were gone. Their low moaning filling valleys, haunting minds like they did to mine. They'd found other pursuits, other pleasures, and other prey, or perhaps each other. A strange sadness settled into my bones. I'd been wrong, so wrong about so much in my life.

I crawled back into the tent. Yanqui stirred as a blast of frigid ice crystals swept over him. He looked up at me and in that stare

I caught the glow of knowing in his eyes. He knew the journey I'd taken, for I knew he'd taken it himself. I turned and looked back out into the expanse of white and darkness before I zipped up the tent. Under the moon's glow I caught the sight of the piss colored angel staining the snow.

The Myzsterious Mr. Jones

"Can't say I've ever seen that before." Mark counted again tapping his double ended pigtail explorer tool along the row of teeth before asking his assistant to take x-rays as he stared at the man's mouthful of teeth. The other thing that struck him as odd was their size, they were about a third smaller than usual. Which would account for his rather normal sized jaw and not some hulking chimpanzee-sized jaw.

"Am I going to be okay, Doctor?" the patient asked in a lyrical accent Mark didn't recognize, and he'd heard a lot of different regional accents in his many years of being a dentist here in Chilliwack, BC, although he was born in Singapore. He liked living in Canada, rather inexpensive golf green fees compared to other parts of the world. Most days would find Mark on the golf course instead of staring at mouthfuls of rotted teeth and mentioning for the six thousandth time, "a simple two minutes of brushing a day and you wouldn't be here in this chair."

Dr. Mark Huang, pronounced Wong, to his clients and customers but, on occasion, his wife would call him Dr. M. HU-ang, because she knew how much he disliked it. When she full-named him Mark knew he was in the doghouse.

The man, rather simply named A. Jones, put him in mind of a Scandinavian or some such; very pale skin with white-blond hair, and a long lanky frame. But he had eyes that were almost Chinese, with slight epicanthic folds.

His voice didn't match any of that. He wanted to pry but knew not to after all these years of dealing with the public.

"You'll be fine. One molar is badly cracked, hence the intense pain you're feeling, but after I fill it you'll be fine. But I can't say I've ever seen anyone with forty teeth. Even with full set of wisdom teeth, you should only have thirty-six. There is a condition known as Supernumerary and another called Hyperdontia that causes extra teeth to grow, but that is on the inside of the jaw, not behind the normal molars."

Mr. Jones furrowed his long white eyebrows, his eyes shifting back and forth as if he was searching for an answer. "I'm, ah, Norwegian. I've a rare genetic anomaly. I'm told fewer than a thousand people have it."

"Yeah, I guess that makes sense, up in the Arctic you'd need more teeth to chew on walrus, seals, and the occasional reindeer. Well, except at Christmas; the big guy in the sled needs them at that time of the year." Mark laughed, trying to inject some humor into the conversation with the dejected and rather sad-looking man.

He glared darkly at Mark. "Let's get this over with. I have to go home to take my meds in about an hour."

Obviously not the chatty, humorous, types these Scandinavians. Mind you, most Vikings weren't known for their over-developed sense of ha-ha.

More for being the rape-and-pillage kind. Yup, let's get him out of here as quickly as possible. Mark checked his patient over. *No sword; this is a good thing. Probably a bit more civilized these days than his ancestor Eric the Red.* He laughed at himself.

Three fillings, one referral to a gum specialist, and an elder that hadn't brushed his teeth since the Beatles were together finished his day. Several cavities that needed attention there. That one he gave to Mandy his hygienist, to clean up first. *Yup, it's good being the boss some days.* But he remembered the days when he was in training and getting the awful jobs. *Glad those are behind me and all I need worry about now is my golf handicap.*

He sent an email to one of the mentors, Dr. Jason Born who had guided him and often helped when he had a difficult case, asking his opinion on this anomaly.

Two days later he received a reply from Dr. Born. "Nope, never heard of any such case. I searched the bona fide journals, even Googled it. Unheard of. Did you by any chance take x-rays?"

"Matter of fact I did. I'll send them to you."

Odd, Mark thought, *either I've a one-in-a-million human or an alien.* He went on with his work for the rest of the day, putting the rather strange case as far as possible into the back of his mind.

Jason called him the next day. "Are you setting me up with a practical joke, like last year?"

Mark and Jason would often play pranks on each other. Jason had never forgotten the time Mark had broken into his office at college, picking the locked door, and making off with the eighteen-year-old bottle of Glenfiddich he had stashed away. For a while they had traded pranks but now they usually only duked it out on the golf course.

"No, this is for real."

"Oh, and I'm to believe this? Did you look very closely at those x-rays? Forty I might believe, but not forty-four. Nice try, sonny boy." He hung up the phone.

"What?" Mark looked at the man's scans again. He counted. "I don't see." But something caught his eye. He hit 'exploded view' until all he could see was the last molar. And there, just beside it, he saw the small outline of another molar. Faint, but there. He went to the three other fourth Molars. All showed signs of another tooth beginning to grow in. "Well I'll be damned! Must be quite the smart man with that many wisdom teeth."

He asked his secretary to make a follow-up call and see if he could get Mr. Jones back in his office. He had a lot of questions that needed answering.

All she got, every time, was voicemail. "Can I see his file?"

Mark glanced at his file and caught the street address. It wasn't far from his place. *Think I'll take Slinky for a walk up that way tonight and see if he wants to chat further.* Slinky was his six-year-old Dachshund that he took on walks after work.

Mark rang the doorbell to the Jones' residence for the fifth time. Only the porch light was on overhead, the rest of the house was dark. He quietly wandered along the sidewalk to the side and caught a figure moving in the light in the garage. *I guess he's working on his car, motorcycle, or new dragon boat.* He smirked. *Well no signs of a guard dog nor a keep the bleeding eff off my property.*

Mark walked up to the garage, but before he could pound on the side door he caught sight of some kind of bizarre metallic contraption he'd never seen the likes of. *Wild! Yup, looks like a dragon boat. But a dragon boat from Mars.* He knocked on the door; the lights went out. "Mr. Jones, are you in there? Can I chat a moment with you?" He tried the door but it was locked and, as he let go of the handle, the sounds of a large dog echoed from within.

Time to beat a hasty retreat. He picked up Slinky before she became Rover The Attack Dog's next meal and sprinted down the sidewalk. Once on the street he glanced back and caught the rather pale face of Mr. Jones in the frame of the garage window, glaring at him.

Not the warm, come-on-over-for-a-spot-of-tea, type then.

His secretary tried for the next two days to get hold of him, but always the same response; only voicemail. Mark walked by the house three days later. All dark except for the newly-placed, large red sign, with the picture of a rabid Doberman on it, exclaiming 'Guard Dog On Duty. Keep Out.'

Yes, not the chatty invite-you-over-for-a-poker-game-and-beer dude. Mark left it for a few days. But the possibility of someone having eight more teeth than normal drew more and more blanks. He had to go back one more time. Mark waited until it was quite late before taking Slinky for her evening constitutional walk.

Mark strolled down the back alley this time. On his first visit, he'd spotted a cement pad behind the garage. *Although how he got a car into the garage with that large weird metal thing in there I'll never know.*

There was no one around at this time of night in the alley. All the lights were out in the house and in the garage as well. There was no sign in the backyard as he walked quietly up the drive. *I've got to see what that crazy looking contraption is. Because he ain't no Norwegian. Not with that accent and the eye folds.* He'd researched dialects, and if any Scandinavians had epicanthic eye-folds, and drew a blank. Mark loved murder-mysteries. He would quite often call out the name of the killer before Poirot is on his reveal-all scene. Sometimes he knew "whodunnit" after the first twenty minutes. It drove his wife crazy. "You're always right. Now there's no point watching". He had always had a fantasy to be dentist-turned-detective. He'd always liked the sound of "Dr. Mark Wong, D.D.S, P.I.".

The puzzling thing was that there was no fence around the yard. Which meant one of two things; either the dog was never allowed outside, or there was no dog.

Mark pulled a dog whistle out of his pocket and blew into it. *Nothing.*

He'd also brought a small steak, just in case he needed to distract the guard dog, if there was one, and he was wrong, but he was rarely wrong. If his second hunch turned out to be correct it would be Slinky's reward for being out this late. *I think it's a recording of a dog barking.* He'd found a number of such security devices sold on Amazon. He bent over, took a small piece of the steak he'd cut ahead of time, and fed it to Slinky, before sliding another piece under the side garage door and tapping on it. Again nothing.

Mark carefully tried the doorknob. The door was locked. He tapped twice, ready to do a runner as soon as the dog began barking. Only no dog. He gambled and tapped louder. Silence.

Okay, captain, I'm going in, because my money's on the fact that he's not Norwegian, nor does he own a real dog. His wife had told him that his curiosity would get the better part of him one day. *I'd better live up to my reputation then. Besides, life, other than golfing, was the same old boring thing day after day. Researching this man is the most exciting thing I've done in years.* He thought of the corkboard on his office wall, the large pictures of the famous golf courses he'd swung a club at. St. Andrews, the old course, in Scotland, considered the home of golf, and Gleneagles, on the same trip. Also Augusta, where the most sought-after prize in golf was presented; the Green Jacket. Besides those he kept a picture of Mt. Kilimanjaro. Ever since he could remember he wanted to stand on its peak and yell 'FORE!', swatting golf balls into the jungle. *One day,* he thought, *it's at the top of my bucket list.*

Mark pulled a leather pouch from his pocket and looked over Margin trimmer, the Ex-probe and the various Endodontic hand files he'd brought along. He grabbed one and began to pick away at the lock. *What says he's also got a bottle of Glenfiddich hidden in there? Don't let me down now, boys.*

In about ten seconds Mark heard the audible click of the door unlocking. *I've still got the old knack. Jason would be proud of me.*

He'd had the foresight to bring a flashlight that strapped around his forehead, a must-have for detectives, and, clicking it on, he opened the door. As Mark stepped in holding Slinky, a slight, but shrill, alarm sounded. A flash like a thousand light bulbs surged all around him and Mark closed his eyes to protect his retinas from the sudden brightness.

Stunned, Mark fell to his knees onto damp grassy earth. Slinky tumbled from his arms as he clutched at wet grass. "What?"

He opened his eyes. Green grass stared back. Sunlight, the hot kind like in the tropics, beamed down on him. "What the?"

Mark looked up and stared into the face of what, for all intents and purposes, appeared to be living and breathing Stegosaurus chomping on the lush grass. *This I wasn't expecting.* He looked around, blinking several times to get the spots out of his eyes from being nearly blinded. A dozen or more of the Precambrian beasts milled about. Their clubbed-shaped tails swinging to-and-fro in rhythm with their chewing. *Like cows on their cud. What the hell? I've just been teleported or time warped? Okay. So Mr. A. Jones isn't a Norwegian, then, he is an alien and, and...man am I screwed.* He could hear his wife already yelling, "you went to two-hundred-million BC without me? Serves you right for being a curiosity hound."

A screech rent the air above him. *I'm standing in a pack of Stegosaurs and there's Pterodactyls flying overhead. Not what I expected to find in the next-door neighbors' garage. A fifty-six Ford Thunderbird yes, Pterodactyls, no.* He seemed to be on a knoll of a plain. Mark glared all around. No houses, cars, nor anything remotely manmade could be seen. Only herds of various herbivore dinosaurs.

The stench of rotting meat assailed his nostrils. He caught Slinky tearing into the massive pile of dead something just below the rise. He barked at a Stegosaur as it sniffed at him and returned to tearing meat from the corpse. *No, not a wise thing to do Slinky. One swing of those clubs and you're mashed meat.* The stegosaurs ambled away from him. A twenty ton stegosaur could do nothing but amble quickly away with its stumpy legs, fear in its eyes. *I guess they've never heard a dog barking.* He thought a moment, his mind working overtime. *The first mammals mostly won't be around for another ten zillion years.* He walked over and grabbed the leash, hauling the dog in, nearly gagging on the stench. Mark tried to pull the meat from between Slinky's teeth. The dog growled and swallowed quickly. *Who'd have thought dachshunds would love dinosaur?* "I just hope you're not allergic to a million year-old dogfood." He stared closer at the large carcass. Overhead the Pterodactyls cried out, circling closer now that the herbivores had eased away from the rotting meat.

Only this wasn't a stegosaur. Mark walked to the other end of the remains, noticing the two small front appendages. The head badly smashed, one eye missing, of what looked like a carnivore. Either a junior Tyrannosaurus Rex, or a close cousin like an Allosaurus, or one of those Raptor things from the Jurassic Park movies, he surmised. Its jaw had been broken, several teeth, some shattered, lay strewn. Mark picked up one of the more intact teeth, an incisor nearly two inches in length, the edges razor sharp. *I'm thinking something got whacked by trying to make lunch out of one of these Stegosaurs nearby.* Just down the hill he spotted another corpse. He could see long jagged tears in its side, but the club on the tail told the rest of the story. *Yup, they both lost.* Overhead more cries. The flying dinosaurs wouldn't hold off much longer before they came down for lunch, and hopefully it wasn't him or his dog.

A mild buzz and a flash of light drew his attention as the mysterious Mr. Jones came into view. He put the tooth in his pocket. *I was hoping whatever the device was he had rigged up in his garage would notify him and send him my way long before either of us became lunch. Yes, trying to explain that one to the wife wouldn't be easy.*

"What are you doing trespassing in my garage?" Mr. Jones yelled, as one of the Pterodactyls began to circle down. In his hands, a rather sinister-looking firearm the likes of which Mark had never seen before. Mr. Jones aimed skyward and a blue laser tore apart the lowest diving dinosaur. Blood splattered the ground as the others lifted higher, deciding to keep away for the moment.

"What was that you have installed in the garage? It sure isn't anything from Home Depot."

"That device, you so aptly call it, is a Tyrolian Security Lock."

"If I didn't know it before, I do now. You aren't from this world, nor is that laser gun."

He aimed it at Mark and the dog.

"I wouldn't do that if I were you. I've left detailed instructions regarding my whereabouts tonight in case I don't return," he lied quickly.

"You are a smart man." He lowered his device. "That just saved your life. Now we must go, as the Pterodactyls can only be held off for so long. The smell of decomposing meat drives them mad in this heat. But it isn't them that worry me."

The shrill screech of a raptor tore the air. Mark looked back and caught several of the same type of carnivore as the one dead before him racing toward them. The Stegosaurs responded by thumping their tails on the ground and formed a tight circle, with the smallest in the centre. So like the videos he'd seen of Musk Ox in the arctic. The raptors approached at an astonishing speed. Drool slavered their jaws.

"They can smell rotting meat from miles away," Mr. Jones said again, as he touched Mark on the shoulder and, pressing a button on some kind of remote control, they quickly vanished from pre-historic Earth back into the confines of his garage.

Mark let out a deep breath, sweat rolling down his face, just realizing how humid and hot it had been seconds ago. "That's some kind of security system you've got, so Norwegian you are not." He let the squirming dog down. "Nor, I suspect, even human."

The man stared at him, sizing up what to do or say. Slinky ran up to him and nuzzled the alien named Mr. A. Jones.

"Well I'll be! He likes you. Dachshunds don't like many people, very protective."

The man looked at Mark in disbelief and bent down to pet the dog, who licked at his hand. "The first being that has befriended me on this world. He reminds me so much of our driggels back home. I had one, probably dead now, we used to go around the neighbourhood and chase kristiax for a laugh." He sighed deeply. "Home."

Mark looked at him blankly. After being thrown into the very distant past, seeing raptors, pterodactyls and staring into the face of a stegosaurus, there wasn't much that could now surprise him. "Where are you from?"

A tear streamed from the being's eyes as he scratched Slinky's ear. The dog rolled on its side and let him scratch at her belly.

"She's very trusting of you. Either that or she's hoping for more dino treats." Mark laughed.

Jones didn't laugh nor smile. A great sadness seemed to emanate from him. "We are a very affectionate race, and I haven't touched nor hugged anything in the twelve years I've been stuck here. All alone." Tears streamed again down his pale cheeks.

Mark thought a moment. "Would you like to join her and me on our nightly walks?"

He broke into a sob. "I would. Very much. That is the kindest thing anyone on this world has ever said to me."

"So, not the rape-and-pillage type, like you tried to portray by being a Viking."

He smiled and laughed. "No, more like the come-over-here-and-let-me-give-you-a-big-hug type."

"Yeah, doesn't fit the alien-invader-wishing-to-wipeout-all-humanity movie stereotype."

They both laughed.

He went over to the wall and turned the lights on. Scattered everywhere were bits and pieces of equipment.

"Your ship, or parts of it, I presume." Mark gasped at the litter of parts that he knew were *not* from a fifty-six T-Bird.

"Yes. You are very observant, not the normally geeky type of dentist. It never dawned on me that we would have more teeth than Earthlings."

Mr. Jones stared at Mark quietly as he bent down to scratch Slinky's stomach some more. The dog licked at his hand. More tears streamed down his face. "You must keep this in strict confidence.

If I am found out, the authorities will come after me. I just last week managed to send a signal to my home-world of Teradorn. It is the third world circling the star you call Alcyone of the Taurus Constellation."

He stood up. "We are known to your kind as Pliedians. But it will take nearly five of your years for my signal to reach Teradorn. I have resources and funding to live comfortably. They will come to rescue me. But I cannot be found out. I have heard of others of our kind being imprisoned and ruthlessly tested on by your government. I would die first."

Others? Mark thought a moment. "You are safe with me. But I see you could use a friend. We could go for walks together, chat and, who knows, grab a beer or even play a round of golf."

"Golf? That annoying game I've watched on your television? Where the object seems to be to lose a little white ball down a hole?"

Mark laughed at the analogy. "Annoying yes, but it teaches patience and is good exercise. Also known as 'a good walk spoiled.'"

"That would be acceptable."

In the next five years, Mark and Alphonivona, his real name, shared much of each other's spare time together. One day after Mark found out that Mr. Jones' people were finally coming for him he told of his bucket list want. "I have a vision in my head of yelling FORE! from the top of Mt. Kilomanjaro, driving those little white balls into the jungle below. Yes, my wife calls me crazy for it, but I want to do something no golfer has ever done ever before."'

The no-longer-mysterious Mr. Jones replied with, "So you want to go golfing where no golfer has ever gone golfing before. I have an idea."

From a grassy knoll under the sweltering heat in 200,000,000 BC both pulled their clubs out, placed their balls on the tees and yelled FORE! Much to the chagrin of the herd of Stegosaurs before them.

Epilogue

Mark walked into a museum months after Alphonivona left. That had been a very tearful day for both of them. Slinky was sad and forlorn for a long while after. Slinky had grown rather fond of the Mysterious Mr. Jones.

He held the tooth he had retrieved from the grassy knoll and walked around the raptors on display, not sure which one it would belong to. A man walked up to Mark; his tag read "Curator". "May I help you?"

Mark squinted at his tooth and at the dinosaur before him. "A friend gifted this to me," he lied. "He knows I'm an avid dinosaur buff but didn't know which one it came from and, being a dentist, I was most curious as to deduce which one it would have belonged to."

"I think that is most likely a T-rex incisor, although I would suspect an immature one, judging by the size. Adult teeth are typically six inches or so in length," he replied. "May I see that a moment?" He squinted at the tooth, turning it this way and that. "Yes, the striations match more closely to a type of Tyrannosaurus Rex than a Velociraptor, which would have more jagged markings, made as they tear into their prey. Only..." He squinted closer with a small magnifying lens. "...yours is not fossilised and still has bits of meat attached to it."

Thunderbird R.I.P.

"**S**ome bird thing on wheels," the old lady sputtered as Elton Norden stood outside her house. The ad in the paper merely said 'Old Ford For Sale. Hasn't run in years. $200.' 'Sold' was plastered at an angle on the 'For Sale' sign on the lawn behind him. "John loved it, drove it only on weekends. I'll get the key to the garage and meet you out back."

Thunder grumbled overhead. *Storm approaching*, thought Raymond Johnson sitting in the tow truck parked on the street. He'd lived here his whole life and was surprised when he took the call to tow her husband's old car. Was it possible?

Elton walked around the side of the house, down the long driveway amid the smother of dandelions and other weeds. The backyard hadn't seen a lawnmower in ages, probably all year. He avoided the thorny grasp of overgrown rosebushes, their flowers spewing delicate fragrances into the air. Now he could understand her selling up and moving to an old folks home.

He didn't expect much, but every once in a while Elton got surprised. She came shuffling out, slow. It was obvious the old lady couldn't upkeep the place on her own and probably didn't have much time left on this world either. "You and your husband were together long?"

"Married fifty-three years last month." She gave him the keys to the old wooden doors. "Can you open them for me? Can't manage it on my own no more. Wanted him to get new electric doors over the years but he thought it was a waste of money. Guess now he was right."

Elton clicked the lock and slid back the old rusty bolt. "Must feel like part of your soul is missing. Sorry for your loss." He'd read somewhere that two people who really loved each other became intertwined over the years and they become one soul, one heart. One very rarely lived long without the other. Although his wife Milly could keep her soul to herself, the old battleaxe. He wondered why they were still together. Other than cooking, which was for her benefit as much as his, she didn't do much else. Didn't clean the house worth beans, cared only to play Bingo and watch 'As The World Turns.'

Elton clicked on the lights and walked up to the covered vehicle. Overhead thunder rumbled again. It had threatened to unload a summer rain all day but had held off for now. He nearly didn't answer this ad, but with the weather he decided golfing wasn't safe. Who'd be stupid enough to wave metal sticks around in a storm? Being more or less retired, Elton enjoyed buying the odd old clunker and fixing it up, usually helped, or sometimes hindered, by his brother. Gave them something to do. Both had made well buying and selling land over the years and had retired very comfortably. "Trust Elton and Bernie to sing you a better deal than that English Bloke," their TV ads always ended. Made them a fortune.

Trying to avoid sending a cloud of dust into the stale air he slid the old tarp off slowly. Having allergies, he didn't want to break into a sneezing fit. It was obvious the car hadn't been moved in a long time. "Unbelievable."

The sleek lines of the bronzed red 1964 Ford Thunderbird sparkled under the incandescent lights. Chrome glinted as if just polished. He walked around the car, drinking it in. Tires, old fashioned wide-whitewalls of course. He bent closer. Firestones! Originals? Amazingly looked like they'd even still manage a few miles. He glanced at the speedo, though the window. Fifteen hundred and sixteen. "Been wrapped around once?"

The old lady didn't answer, maybe didn't understand the question. She stood there, unable to enter. Probably forbidden territory for her when he was alive. Even now she didn't want to enter the sacred place of his garage, disturbing his memories. "Nothing's been changed since he parked it for the winter, after that first summer."

"But if this is original, then this thing is probably worth ten, twenty grand, or better." He tried the door, expecting stiffness or the hinges to sag but it opened easily, not even a squeak. It clicked closed like it had just come off the assembly line, which it virtually had.

"Lady," he said as he walked around the car and opened the other doors. All smooth, like new. "I can't take this for just $200. It's worth much more."

She shook her head. "I shouldn't tell you this, but he had a bad thing happen to a student. He parked it after graduation, '65 I think, didn't drive it again. So, it's what it says it is. He loved the car, I didn't care much for it, couldn't see barely over the dashboard.

The house is sold and if you don't take it, I'll just have it hauled to the scrap yard. Already called a tow-truck, he's waiting out front. He'll tow it either for you or for me. Everything else including the house is off my hands tomorrow, want this gone too."

"Okay," Elton said signaling the tow-truck driver to pull into the yard. "I'll take it, but I sure feel guilty about it."

Raymond Johnson winched the old red Ford onto the flat-deck. The chrome and red glinted under the far-away crash of lightning. He knew the house had been for sale for awhile and but had no idea that the old car would still be here, he thought the old bastard would have got rid of it long ago.

Head throbbing, old nightmares singing to him anew as Elton jumped into his car and he followed him home.

"Cindy and Tyler. Sit down and be quiet. You know I can't have kids running around in the diner," Sandy Two-Moccasins yelled, looking up from her paper. "The papers say another wave of red tide is sweeping across the North Shore, looks like we can't go clamming again this summer."

"Wouldn't happen if Thunderbird were here, one of his jobs was keeping the waters clean for his people and the salmon." Her uncle Charlie spoke from under his well-worn, button-festooned Montreal Expos Baseball cap.

"Thunderbird, Raven. You keep talking on about these fairytale creatures as if they're real. The red tide is just from the white man polluting our waters and overfishing our fish. Hey, didn't I say to settle down?" she bellowed again.

The two kids continued pushing and tormenting each other, nearly upending a waitress with arms full of plates, as one tore off up the aisle.

"She pushed me."

"He pushed me first."

Charlie frowned, "nothing to do with the white man, he doesn't understand native spirit. It has to do with Thunderbird not being here. His job was to keep the waters clean and pure, keep the salmon safe from the Water-Spirits and the Orcas."

His niece glared back. "Not sure who's more whacked-out, you and your crazy ideas or the white-eyes who think they know better."

Charlie simply smiled back. "You pay the lady and let me talk to these two misbehaving youngsters. They remind me of an old tale about no doing good."

He rounded up the kids roaming in the aisle. "Come outside and let me tell you what happened to a young thunderbird who didn't listen to his parents."

"Whoopee! A story!" They followed happily. Unlike their mother, they both loved the old tales their great uncle told them, especially as they were always accompanied by chocolate treats.

Midday found Elton draining the fuel tank. Fresh fuel has a strong acrid tear to one's nostrils; the fetid waxy aroma of this gas told him it had been in the tank a long time. He'd already primed the carb and drained the oil. He was excited; this was quite the discovery and he wanted the car to fire up for his brother when he arrived later that evening.

He turned the engine over by hand several times with the spark plugs out, putting two squirts of oil in each cylinder, hoping the rings hadn't seized in their bores. He knew the old Holley carb could be quite finicky, with a good chance the floats would stick and flood the engine. He'd cleaned and re-gapped the virtually new looking points.

Elton sprang the bottom half of the back seat up. He'd bought many cars in his days and there was always a story under each one. Treasures like old coins, plastic toys, hair bands, tickets to events, memories of people, of lives lived in cars. Although with such little mileage he didn't really expect to find much under this one.

In the dust and crunch of old vinyl, a plastic card lay.

Elton cringed as he held up the yellowed school ID card. A young native boy's face stared back, vaguely familiar. "St. Mary's Residential School, home of the Thunderbirds. Grade three, Raymond ..."

"... Jones."

He jumped at the sound of someone's voice, highlighted against the light streaming in behind him from the open garage door. The tow-truck driver. What was he doing here? Although, now that he thought about it, he'd seen a tow-truck drive by earlier.

"My card." The rounded, morose face of a native man, about forty years older than the picture he held in his hand, stared, back at him. Devoid of emotion, so unlike the smiling face of the young lad.

"What?"

"You've my ID."

"Raymond?"

"Jones. Yeah, hand it over." Elton blinked. Technically he owned the car and everything in it, but what would the owner of the old card he'd only just found be doing here right now? A coincidence?

"Sure. I'd probably just chuck it out anyway. How'd you know it was here?" *Didn't the old lady say something about an incident regarding the car?*

"Lost it," he said, staring at the yellowed plastic. He closed his eyes, sweat beaded his face and darkness moved inside his eyelids. He watched him shake a little, Elton knew memories were going off like bombshells inside the man.

"It must have been under that seat since ... when?"

"Class of '64."

Elton added two and two together and was just wondering if he should ask the awkward question of how to make four.

"What you pay for it?"

"Two hundred. A steal. I wanted to give her more, but she refused. I think once I fix it up I might give her a cut, don't think the old gal is hurting for money though. I was just about ready to start it up. Care to stick around?" Elton managed to avoid the hated question, but thought that if he stayed, perhaps he'd volunteer the information. He had to admit his curiosity was aroused.

Charlie sat the pair on a bench just outside the restaurant. Amazingly they listened quietly, each munching on half a KitKat as he spoke. "There lived a family of Thunderbirds, once, up on Northern Vancouver Island. They had a very young son who, like you little tykes, didn't behave. He used to transform all the time into a human. He'd tilt his beak back like this." The old man opened his mouth widely trying to stretch his skin back. "And pull back his face and shed his feathers."

"Cool," the boy said.

"Gross." His sister grimaced.

Charlie shivered and shook himself, all over, showing them how the young creature would wash its feathers away and become a little boy. "His parents warned, 'Do that too many times and you could become trapped in a human shell'. Only the boy wouldn't listen, he enjoyed pulling pranks and every time he remained longer and longer as a human.

"Kinda like Raven, the trickster, right Unc?" the boy spoke up.

"Yes, but Raven was born to pull stunts, not Thunderbirds. Their job was to hunt killer whales and ancient Water-Spirits, beings so old no-one remembers their names. If the Orcas got too many they'd eat all the salmon, and the Water-Spirits loved messing up the water. Loved to live in slime and filth. Kinda like your rooms."

The two kids frowned at him, not liking being told off.

"One day the Water-Spirits got together with the killer whales and vowed between them to get rid of the Thunderbirds. 'They are too strong for us, they are fearsome hunters. We grow weary of always searching the skies, looking out for them. If we get rid of the young one, who likes to tease the humans, then his parents will become depressed and return to their own lands.'

So killer whales and Water-Spirits together transformed themselves into children and befriended the young boy, telling him the things they learned from the humans in a place they called school. 'Teachings. We learn much from there. The humans are very smart.'

Hearing the wonderful stories of this place called school he decided to join his new friends, relishing the opportunity to play even more tricks.

Only the Water-Spirits and killer whales placed a spell on him, and he couldn't remember that he was really Thunderbird. The white man took him to the Ministry, where discovering he had no parents, at least none that he could speak of, they declared him a orphan and took him far away to one of the residential schools on the mainland. There he stayed for the whole year before being allowed to return. Only he never did return because his parents were right. Stay in that form too long and you become like them and forget who you are and lose your powers.

'He's trapped in human form forever now', it was whispered among our people.

The Water-Spirits and the Orcas were correct, their plan had worked. His parents were heartbroken and left the island, but not until they had discovered the trick played on their son. So the Salmon people disappeared, rumored to have been taken by the Thunderbirds as a way of torturing the killer whale people and the Water-Spirits.

In grief they transformed themselves into mountains along the coast, dark brooding mountains that always had clouds and thunder gathering around them in sorrow."

"Didn't know he still had this car." Raymond walked around the cold Ford, admiring it, but it was obvious to Elton he was afraid to touch it.

Elton popped the back seat down, feeling tension in the air.

"Get it running yet?"

"Just got to put in the new battery and crank it over."

"Think it'll start?"

"Most likely not, even with the carb primed and everything. There's things like the fuel pump diaphragm that I don't know about. Most likely will crack and the carb's floats could stick, but we'll soon see."

"Some things shouldn't be disturbed," Raymond muttered, pacing back and forth. He reminded Elton of a grave digger uprooting an old coffin, nervously waiting to see what was inside, like Howard Carter opening King Tut's coffin, sure it would release some plague or curse on this world.

"So you knew the Bamfords," Elton enquired amiably as he pulled the old terminals off the battery, trying to alleviate some of the tension in the air. He concentrated more than he needed to on removing the green acidic fluff from where it had grown slowly over the decades. He'd take baking soda to the battery terminals to kill it all off later. First he wanted to see if the old gal would start.

"Could say that. He was one of my teachers." Raymond gritted his teeth, growing paler by the second as Elton pulled out the old battery and hooked up the cables to a new one.

"Probably have to polarize the generator. Most likely lost its charge after all these years." Lost in the thrill of having the ability to bring something this old back to life Elton missed the fire seething under the native man's tortured eyes. "But for now, let's hear this baby run." He slid behind the seat, pumped the gas pedal twice and turned the ignition switch.

Raymond cringed and closed his eyes, the same visions haunting him again. What Elton said about polarizing had stirred something. He reached out his hand, swearing a spark flew from his finger into the old generator.

The engine cranked slowly, dislodging four decades of rust and neglect. On the third revolution one cylinder coughed, catching, then another. Elton pumped the pedal again, "come on baby." The nearly four hundred cubic inches of displacement thundered to life, spewing black and blue smoke.

Elton held the throttle down, keeping her at about two thousand rpm's, coughing in the acrid stench of the black smoke, the oil he injected into the cylinders earlier, dispersing. After about a minute he let go of the throttle. The car purred like the day it came out the showroom. "Nice." He opened the garage door some more allowing the smoke to dissipate. "Don't get that often. She's a good one."

Within a minute of running Elton kicked down the choke on the old Holley carburetor as he snapped the throttle from under the hood. "Like new." He smiled as the engine sat running at an idle. "Hey look at that, she's even charging." He glanced at the dash, excited as a kid in a candy store holding a twenty-dollar bill.

Raymond stood quietly, tearing at his lip as Elton kept an eye on the coolant level. He'd already drained the antifreeze, he'd told him, and put in water. He'd allow that to circulate through before draining it along with any built up rust, then he'd add some new antifreeze. "So that raises the question, why are you here? 'Cause it sure wasn't to retrieve an old ID card, was it?"

Sweat beaded on Raymond's forehead. How could he tell anyone after all this time?

"Looks like the thermostat has opened. Unless it has to do with that card and where you lost it?"

Raymond clenched his fists, balled-up memories unfurling. "He'd take young boys for a spin. We were native. No-one cared what happened to us, what the teachers did. We were nothing, less than dirt. We couldn't call our parents, nor run away and were only allowed to see them twice a year. It was worse for me, I was an orphan."

"His wife did mention he loved his car. Took staff and students for rides. Then something happened and he stopped."

"That something was the day he took Tommy Johnson and me out for a Sunday afternoon drive. His Lord's holy day. Only what he did wasn't sacred, nor remotely holy. More like hell's playthings."

Tears streamed down his face. Elton hadn't seen many men cry. He swallowed deeply, realizing as much as he didn't want to hear it now, the man had to let out the rest of the story. He'd kept it in him too long.

"After he had his way with us, he beat us silly, saying we were evil temptations. That's what we were, children of the devil, he kept telling us as he whipped us." Rage lit up Raymond's face as he screamed in realization for the first time. "Only it was him. He was the devil's possession. We were kids. Helpless kids."

Lightning crashed heavily outside as the storm blew up. Daylight faded against the ferocity of nature crashing down. Thunder hammered the garage. "Wow, big storm coming." Elton moved to close the shaking windows.

"Kids, we were just kids!" Raymond lunged at Elton, screaming, the festering anger of the boy inside tearing away at all the years of counseling.

Elton fell backwards, his head contacting heavily with the cement floor. When he awoke he rubbed the large lump throbbing on the back of his head. Scattered on the empty garage floor was three one-hundred dollar bills. The Thunderbird was gone. "Not quite what I was expecting." He scooped up the money, contemplating calling the cops, but decided he didn't want the car back now anyway, knowing its history. "Poor Raymond's got enough to deal with right now and technically," he stuffed the money in his pocket, "he didn't steal the car."

Raymond checked for breathing and pulse. The man was okay, just out cold. He grabbed his wallet and flung two hundred, then an extra hundred, down beside him. Taking a deep breath he touched the door handle and slid into the seat. It was like touching *him*, those slimy hands, all over him. Memories of the skin didn't lie, his medicine man grandpa once told him. The whites don't understand that. But your body never forgets certain things.

Never, he muttered. Visions floating before his eyes of Tommy getting beat across his bare rear end and trying to escape out the car, managing only to run into the road, pants tangled around his feet tripping him. Someone ran him over, crushing his spirit from him.

He could see it hanging there, his soul, hovering above his body. He never did tell anyone about that. "Why?" Tommy's spirit kept asking, until it slowly dissipated into the wind. "Why."

Raymond eased the car into gear. He closed his eyes, the man's hands all over his body, his slimy touch, kept coming back to him. Like being caressed by the devil's own bony fingers. He was beaten to keep him silent, threatened with worse should he ever speak up. Still, he could never understand how he got away with it, Tommy dead in the road like that. But no-one asked any questions. It all got swept under the carpet. After all, they were just native.

Re-living the horrors, as he had so many times since, Raymond turned the corner and headed for the park on the bluff above town. Mr. Bamford's voice still inside his head, haunting him.

Minutes later he walked to the edge of the cliff overlooking town.

"Yes, do it jump!" A wavering voice told him. "Come on, join me and Tommy. We'll have fun every Sunday, together."

"And that's what will happen to you if you don't listen to your mother. The Water-Spirits have large teeth, bigger than the whale's. Very sharp, and they use the young children to floss between those teeth before swallowing them whole." The old man made a large gulping sound.

They stared up at their great uncle with eyes as big as saucers.

"Are you scaring my kids with native stories again?" Sandy said as she walked up to them. "And feeding them chocolate?"

Charlie winked, "Sometimes the old oral stories my granddad told me when I was their age had more than one purpose." He smiled at the two, now walking quietly with their mother, clenching her hands as they walked to the car.

"When Thunderbird has returned to his people, go to the river and listen to the waters. You will hear the rush of the salmon people returning, like no sound you ever heard before. But be careful. Watch the skies for him. He'll use the lightning snakes that live under his wings to hunt for Water-Spirits or killer whales to devour, or," he whispered "bad boys or girls to snack on." Charlie bit down hard at them and as he did thunder crashed in the background.

The two hung onto their mother's legs screaming. "Now look what you've done! Scared the crap out of them."

Elton watched the thunder and lightning explode in the sky like livewire snakes. "Looks like one helluva storm brewing, better shut her down and get in the house." As the first drops began to fall like fat tears and the wind slapped the trees with its condescending hand Elton retreated to the house, only sorry that his brother would never witness his greatest find.

Raymond jumped in the car, behind him Tommy crying in the back seat. It was here he died all those years ago, trapped in the body of a boy. Currents of fear ran like live wires through him, wriggling inside. Old memories returning. He slammed the throttle to the floor, tires smoked. The car leaped forward. "This has to end now." He tilted his head back, feeling as light as a feather as the car arced through the air.

Charlie read the headline from the Vancouver paper Sandy threw on the back seat. 'Unprecedented Salmon Run entering the Fraser River. Largest since 1915'. "Well I'll be, maybe there's hope in this world yet."

Lightning danced across the sky.

Santa's Wizardly Christmas

I came from salt water and will return there one day, dreaming of past lives as the oceans move in their mysterious ways. Other lives, other worlds away.

Thomas woke up and shook his head; the same nightmare. Again. Of a place he no longer was and never will be. Ever again.

Thomas Andrews, no longer the Great Magix of Magixes of Cramadran, got out of his warm bed. Splattering water on his face, he closed his eyes and lent his tears to the waters of the faucet before him. This house on Earth so cold and so very alone.

A shrill scream and several growls rent the air.

In his head, he saw the young lad from two doors down, Dayne, in trouble. The neighbor's dogs, they'd gotten loose.

Thomas grabbed the five-foot hardened shaft he'd spent many a night carving some years ago. Flinging his front door open he tore down the street as fast as his elderly legs could propel him. *I shouldn't be doing this.*

The two black dogs barking viciously, he knew, were Dobermans, about to attack the child again, one on either side of him. Blood streamed from his pant leg as the lad tried to protect himself.

One dog growled as the old man ran to them, twirling his shaft before him with the agility of a cheerleader, mesmerizing the animal. It lunged towards him, ready to assault the new foe, only Thomas yelled a war cry from his former days and struck the canine three times before it knew what hit it. The dog fell to the ground. Thomas hammered the end of his shaft in the middle of the beast's skull. A crack resounded. The other, wanting to defend its mate, ran towards Thomas with jaws slavering. Thomas stopped and let out a bellow that would have graced most lions of Africa with humility.

The canine stopped, unsure. Thomas bellowed again with the rage of a bull elephant in heat. The animal sensing its master beat a hasty retreat. Thomas slumped to one knee gasping for air. *Man, I gotta remember I'm nearly two hundred years old, not a young nobleman anymore.*

Dayne grabbed at his leg. "He bit me! That was amazing! How did you do that?"

"Just my military training from the days of my upbringing." Thomas inhaled deeply several times. "It takes a lot out me though. I haven't much energy these days."

"That is from no army that I know of. My dad was an ex-marine. You are a wizard and a warrior."

"I do not lie young Dayne of the Smiths."

"How do you know my name?"

"There is much I know about you. For you are correct I am indeed a former wizard. You must not let anyone else know this."

Dayne nodded in agreement. He knew the old man lived alone and kept to himself. *Dad said some people were like that. A harmless recluse he called him.*

The old man smiled as if he could read his mind. "Now let me take you to my house. I can fix your leg, but not here in public view." He gently picked the lad up and carried him home.

"My mom says I shouldn't talk to strangers."

"Your mother is very smart. But I am not a stranger and I saved your life."

Thomas closed the door behind them and deposited the lad on the carpet. "Now let me see your leg. If you go home like this your mother will not let you near me again."

With that he clapped his hands together three times. Sparks flew between them. Dayne watched as he held them to either side of his leg; instantly the pain stopped as sparkles transferred between his palms. The blood ceased flowing, skin began to heal over. "You must never tell anyone I use Reiki on you."

"That isn't Reiki. I saw it on a movie once. The Karate Kid."

"Okay, call it magic. But you must never tell anyone. If you did I would have to leave this town. It has happened to me before."

Dayne nodded in agreement.

"Now, the magic. Watch."

Dayne stared in disbelief as the ripped threads wove themselves into each other and all too soon the pant leg was whole again."

"Wow! How?"

"It is a little of what I once was. But I must go now, my energy is weak. I will need much sleep to recuperate." With that the man rose, staggered to his couch and fell asleep.

Dayne blinked, picked himself up. His leg felt normal, he stared at the man, who'd already slumped into unconsciousness.

He glanced around the room. Little soldiers walked, patrolling the grounds of the lintel over the man's fireplace. As he stared, they walked to the edge, lifted a leg, turned and went back in the other direction.

"Cool."

Dayne opened the front door, "Thank you, mister."

He walked towards home. Already the fat balding man from across the street was yelling into a phone about his dead dog to the police.

Dayne walked up, "I saw it happen. Your dog ran across the street, got hit by a car."

His mother came running up to see what was going on. "My husband told you last year to keep them vicious dogs of yours on stronger leashes." With that the two walked away.

Later, Dayne lay in bed staring into the ceiling. *How do I explain this? What had I just seen? He's either not of this world or a magician. Wow! I've a great wizard living next door to me. Just like the Potters. Cool. So freaking cool.*

Dayne returned the next day to visit the old man, taking some of his mom's homemade cookies.

"You really a wizard?"

Thomas nodded. "Once was. Not now."

"Yeah? What can you do then?"

"Well, small wizardy things."

"Are you kidding me? So do you, like, transform lead into gold, make ugly frogs into princes or blast holes through time and space?"

Sadness streamed over his face. "I wish. That's how I got here. Look, forget I said anything." He walked off, a sad look on his face. "That's what got me here, being cocky and boastful. I thought I was powerful beyond belief. I lived in a large castle near our equator on the seashore. My sworn enemy was Hanus the merciless, also a Grand Magix Inquisitor of Cramadran."

"The what? Sounds like a character from one of the old Saturday morning cartoon shows."

Thomas sat quietly for a moment. "If you keep interrupting me I'll zip your lips shut and turn you into an aardvark or something. Could spend the rest of your life licking up ants. Well, could have. If I still had the power."

"That's an anteater."

"Whatever. Anyways, before I got interrupted, I was going to say I had been on my guard knowing he would try a trick of some sort to best me. Only I didn't have any fail-safes in my washroom. When I sat down on my toilet seat it triggered a dimensional spell and next thing I knew I was here."

"Caught with your pants down." Dayne smiled.

"Literally. Very humiliating as well. Only we don't wear pants back on my world and since in this world magic is very weak, I've no way of finding my home-world or generating the kind of energy I need to open a dimensional portal in order to return."

"You are kidding me, aren't you?"

He looked sadly down. "I wish. I've been here for nearly two hundred years and judging by my slow aging, probably will get nearly three hundred more before I pass away. He knew my aging would be slow on this world and obviously wanted to prolong my torture. Everyone I knew is now deceased and with the billions of realities and dimensional time shifts, there's no way of returning, and even if I did, everyone I knew would be gone."

"Well, that really sucks," he said, trying to cheer him up. "At least you ended up on a planet where the air isn't poisonous and there aren't nothing but dinosaurs running around."

"I guess there's that. Just annoying neighbour kids. Probably better than being chased by hungry T-rex, I suppose, like I was once as a kid."

"Really? So cool."

The little plastic soldiers marching back and forth on the mantle caught his eye again. He walked up and reached out to pick one of them up; it waited, leg raised, and fell to the ground.

"What the ..." He picked up the toy soldier and looked closely at it. No sign of any place to put a battery or a wind up slot. It looked for all the world like a cheap one-piece molded toy. "How do you do this? His legs can't possibly move."

The old man reached over, put it on the mantle and snapped his fingers. The soldier winked at the lad and began to patrol once more. Only this time it lifted its gun and moved it to each shoulder as it did and saluted him. "How, I mean, what the ...?"

The old pendulum clock chimed five times. "Oh! I've gotta go. Would you like to come over tomorrow? Have dinner, meet my parents? We're going to have a Harry Potter movie night."

"A movie of a pot of hairs? Even I know on this world that doesn't grow in clay. Potted or not."

"No I think you'll like it. It's about a world where magicians exist along with humans."

Thomas scratched his chin. "I have no one or nothing in this world. Somehow I believe you are indeed sincere. I shall go with you young Dayne of the Smiths."

"Okay, no wonder you haven't many friends. It is Dayne Smith. We shorten everything here. I can help you fit in better."

"A young escort into the workings of your planet. Agreed."

"Man, you are a strange dude, Thomas. I'm almost beginning to believe your story."

"What is that TV series where at the beginning they say... Oh, yes, 'The Truth Is Out

There.'"

"X-files."

"A lot of truth in those shows. I enjoy them. The female is quite strong and attractive."

"She's a girl. Yuck!"

"You shall change your views on the opposite sex soon, my young man. My betrothed had manes of crimson hair. All curls. I loved running my hand through as I kissed her." He sighed deeply.

After the movies Dayne asked if he could walk him home.

"Sure. But be back in time for bed. Get it?"

"Yes, mom," he said with a groan.

They put on their jackets and slipped into the night. "Mom is so controlling."

"Your mother loves you and is protective, it is what mothers do."

"I can look after myself."

"You think so. I was also a cocky youth. Grew to be a most powerful man. Now look at me. Only a housebound old man too afraid to go into the world."

They walked the four houses down to his place. Thomas snapped his fingers and his front door opened as they strode up the steps. "I thank you, my noble knight of protection."

"You are a most weird man, Thomas of Cramadonut."

"No, of Cramadron. Oh, it's okay I'll never be there again. Just call me Thomas."

"You know with that grey hair you'd make a good Santa Claus in the mall. My dad works there and says they are looking for someone as the last guy just quit."

"A saint of good will and helping others?" He ran his fingers through his hair. "I have been here too long alone. I agree, I shall do your bidding."

"Goody. I'll let Dad know."

"I have begun to like your company, young Dayne of the... Smith, Dayne Smith." He laughed deeply for the first time in many years.

Thomas shut his door, lent his head back and shuddered. It was so hard to be out there in the fresh air. All these years of being shut inside sent shivers of terror through him. *How did I become a scared old man, when I had a kingdom, legions of trained soldiers at my fingers?*

Two weeks later Dayne smiled as Thomas sat on the plush red chair. A line of kids waited to tell Santa their desires and wishes.

Behind the fake beard Thomas smiled at the lad. He'd spent many an afternoon with the old man listening to his tales of his home-world. Of the woman he loved and would never hold again. Of the men he battled and slayed.

Oh man, I've my own Harry P. living next to me. This is the neatest. Only he's so lonely, I hope he can help Heather's mom, Anne.

"That is one of my best friends, Heather, in the lineup. Her mother is alone, the husband left her years ago and she is battling cancer." Thomas stared at the older woman in her mid-forties. Her red hair hung loose over her shoulders. She leaned on a cane trying to stand, but in obvious pain.

The little girl sat crying on his lap when her turn came up. Her only wish was to have her ailing mother healthy. He stared at her, their eyes locked. He saw her pupils widen, as did his. Dayne watched as Thomas gritted his teeth not taking his eyes off her. "Bring her here to me. I shall try to grant you your wish."

"Tell the others to come back later. My time today is done, but I will talk to Heather's mother alone."

The two went behind the paper decoration ice castle. "You cannot help me. I haven't told my daughter that I am dying. I have cancer throughout my body."

"I know, I see its claws eating and digging through you." Her eyes so reminded him of Elouise

"This will be the last Christmas I shall have her."

He stared at the two children joking and playing with each other just outside.

Thomas closed his eyes. "You shall live a longer life than you know. Will you trust me? If this is to work you must believe in what I am about to do."

Anne looked deep into his eyes. "There is someone more saintlier than Santa inside there. I don't know why, but I trust you."

"Good. Now, set aside the cane and stand still."

Thomas clapped his hands together three times. A blue glow issued from between his palms.

"What?"

"Do not ask, just trust the process. I call it a deep form of Reiki. This will hurt briefly. The demon will not take lightly to being pulled from its life giving host." He thrust his hands on either side of her body. Anne cried in pain. Thomas ran his hands over her stomach. "Gotcha."

"Mom?" Heather yelled.

"I'm okay, darling." Anne gasped back.

Very quickly Thomas pulled a hideous serpentine beast with slavering jaws from her. It spit and twisted in his grasp trying to return to the meal it relished. Thomas sneered at the vile beast. "Destroyer of life and goodness I commit thee to the depths of hell."

With that he grabbed it by the throat and twisted hard. A crack resonated and the creature went limp. Thomas flung it to the ground and crushed it with his foot. It exploded into blue mist and vanished.

"MOM! Mom, you okay?" Heather and Dayne ran to them. Anne stood up, flexed her body, smiled and breathed deeply. "It's gone, I mean I'm .... Good. I'm so very good."

She straightened herself and hugged her daughter. She turned to the old man struggling to stay on his feet, his body trembling. The ordeal too much for him.

Anne, without thinking, put her arm around him and pulled him up as he slumped into near unconsciousness. "Help me with him, we must get him home to rest."

"Mom, how is this possible? You can't even lift me?"

"I don't know darling, but we must get Mr. Claus home. He will need to rest after working this miracle."

They all pulled Thomas, struggling to stay conscious, to her car. Once seated she put on his seatbelt. She held his hand. Sparks danced in her eyes. Her hand warm, the connection instant. The knowing of what could be.

The drove silently for a while, then she ventured, "Are you single? I don't even know your name."

"Thomas. And yes."

As they lay Thomas down on his couch, Anne looked around. "You two go outside and play. I think I will stay and look after my man, er savior." She smiled and stroked his forehead. The touch ringing familiarity inside, tissues longing to be together, and dreams of Christmas future.

On the floor of the shopping mall a forgotten cane lay. Unneeded. Victim to the magic of Christmas past.

"Thank you." Anne leaned over and placed a gentle kiss on his forehead, "this is for the Christmas present."

Sylvia's Sun-catchers

White glistens off the ocean's waves crashing to shore like a line of marching angels crying to heaven in thunderous silence. The distant lighthouse blinks its one eye at me as I watch an old man playing with his white dog on the beach. Decaying tang of salt air wafts indoors as I shut the window of Amy Tan's room. Comforted by the eerie presence of all these authors cradling me, I walk down the hall and fade from the ocean's shimmer.

A night in the Nye Beach Hotel in Newport, Oregon. I check in and glance at a cat curled on a chair warming in the sun. "That's Shelley and she's not a mouser," the innkeeper states, "she's a sun-catcher cat. Wherever the sun is, she catches it."

"Much unlike the author," I add. The smell of musty volumes hangs, I'm in a very familiar place. "My friend suggested be careful, this place either comforts you or spits you out."

"Your friend is right. You either love it or hate it here." She smiles.

I hear light sobbing and turn but there is no one there. Mere literary sniffles I assure myself, it is after all an old building. "Do you have Wi-Fi?"

"Phhh. We don't have internet, phones or even TV. Instead, at night, the sound of old bards' footsteps creak in the hall reciting their next novel, and you fall asleep to the lullaby of ocean crashing to the beach. Upstairs, there's games and puzzles to play, along with coffee, tea and mulled wine in the library after ten pm. Will that do?"

I can already taste the sweet tinge of cinnamon and heady musk of cloves going down my throat. "Well as long as I don't have to drink Dickens under the table this is my idea of perfect."

Again, tears on cheeks, shedding somewhere in the backdrop. I sign in.

"I warn you Dickens isn't the worry." She leans closer. "I'd stay away from playing cards with Dr. Seuss. He keeps changing the rules to three eggs and ham and even if you win you don't want to have to eat anything green." She laughs as I grab my bags and head for my room.

I pass Jules Verne as the ocean crashes in the background, hopefully not from his room, and wink at Mrs. Jo Rowling as sparks flutter from wand to wand in hers, The Gryffindor. Should be the name of a hotel not a room in an inn, I mutter. If you haven't figured it out yet, every room is dedicated to an author or a novel and yes I will lie with Amy Tan tonight. Well, okay in her room. As I unpack, my wife is shedding old memories in the Irish pub up the street. She hates travelling and Austen or Hemingway do nothing for her. This was my idea for a holiday.

Gentle cries rent the air calling; I stare down the hallway, no one. I decide to go for a coffee upstairs. On the third floor little ceramic suns dangle in the library, rooms of unfinished puzzles, sofas and a fireplace. Outside seagulls squawk in mock soliloquy, while the heady robust of coffee keeps me company.

From nowhere, she's there. Tear-filled eyes tremble on the face of a dark-haired lady, younger than me but that isn't hard to do these days, as everything seems younger to an aging man.

Smelling of lavender and patchouli perfume, while bitterness oozes from her.

I stare side-to-side, wondering where she came from? "Sorry, didn't mean to disturb you." Eyes of red puffiness radiate her misery. She doesn't answer.

"I was just beginning to wonder if the seagulls were squawking at me. But I see most likely it was you instead."

"At me. Why would you say such a thing?" Eyebrows frown.

"Got your mind off the pain didn't it."

Fire steals through those puffed orifices; I'll bet she wants to rake her nails across my face. As a man I think that always translates to lust. There's nothing quite like a lusty woman, ask Shakespeare or Yeats or a lusty female like Mae West. Or is she simply someone that doesn't back down from confrontation?

"You bastard! Can't you see I'm in pain? Grieving?" Lightning shies from her glare.

I've a live one. "Can't you see I'm here laughing and enjoying my holiday? Good day Lady Whatever-you're-royal-highness-is?" Oh, I think she has a lot of lust inside. Lust is good, makes you want to possess life from death. It drives you to not want to give up.

"Jane!"

"What?" Ah, I've cast rod and I've a biter.

"I'm Jane Stevens. I hate being called lady. My ex used to always say that." She sniffles.

"Whew thank god. For a second I thought you were going to say something like Austen or Eyre. Thinking I'm seeing ghosts and actually talking to one is another wholly different thing." She smiles slightly, on lips that don't need lipstick to look luscious. The round doe-like eyes and high cheekbones; add twenty more pounds she could resemble Raquel Welch. Why did so many women think pencils and coat hangers are attractive these days? "Ah, so you've lost someone then." I sip at the deep earthy aroma of my coffee.

"Isn't that why people cry?"

"No, sometimes they cry over a good movie, their pets dying. Some cry over eating the best chocolate cake they ever ate. I knew a lady, err woman, sorry, that cried with every orgasm she ever had."

"What? You're rude." Brows furrow. Eyes widen. Lips pout. I taste the salty pain of her on my tongue, like the tang of ocean crashing outside.

"No, Tom. Rude was my brother. I grew to truly appreciate rudeness from him. He could say things that would make priests blush and nuns wet their habits."

She blinks, caught off guard, mouth agape like someone loudly interrupted turning pages in a library book not knowing what to say. "I, er I . . . Are you here alone?"

"Well if you call a suitcase, dozens of seagulls, two people on the beach both badly overweight, thin on financial resources and long on lovemaking. A porter who doesn't give a rat's ass about his job and only wants to catch the next Seattle Mariners' game, then I'm alone. Oh, the cat. I forgot about the cat. She chases mice on crutches."

"He what?" The tears are drying away as she grinds the Kleenex in her fingers and another smile threatens to break. She is beginning to think I'm nuts when I already know I am.

"Old friend once said, I've learnt to chase fast whiskey and slow women in my maturity. So you call me alone if you like, but no one is ever truly alone, depends on your perception. It's a big, beautiful world out there. Wait. I think I did forget something."

I pat my pockets, "left it somewhere, now what was that?" I look up frowning.

"Left what?" Jane watches my hands, expecting a cheap magic trick.

"Ah crap! My wife. I must have left her back in the pub." I laugh. Jane tries but fails.

I wait, as she wipes aside her tears on the well-worn Kleenex. "Sorry, it's like being in hell right now."

"Hell passes."

"Feels like forever."

"Yeah, I'll bet they said that at the Alamo."

"You're a weird, off-putting man." She rudely stuffs the Kleenex in her pocket like a heavyweight boxer denied his knockout punch.

"Better than a sad excuse for a happy full of life woman." I grin ear to ear.

Jane eyes fire venom. "I think this conversation has ended." She storms by me.

"I think it has just begun. See you tonight. Mulled wine, fireplace and me. Couldn't get any better."

"Not in a million years." She harrumphs in disgust. But I know she'll be there.

I stare out the third story window, the sun recently set, listening to the dull thunder of surf angels crashing to the beach as the sky darkens. Ocean's coldness licks at me through the single-paned glass as the cinnamon infused spice of the wine tickles the nose, addles my mind and warms my belly.

A sniffle. Jane magically appears again.

"Ah, I see you found the mulled wine they brew every night. Lulls the guests, staff and ghosts to sleep." Well most of the ghosts anyways, I thought.

"Ghosts? You think there's ghosts in here?" She speaks, her face a little lighter, eyes less puffy than this morning, and no tears. Perhaps my tirade helped after all.

"Only good 'uns. Most are probably pondering their next book. Some literary great like Left Me in the Wind, a sequel where he did give a damn and falls in love with the Aunt Jemima housemaid. Or Bridges of Jefferson County, the modern-day version of the story where a travelling camera guy realizes he needs more pixels on his digital camera and falls in love with the blonde at the photo shop, only she's into bondage and leaves him tied up in a hotel room. Or even Frankenstein's Monsterous Inventions, tales of organic experiments gone wildly wrong, in triple XXX of course. Wouldn't want to watch your kids viewing drooling cauliflower cohabitating with lecherous broccoli." I'm on a roll, the wine is starting to kick in.

She laughs with her eyes for the first time, smearing away the tatterings of bitterness clinging to her. The streaks of tears are gone, as well as the lavender and patchouli perfume she had on earlier. Darn, must have washed it away in a shower during the day. No odor, no perfumes, no makeup, this is Jane stripped bare. I envisage what she would look like naked and wet. Well, how I could only wish anyways. She's actually dressed in a simple flowered dress that hangs to the floor, not giving me a hint to the fact that her knees might be knobbled or dimpled. Or if she shaves her lady-garden like so many these days.

"No I was born a little more dexterous than that. Spent most of my life changing spark plugs and oil. They do say mechanics have great hands. As for books and writing I'm more of a reader. I believe for every great book ever written there's got to be someone or several someones to read it. Or at least someone to appreciate great literature and clutch the covers after they've read the last page and say something profound like, 'Damn good book. So good, in fact, if I was stuck out in the woods with no toilet paper and had to do a number two, I'd use my fingers instead of these pages. It's that good.'"

She makes a disgusted face, lets laughter adorn her face like bridal lace and chucks her wine back. "Your wife doesn't mind you talking to other women?"

"Oh, chatting is okay, but if the talk turns to baseball and getting to third base, she gets a mite cranky. No, at my age, cheering a beautiful woman up and making her blossom like a gorgeous flower is about as close I'm going to get to open any of your rose-petals I'm afraid. The younger generation only thinks of sex, sex, and sex. I once got slapped in McDonalds for saying lovely pair of buns to the waitress picking up her burger tray. Nobody appreciates good well-rounded food these days. I tell ya."

She giggles and goes to get another glass of wine. I sip mine in slower quantities, knowing warmed alcohol hits you pretty quick. Jane returns and I decide to stir the pot again. "I think this is more you. Laughing, enjoying life, chatting up older, more mature and debonair men, over wine. But if I can ask, your ex? What happened, he absconds with the nineteen-year-old buxom next-door neighbor from the local Hooters restaurant? Turn raving gay, or offed himself in the garage by leaving the car running?" I was never great at being delicate about death, or splitting up, but how can you really approach the subject with etiquette. "Or maybe he died while walking the dog across the street by a . . ."

"Car crash while texting. Only I found later it was to spend the weekend with a co-worker and, yes, she was buxom. Bastard. I thought he was a good'un, as you said. Kind and honest. I would have borne his children someday. Now thank goodness I didn't bear his last name and kept my maiden name. We met here nearly ten years ago."

"Here? Didn't see that coming." For once she threw me a curveball.

"My girlfriend thought it would be cool to attend a writers' convention held here annually. I was into Chic Lit and thought why not. Always wanted to come back here with him, but we never did and now I'm here on my own. Starting out all over again, I'm afraid."

"So you've come to bury his memory or at least pitch it into the sea and let the surf angels take him away to the sun-catchers."

"Never thought of it like that, but I suppose you're right. How do you know so much?"

"Been around. My skateboard is on its third set of wheels."

"Or a long childhood," she quipped back. "Look, you make me laugh and that's quite a gift to this sad woman that was pretty angry with you earlier." She stops and looks at me strangely. "Surf angels? How funny, never viewed waves in that way."

"Yeah, that's the third glass of hot wine talking, makes you appreciate illusions in a better light. But laughter is good medicine, cheaper than Viagra and consumes fewer calories than frowning. Usually makes for better pictures as well. But it's late and I must check up on my wife Cynthia. She's probably still at the Irish pub telling rude Irish jokes or chasing leprechauns, or ruder Irish men." Jane stares at me, lips plump, eyes wide with desire. I have her and if I were Rhett Butler or Austen's Willoughby or Bridget's Cleaver, I'd reach behind her head, pull her to me, holding her while I kiss those waiting lips. Unfortunately I was born a gentleman.

"But I must bid my adieus and go find my whisky besotted wife."

"Wait! You said a minute ago something about the sun-catchers. Are they those?" She points to the ceramic suns, etched with native designs, dangling in the corner of the library.

"Yes. The little sun-shaped ceramics you see hanging around here. Me, I take them to be the opposite of the dream-catchers of native beliefs. These give you dreams and instill the faith to grow better things in your life. Or at least cheer you up with positive karma. I guess they give a little sunshine out to those that need it. Hey, maybe they also give you fantastic writing thoughts. Like, man, after I leave here I'm going to starve myself living off only Can Hardly Soup for weeks on end and write insanely like a madman."

"Don't you mean canned hearty soup?"

"Nope, soup so good I can hardly stand it."

She laughs again nearly choking on the wine, "I really fell for that one. Thanks Tom for cheering me up." She reaches her hand out, I shake it and she lets it hang on my skin for a second too long. Lingering. Like I said if I was dastardly those lips would be crushed to mine.

"You're welcome. Some of my stuff is kinda hooky, but then so am I. The wine has wiped me out and I'm not much for breakfast, especially Cheerios. I'm a late morning type of guy, kinda like get out of bed around two pm and see what the day drags in. I leave it to others to kick-start it. So good night." I leave her pondering, watching one of the sun-catchers as it begins to twirl when the heating kicks in.

I walk down the stairs before she can reply, turn at the last step and look back. She's vanished again. The ceramic twirls, gleaming back at me, I didn't tell her about the other side of them. Cynthia will probably get jealous knowing I chatted up a 'young bird', as she calls them. Still, Jane was in pain. They say even deep hurt is temporary, while madness is a lifetime sentence. Just ask Van Gogh or Picasso. Only madness doesn't hurt as much, unless of course you're trying to express or find yourself. Then there just isn't enough canvasses to paint or water colors to suffice.

I grab the dog instead and go for a walk along the beach. Mist hangs on the ocean's tendrils like in the movie The Fog and begins to drift thickly inland. I wished I had Adrienne Barbeau to chat up on the beach or walk hand-in-hand with. Instead the dog barks and scatters seagulls. I laugh as the mist curls around us, knowing my hands would sooner be cupping other body parts if I had her in the room.

Jane gets up early in the morning. Looking in the mirror, a smile graces her lips. It was him, he made her laugh last night. She must thank Tom before leaving.

She peruses the gift shop next to the front desk before leaving. "I'm checking out now, but excuse me." She interrupts the porter listening to the last night's Baseball highlights in a small room adjacent to the desk.

"Damn! Mariners lost again." He shuts off the TV in the private room and comes out to attend to Jane, closing the door behind him. "Sorry about that, not supposed to let guests know I've got a TV here. But screw the owners, I don't really care. We're talking important stuff. It's the playoffs." He glares at her. "Was everything alright? Was your stay okay? Which room?"

"Yeah great. The Hemingway room. Say, are there any more of the sun-catchers for sale or have you sold them all? There were a few out here last night. Don't see any for sale this morning."

"What the hell you talking about lady, we've never had any . . . Damn." He stops and looks hard. "Old guy, dark green suit jacket, khaki pants and red wooly socks?"

"Lacks fashion sense but yes, that's Tom. He stayed in the Amy Tan room."

"Ah crap. We keep trying to flush him out, every other year, but he keeps coming back. Like locusts, always hanging around."

"What to you mean, every other year! How long has he been coming here?" Jane sighs deeply as shivers range down her back with his answer.

"Since the forties. I'm told."

"What? That's impossi. . . Him and his wife Cynthia stayed in the Amy Tan Room last night."

"Lady, no one stayed in that room last night."

"No. You're lying." Jane throws down her luggage and storms up the stairs. The door to the room is open and bed neatly made. "How?" Shelley, the cat, meows, lifting her head from the middle of the bed where the sunlight is streaming in and glints off dust specks swirling in the air.

In the hallway no ceramic suns hang. She runs quickly up the stairs to the third-floor library. None hang there either.

Jane weakly staggers back down the stairs. In the dining room a lady is cleaning up the cups and setting more coffee for the morning breakfast. "Do you work here?" The older lady nods back. "Sorry, stupid question time. But have you seen any of the sun-catchers for sale?"

The matronly lady blinks several times. "No, we don't sell such things."

Jane walks numbly away and waits as the porter finishes with another guest at the front desk. She pays quietly as the older lady comes down the stairs and pulls the porter aside. "Did she?"

"Yeah, in the Tan room this time."

The lady glances over at her. "Sorry, you're probably wondering what the hell is going on. I'm the owner here since the eighties and

James here is correct. Legend has it that one of the earliest writers put a sun-catcher up in the library. I've heard people say they've seen them around over the years. I haven't, but then I guess I never needed one. Not bad things, they seem to give people hope and life before they leave. Is the old man Tom with a wife named Cynthia who hangs out at the Irish pub?"

"Yes?"

"Cynthia is his dog's name. He used to go for walks with her out on the beach. I was told he died in the early forties. Sorry. Nice guy everyone says, but then all of them are here. Good day." She walks back up the stairs.

Jane stands stunned. He seemed so real. She touched him, even.

"You okay?" the porter asks, as another guest arrives to check out behind her.

"Yeah." Jane breathes in deeply several times to ground herself, "Chakra breath! Chakra breath!" and looks down counting three to herself. "I'm good." She grabs her luggage and walks out into the morning sun, as it casts its warm blanket over her. "Too bad really, if he kept talking and prying me with more wine, he might have got a homerun out of it. Then I can appreciate a true gentleman." She laughs and stares at the beach one last time.

An old man with his back to her stands studying the lighthouse on the cove next to them. His white dog runs madly about trying to catch the seagulls. She watches the gulls squawking away tormenting the frustrated canine as he tries to desperately catch them. "He'd probably say something silly right now like, old Cynthia, thank God she doesn't have any wings otherwise she'd end up in Japan chasing dragons. Well small ones anyways, before they grew little Bic lighters in their throats. Crap! His humor is rubbing off on me. Oh, I hope this doesn't mean I'm going to cut off one of my ears and begin writing like mad. I actually hate canned soup." She laughs out loud. "See you Tom and thanks for that butt-kicking. You were right, I sure needed it."

The line of surf angels thunders its reply and the old man in the distance lifts his arm waving offhandedly over his shoulder as if over the ocean's drone he heard her.

Overhead the hotel's sign creaks on rusted hinges. The smell of hibiscus and roses from the small garden fills her nostrils. "Looks like it's going to be a beautiful day after all."

Nights I've Lain Awake, Alone In Another's Dreams

"Follow me if you're ready to begin."

"Ready? For what? I don't understand." Yet inside I knew what this being was asking of me, what Tiyah had asked. Only who the hell was Tiyah?

As I walked calmly behind the lithesome being with the flowing robes, I knew I was changing my life, going down a path that would make everything I had learned so far meaningless, yet give me more meaning than I'd ever known. How messed up was that?

He called himself a Hathor, I'd seen pictures of them scrawled on somewhere in Eygpt. Whenever I get there to visit, which I must at some point in this lifetime? He, by the way they didn't give themselves names, guided me through the grounds of the complex. At one point I turned and stared at the imposing structure of a step pyramid a mile or so off in the distance. Jungle surrounded the area, although it had been cleared from the courtyard we walked in. Temple of the Sun complex at Teotihuacan. In one stride we were halfway across the courtyard, in another at the base of the pyramid, and as I put my foot down to climb the first rise we were on top of the three hundred and sixty five steps and overlooking the entire jungle. For all I knew we could have been there sometime in bygone centuries. "How?"

"Time is the constant of the third dimension. Not so with other realms." It spoke inside my mind.

"But it is so bewildering, confusing."

"Only those not used to it, they only see chaos here. Everything the way it is meant to be. Order is a matter of perception."

I shook my head. "Things happening so fast. This is so hard to wrap my brain around." I blinked, gripping the edge of a stone railing, staring down from the dizzying heights of this pyramid. "Is that why you are here? Are you to teach me something about the other dimensions?"

"I am a teacher and your spirit guide from the realms beyond this one. But don't get me wrong, it is not I that called you. It is you that called me."

"Say what? I didn't call you."

"Think again. Did you not summon the one your kind calls a shaman of the wood stick with the fish of many teeth?"

"Charlie?" Memories floated upward from my subconscious depths. "But I met him only after watching an article on TV. He was just there by ..."

"Coincidence?"

It had picked the exact word out of my head. "Hey. Are you reading my thoughts?"

"No. It's just that your thoughts spill out faster than a torrent. It is like a waterfall, shouting so loudly in my mind. You called the shaman, you called Tiyah, and you called me."

"You, I don't know you or any of the others. Tiyah?" I paused. "Egyptian lady at the pyramid and Stonehenge? I met her, yet I've never been there. How do I know these people before I met them? It's not possible? This is madness."

"It is both. Tiyah knows these power centers well. Tiyah was originally a keeper of the crystals, she helped build them."

"Say what? Helped build? But she's young, couldn't be much over —"

"Sixty thousand years young, of your Earth time, nearly half her lifespan. She is a teacher of your places of learning called the Mystery Schools."

"Obviously not human then either. She mentioned the Mystery Schools. Are they related, then, to the pyramids?"

"There is much that you will find out, and much that I cannot tell you. It would wreck the learning and the journey."

"I'm beginning to see that patience is a good thing to have out here."

"You are learning fast. But I've said enough. We are not here to speak of other matters today. My purpose is to teach you of the fourth dimension. We begin by understanding the centers within you."

"Centers?"

"Power centers. The energy that spins inside that keeps you in touch with the rest of the universe. You must become knowledgeable of your internal chakras, as they are called here, before you can walk in the gateways to other worlds."

"How did you know about the gateway thing? Let me guess, I called you, so you must be a teacher of gateway walkers."

"Ah, you are perceptive."

He may have thought I was perceptive, but I didn't have the foggiest idea what was remotely going on here. As my dad once said, I was talking out of my ass. But what the hell, I was here and he didn't seem like he was about to mug me or have his way with me, so let's let this whole messed up experience get rolling.

He started to walk and before I knew it we'd walked down into the heart of the pyramid from a flight of stairs located in the small room on top. Protrusions of shell-like objects glowed as we walked, the energy of our bodies, I assumed, causing them to turn on. Yet, this place was vaguely ...

"I've ... I've been here before," I blurted. The Hathor said nothing as I stared harder at the walls. Some of the blocks were inscribed, or chiseled. I peered closer. "This corridor, these carvings on the walls, this is a classroom."

"Yes it is. And in other lifetimes, you have been here."

"But that's impossible, I've never been here before. I've never seen ..."

I stopped, peering at a certain inscription. The brief vision of myself, chiseling away in a feverish pitch, trying to finish the plaque before ...

"Before what?" The stone figures gazed out with large eyes, so much like the beings on the shaman's totem. "Why was that so important?"

"Something to ponder over another time. You did chose to stand next to the tablet of the Muladhara Chakra. The first chakra. This is where we begin the journey."

I stared up at the tablet above the one that had triggered the flashback and ran my fingers over the carved edges. "I know these." Four lotus petals touching each other and within a square. Each petal had symbols, sacred symbols, inscribed within. Soft vibrations began in the background as I ran my fingers over them, returning to the first and beginning again. Words, some sort of chant, wanted to echo from my lips.

"The touching and repeating of these are designed to begin the necessary vibrations to open the root chakra."

"I know this." Sounds, like the calls of whales, echoed in the background. A xylophone-like instrument chimed, playing one long note after another.

I turned and the being known as the Hathor was gone, its voice drifting like mist on water. Still I ran my fingers over the stone over and over again.

"You carved those also." From the darkness came one final echo. "More than any, this chakra is of earth."

"Of grounding and survival," I muttered. The root that anchored all others. Without this one as a solid foundation, like the basement to a mansion, nothing could withstand, nor stay together. The fragrance of cedar filled the air as I ran my fingers over this tablet, which began to glow a dull red. All the other chakras flowed through this one. Without even knowing where the image sprang from, I visualized the elephant god Airavata with its seven trunks. More than any of the others this one was dense, the cement that anchored.

Uneasiness grew within, compelling me to utter a word. The one inscribed within each of the petals before me.

"Lam," I whispered. Women's voices began echoing and chanting all around me. Some spoke in tongues, ones I'd known once in the ancient languages of Lemuria, Atlantis and Mu.

"Lam," I uttered louder.

Wind chimes clinked in the breeze. Flutes breathed in sequences and I turned, knowing I was no longer here.

I stumbled, falling head over heels, over the furs I was dressed in. A crude wooden spear fell from my grasp. My heart raced, weariness seeped into every muscle screaming for rest. I was being chased and had been running all day. Memory seeped into my head. I was a caveman, dodging from the hunter. My family and others had been killed by a pack of saber-tooths. Some, like me, had escaped into the forest. Separated from the tribe, we were now easy pickings, a gruesome dinner. One of the large cats was tracking me. Intent on finishing me off, or just playing with me, I didn't know which. The thud of feline feet that haunted my every breath drove rational thought away, leaving only the slobbering fear that death stalked on four razor sharp paws.

I picked up my spear and looked around. I'd run into a canyon and before me a sheer stone wall stood. Behind me? The thump of paws as my hunter approached.

This was it. No escape. Shaking, I pressed myself against the cold stone, more to keep myself standing as sheer exhaustion sucked at me with its vampiric appetite. Seven-inch teeth glinted bone-white, coursing with the blood of my fellow tribesmen, as the big cat parted the bushes. I gripped the spear in rage, but no malice, no hate, stared at me from its eyes. It was merely doing what it must, what it was designed to do. To hunt and kill those weaker than itself. Just as every carnivore had been put here to do, it was about to cull the herd. Bring balance to the equation they called life. More importantly it was ready to eat.

I shook, my spear suddenly feeling flimsy. This great feline would take on the huge cave bears without fear. No survival here. I was about to die. Still, it was nature to try, to not give up. Struggle to survive. The saber-tooth charged and I yelled, my last instinct, screaming revenge as I raised the spear.

The big cat swatted the weapon aside in mid-leap, breaking it and then me like a twig, piercing my windpipe with its fangs. Blood, mine, splattered the rock. At the crunch of jaws I gurgled, staring at death through the killer's eyes. Nerves severed, jugular vein gushing my life fluid onto the soil, onto itself and myself, as it dragged my limp body off to dine in safety.

I picked up the spear-shaped stick that had been a piece of furniture until the bombs began falling, and wedged it into the door. The thud of explosions, rocket-fire, bombs falling, reverberated in the background. The Germans had surprised my people by attacking and now they were before the very gates of Leningrad.

As I turned from the doorway a mirror caught me in its sight. Sixteen and toting a gun, a soldier, raised to be a killer. How glorious the communist teachings were, an honor to fight for the Motherland. The Motherland, my mother, I only wanted to know if my mother was still alive. If she could hold me, like she did when I was six. Summers of lazy days on the farm, playing with my sister, being tucked in at night. Gone, all gone. I clenched the only comfort I knew now, the cold caress of my gun's muzzle.

Only now the snow was falling, or was it soot and debris, and the thump of boots in the hallway. Real soldiers bearing sub-machine guns and the gray uniforms of the swastika, the former Buddhist symbol of the wheel of life stolen. I knew this, not from this lifetime, but from another. Now the war engine of destruction, of Aryan invincibility. The wheel that crushed all who opposed. No, I wouldn't give up. I cocked my single-shot rifle and waited. Boots, scurrying like rats, in the hallway. Gunshots, screams, gurgled gasps. Sweat poured from my brow.

A kick sent splinters of shattered spear flying. Bullets ripped. I aimed as the door exploded inward, wishing I were shooting groundhogs on our farm on peaceful days in summers past. My bullet punches square between the eyes of the cold-hearted soldier's stare. I cheer inside at ending the life of another human being and reloaded the cumbersome rifle as the intruder fell in a heap.

Another appeared behind him, hot death stinging a rain of acrid gunpowder. Soon winter would be here, freezing everything, even them. But not soon enough, not tonight, as a dozen points of lead mushroomed inside, scattering my flesh like confetti into the floral nursery wallpaper behind me. I fell back, shattering a crib that could have been mine, in a mist of red.

Mist swirled around. It would hide my escape with the dawn. My dark skin blended into the murky waters of the Derwent River. The dreamtime of my people was ending, now to be renamed. Tasmania, land of new hope. But only for the white-skinned. Not for my kind, even though we'd dwelt here for tens of thousands of years.

The two Amerjigs stood on the bank of the Derwent. Caverns just behind them were adorned with pictures depicting all my ancestry, overlain by others and others still, this I knew. The trials, the important times, the good things. After I died, these would become eroding pigments, to be stared at, wondered and studied by ignorants that know nothing of us.

"Come on Jim, I've skinned these two abo's. I reckon we'll drink good for the next couple weeks."

"Shh. Don't you smell that stink? There's one we missed nearby, in the water I think." Jim stared into the sky at the sun beginning to rise behind the mountains.

I cursed. That one had good hunter sense, like mine. He knew what was there when nothing could be seen, a common trait of my people.

"Another? Hey, maybe we'd have enough then for a spot of fun with one of the sheilas back in Hobart. What d'ya say?"

"I say he's watching us. Crazy abo's, they can talk to each other in their heads, I tell you."

"You're nuts."

"Can't say if that's the truth, but I tortured one once for days and he told me so, before I cut out his tongue." Jim rubbed the dried appendage dangling from the rawhide around his neck.

"Here we go again, mate. You're as bananas as the savages. Thinking its tongue gives you special powers like some ... what d'ya call it? In the East Indies. Oh yeah, voodoo charm."

"You forget, I lived up in the Vancouver Island colony for a while. Their shamans would battle certain animals and wear their tongues around their necks so as to control their powers. Don't forget how many it's led us to. We took more skins than all the other bounty hunters combined, and right now it's telling me there's one more alive in this river." Jim held the talisman in one hand and stared out into the water. "Yes sir, right now he's fearing us, hating us. Dangerous as a cornered croc."

"You scare me with that hoky-poky stuff. Stick to the good book, that's what I've been raised on. The good Lord will never steer you wrong. Besides, what's so dangerous about them? We got lead on our side, they got spears and those crazy throwing sticks."

"Boomerangs they're called, and they can take down a 'roo from 'alf a mile."

I rose from my sinkhole, knowing the mist would dissipate and leave me visible from the riverbank. I cranked back my arm and pitched the boomerang. That dumb mutant would never defile another body of my people. Kill only for food and never for revenge. But the other one, the smart one, was right. There were no others left on this dreamtime.

Jim dove as soon as he heard the swish.

"What's that?" Bill turned, his last words faded away to the boomerang's hiss, ceasing completely when its edge clove into his skull. He pitched forward, falling into the murdered corpses.

Shots rang out. Pain ripped into my body as I ducked back under the water. Blood gushed from my throwing arm, staining the water with red. The arm was useless now. My people always said revenge never paid. Maybe so but for once if I was the last of my kind I would take a soul with me.

"Bloody hell. Knew there was at least one savage left in this province. But probably no more, I think." Jim approached the river's edge. "Yup. I think you're the very last one, aren't you?"

He was right, dreamtime was over and now there was no one to sing me away on my journey back home. Alone. I smiled. At least there would be one white-skinned one to ease my passage.

I sank to the bottom and crossed my legs, found a couple of rocks and propped them over me as best as I could. I waited, water humming in my ears. I smiled. Something to sing me home, until the pressure got too great to hold my breath. No, this one would not get me. I would survive to journey to the real world.

"Damn crazy savage." Jim stared down into the sinkhole, watching the stream of red rising as the sun crested the hills. "He's down there and I can't get to him. Knew I shoulda took up swimming in Sunday school."

The large burst of bubbles surfaced; the body did not. "Probably lashed himself to a rock or something. Crazy bugger." Jim ripped the necklace from his throat and threw it into the water. "Don't need you now, mate. There's none of them left." He studied the hides. "Well, since there's double the money for me, might as well get myself a good slow Sheila and some fast whiskey."

The tongue talisman settled into my lap as the last gasp of air left me and I rose with it from my body, releasing my hand from the tile in the pyramid, and turned over in my sleep.

I awoke sweat pouring from me. I see from above my body, my wife crying beside me. I remember the accident. My head colliding with the rock. My arms, my body doesn't move. Behind me something dark, prowls. I retreat to my shell.

We stand on a mountain escarpment overlooking a high plain. Below us dozens of old stone buildings. Greenery falling away on steep, once terraced, slopes into mist rising. Machu Picchu?

Perhaps, I wasn't sure as a single step covered hundreds of feet in dizzying fashion. We tread on cobblestones, echoing of age and antiquity, as cold to the touch as the still mountain slopes shivering up to the deep blue sky all around us. Air, nearly devoid of oxygen, pulled at my breath. Entering the sacred city, beams of light danced between the streets and the buildings.

Seamless walls of precision fit gargantuan blocks hide not even a cranny to slip paper money between them. I study the blocks as we walk by, cut with so many sides I lose count, and gasp for breath. My body hungers for more than the scant traces of oxygen here. How? Could they build in these dizzying heights? I surmise. How?

Only this town isn't deserted. What I thought at first were beams of light dancing I realized now were spirit-like beings with gossamer wings. When they land invisible bodies reappear. Expanding wings caught the light and glowing like firebugs, they take off and flit about again.

Overhead three suns glow, each one dim, but together they cast about the same brilliance as ours. So full of joy, the odd sprite, for lack of another term, smiling always smiling, would glance our way.

"Content lot, aren't they?" I finally spoke.

"Very. Your legends of pixies and fairies sprang from these folks. They still visit, but not as often as they used to."

"Why not?"

"That will be up to you to repair."

"Repair?"

"No more said, we go to the lowlands, now."

"We're not on Earth are we?" I asked as we walked.

"No. Your sun would be rising into view around midnight." As it spoke the sky darkened for a moment. I gasped and looked up into the sea of stars. There were millions, but they looked so unfamiliar.

"Where?" I asked. "All I see are st…"

"In that grouping of seven stars, which the dwellers of this world call Gaymede, the seeder." It pointed over my shoulder.

As I gaped the night sky ebbed and we returned to daylight. I continued to walk. I stumbled along in shock.

Another step, we left the town and began down a pathway dug by the tread of feet over millennia. I stopped, listening to the echoes of water drops formed from moisture-saturated air dripping from branch to branch. I caught a glimpse of something flashing and noticed another smaller trail. "Wait."

The Hathor smiled, "go ahead, we have time."

"I guess we do, in the fourth dimension." Time was irrelevant here. I laughed, the bastard, he knew if I got it right last time I'd have sensed this side trail. Otherwise we'd be at it again.

I stepped down the trail, through a ring of trees and stood in a clearing. It was well kept. In the center was a fair sized area of white sand carefully raked and polished, like a Japanese Zen garden. A single monolith stood in the center, concentric raked circles radiated from it.

I walked around the outside perimeter of the garden, realizing that something was scrawled into the surface of the rock. Writing, it looked like writing, only it was so hard to see, as water was slowly dripping down its sides and disappearing into the ground.

The Hathor stood quietly. I asked it, with my mind, "is that writing?"

It didn't answer my question, instead merely said "trust, you simply must trust."

I looked round, there were no spirit beings to ask and I knew he was of no use. I took off my sandals and stepped into the sand, which was surprisingly warm. I could hear the trickles of water now and as I stepped closer the sound of water increased until it sound like a stream. I took another step forward, past a ring of carefully tended sand, and the stream grew in strength, water flowing. I took another step. The stream wound over rocks, sounding stronger, yet still only bare trickles fell down the surface of the boulder.

As I stepped closer, water cascaded into my ears until it became a wall of white noise. A mighty river pounding down a steep mountain valley.

I turned and stared behind me, no footsteps were to be seen, as if the water in waves of vibrations corrected my passage. Either that or I simply couldn't see the water flowing all around me. Water flows in the path of least resistance, growing until it gains enough strength to cut mighty canyons. I turned back to the monolithic rock and noticed for the first time six lotus petals inscribed in a pattern around a circle.

"This is the garden of Svadhisthana, the second chakra. Water rules here." The Hathor spoke over the thunder of cascading waters. "Liquidity. Energy is never static, like the ocean it ebbs and flows."

I squinted closer, sacred symbols were written on each petal. Two figures sat cross-legged, one a man and the other a woman. Each held objects and as I stared I could feel the heat from inside my lower abdomen. Hunger and passion.

"It is also the sexual chakra, all desire erupts from here. Yin and Yang, each part of the whole, each incomplete without the other. The petals surround the moon. The moon instills emotions on all who gaze at it. The moon pulls on the waters, tides form and energy releases. The circle also represents the womb, this chakra is very feminine as the seed of life springs from passion. All desire, all movement, begins here."

Was it me? Heat, intense, burning arousal erupted as the Hathor talked. His words blurring away, passion erupting on sensuous whispers. "Hear the urge, tremble in the want." Embarrassed, I turned away, trying to hide my hardness.

"Many get lost on the duality of desire. Like everything else it bares a positive and a negative aspect. Balance for some is hard as the edge is thin."

I reached forward, hoping to ground myself against the coolness of the rock, wanting to release this damning throb building inside. Instead my hand encountered another hand. Soft, warm, it was the woman of the drawing and I was he. She smiled, sparkles of crystal dust flew from her eyelashes. She smiled again and joy sprang as she touched my chest. Naked, I was naked. As I looked over, I realized she was too. The electrifying heat of her hands caused moans to erupt from my throat. Another caress, but of want, not closeness.

I closed my eyes. I wanted her, but I wanted more than just base sex. What I really wanted was the deep connection I felt when making love with Beth.

Beth? My wife? Why isn't she here with me?

Her lips drew against mine yet those lips felt so familiar and I opened my eyes and those of my Beth stared back at me. We kissed deep from the soul, like so many times before. I washed away into the realm of lovers. Her breasts, fire-points of erotic energy, swayed back and forth. Gasps, moans rang out, more hers, then ours. I reached down, wetness flowed from her. A sweet river of desire. She gasped in her need and licked at my ears, my throat.

I fell backwards into the dew of a soft forest grass, wildflowers speared scents into the air, showering us. Aromas of delicate sensuality, chamomile, honeysuckle and jasmine flooded the air. Beth slid on top of me, inserted me into her wetness. I shuddered, every inch of my hardness searing against the heat of her, while her skin, cool to my touch, sent shivers of electricity across me. Fire and ice, heat and water. Passions embracing each other, racing into desire's maddening headlong lust.

We made love again and again, until, totally spent, I lay in complete contentment. Where I could lay forever. She rose and

I realized I was in a room surrounded by curtains of silk. All around many other couples were moaning, making love. Lost in their passions, consumed by desire.

'Lost in passion's embrace.' Isn't that what the Hathor said? I rose limp, weak, she brought two glasses and offered one to me. It contained heady red wine. I wanted water, something to slake the thirst, not sap my will even further and stir what I didn't have left inside to stir, to pull me under.

I reached for the other glass. It contained a clear liquid, which I knew was water, sobering, revitalizing water. "Come, instead, to me, my love."

Beth lay on a bed of silk, rose petals spread all around. Smelling of earth and rain forest. "No, I can't."

I'd already stayed too long, any more and I'd become slave to my own lust. Other women slid past the veils of silk and entered the room. Tall voluptuous blondes, petite oriental ladies, luscious dark beauties.

"Let us give you pleasure, massage you." They held bowls of oils, smelling of patchouli and ylang ylang.

"No, I can't."

Two began to kiss each other. Shedding their clothes, hands fondling breasts with erect nipples, stroking each other between their legs. "Then stay, watch us instead."

One of my strongest fantasies, most males. "I … I …"

Arousal began again. Two other women joined them and kneeled. They began to pleasure them with their tongues between the curls of softness.

Beth reached for the cup of water and offered me the wine. "Stay just a little longer."

The two women threw their heads back and moaned as they pulled closer the two on their knees. Moans of other lovers ghosted through the room, calling to me to join them or watch. I had to go, to stay and drink the wine would be too much. Lost in sybaritic pleasures.

"Yes, stay and let me do the same to you, as she does to me." The tall blonde pulled at the back of the head of the dark skinned girl licking at her. Sights of pink tongue darting through the dark triangle, shuddering as the throes of orgasm ran through her body.

"No, I can't."

I grabbed the glass of water, drank deeply and looked up. No longer in the room.

Green, rampant and riotous abounds everywhere, filling me with humidity and freshness. Jungle, this could be South America, only when I look up, two moons glow overhead. Something glistening with a gold tint catches my attention. A building, in the distance, a temple topped in gold.

After about an hour of walking the jungle parts and before me is a courtyard with four glistening pyramids. There, sitting before them, is a bizarre creature carved of stone. I stare up between the two paws up at the leonine face. Just like the sphinx at Giza.

In a few scant steps we were inside the Sphinx and walking down a dark corridor with hundreds of paintings.

I wanted to ask if this place was like a school when the being said, "This place has been called many things, but a school would be the term most appropriate for you."

Before it could respond my thoughts betrayed me. "A school for what?"

"The mysteries."

"The mysteries of what?"

"The mysteries that are unfolding."

There was so much I wanted to ask, yet this wasn't the time. Now was the time to begin and do. "I don't understand. You are so vague."

"Confusion is a good state to be in, like chaos."

"All you're giving me is riddles and psycho-babble."

"I can only say this. When you go through any transformation there is always chaos, disorganization. As one thing transmutes to another the fear comes alive, awakens. Why do you think people become trapped in unhappy lives?"

"Don't know. They can't like it, yet they stay."

"The fear of the unknown, the chaos of not knowing, stops them advancing from the lesson before them. They do not have the necessary ingredient to want to continue their development as beings of this universe."

"And what is the necessary ingredient? Is it to learn and advance?"

"This is for you to discover, as you begin the journey. Enter the picture when you are ready."

"Enter? It's only a picture." I turned and the being was gone. I was alone in the vast hallway. Hundreds of pictures lined the walls, each depicting some sort of happening or scenario. I walked slowly until one picture in particular caught my eye, a woman crying at her kitchen table. Dishes were piled in disarray behind her; before her on the table sat a bottle of liquor nearly empty and another strewn on the floor. I lurched as the stale must of old beer flooded my senses. Her despair, her hauntedness. Such sadness seeped out at me.

Pigments danced before me. Painted in such a fashion, they drew me in, Mesmerizing, drawing me.

She was so utterly miserable.

I reached forward. How could the artist do that? With what medium ... oils? I swore the paint was still fresh. Touching her eyes I stared at the bottle before me. Stale alcohol wafted upwards in stenches of grapes and rye, fruits and grains of the life-giving earth, perverted into pleasures to numb the mind and corrupt the pureness of the soul, steal at my will.

My guts burned, not enough food inside. My head throbbed as if I was hung-over. Was hungover? I suppressed the brief urge to puke, only because there was nothing inside me to release. Light from the outside world hurt my eyes. Eyes so heavy and swollen. Water, I needed water.

Is that what this picture did? Made you feel everything the subject felt?

I rose, my body moving yet it was not me that seemed to move. As if I was in a dream state or one of ...

Lighter, I felt lighter. I turned around and instead of the hallway saw the rest of the kitchen. I clutched at the countertop, heard the click of nails on formica and stared at my hands.

Fingernails, on long slender fingers. Varnish chipped, manicure overdue. Delicate fingers.

No, this couldn't be. I closed my eyes and pinched myself. I opened my eyes and stared into the same delicate hands. I stared down at myself, saw my small breasts, the flare of my hips, the torn skirt. Again I closed my eyes, yet no matter how hard I shook my head and how many times I opened them, it was the same.

"No, this can't be happening." A woman's voice spoke, my voice.

"Oh, but it is baby." The sound of a male voice behind me. I turn and stare at my husband of the past seven years.

Memories of drunkenness, of drugs, of mixed-up days and nights. And worse things. I stare into his eyes and see his hunger, his need for release, glinting in the darkness of his soul. The damning passion for dominance, for gratification from pleasures of the flesh.

"I found the stuff." He smiled in a lustful sneer.

I stare at the jar of petroleum jelly. Eye the twist from the bulge in his pants and knew that the horror was only going to get deeper.

"I — I can't, I've changed my mind." Pleading, surely I could make him change his mind.

"Too late, besides you like it with lube, you know that baby."

"No, I don't, I don't want this, not this way."

He grabbed my arm and pulled me forward.

"I should teach you a lesson and not use any lube, but because I love you I will this time."

This time. It had happened before and perhaps with compassion and connection between us it could be enjoyable, but not like this. This was degradation of my soul, marital rape. I couldn't break from his grip.

I was so weak. Is this how most woman felt? Overpowered in the face of male aggression?

He flips me around and slams me against the table. Bottles rattle a grizzly tune. "Come on baby, you love it from behind."

Love, this wasn't love, I thought as his hands pulled my skirt aside and yanked my panties down. Love had nothing to do with the slather of jelly along my rear. His one hand holds me against the table while he fumbles for his zipper with the other.

I want to throw up, the alcohol in my system turning sour inside. I feel I'm going to be sick. Am sick. This shouldn't be happening, but it is.

Searing pain fills me from behind. I feel him inside me, deeper, until I feel his coarse hairs rubbing on my rear. His penis buried deep in my anus. Perhaps another time this would have been pleasurable, but not like this.

My wifely duty, to satisfy my man, my mother always told me. Some perverse part of me had always accepted this. Close off my heart from the pain, and it will all be over soon.

The lube helped.

"Oh God, you're tight. Just how I like it and I know you do too." He laughed, his sour breath washes over me, gagging me. He leans closer, reeking of booze and tobacco. I am trapped beneath his bulk.

Pain splashes all around. My head hurts, he doesn't care, doesn't love me. I want this to be enjoyable, like I know it can be, not like this.

"Stop, please, it hurts."

"Only at first. You enjoy it rough. Don't deny it."

"No, stop."

"I said, shut up and enjoy it."

He slams my head into the table. I feel myself going limp, wetness oozes from my mouth. Blood?

He thrusts again and again, I am a mere rag doll bouncing back and forth. "Oh yes, here it comes, just for you baby." He grabs my hair and pulls my head back. I scream in agony as he thrusts deep and heat explodes inside me. "Oh yeah, you get better each time."

The cry of a youngster. My daughter, woken by the commotion. "Mommy, are you okay?"

No, she mustn't see this. I can't have her know the degradation I will allow myself to be subjected to.

"Damn," he laughed as I feel his bulk rising from me. Only the stabbing pain remains as he pulls out and zips up his pants. "That was great. Hope you got off too."

Not caring, nor wanting to, he'd had his pleasure. No, not loving. Why do I do this to myself? My knees weaken and I fell them buckling. Bottles rattle as I slump over and fall into a chair. A drink, more than anything I need a drink right now. My guts burn.

"You know, she'll be ready soon." He smirks as he digs in the fridge, pulls out a can of beer and pops it open with a hiss.

"For what?" My guts heave and I turn, and spew what I have into the kitchen sink. Horrors of my childhood scream past taken my father. He lets out a large belch.

"For me to teach her how to enjoy it like her mother." Calmly he turns and saunters out of the room. "I wonder what's on the sport channel."

I slip to the floor, jelly, sperm and blood oozing from me.

"Are you okay, Mommy?"

I pull myself upright, and straighten my clothes as much as possible. Numbness threatens to take over, to erase the sensations welling inside, like so many other times.

Angela. I'd been named after angels. Only I'm not one and there aren't any around to help me now. Bile burns in my throat, sickness threatens to erupt again. How long? How many years will I allow this? And soon to my eight-year old daughter. The stark guilt slams into me. How did I attract this man into my life?

I love my child more than anything, more than I love myself.

That's the problem, isn't it? I don't love myself enough to want this to stop.

"Mom, you okay?" My daughter walks into the room, puts her arms around me and simply holds me.

"Ah, just feeling sick, a flu or something." I lie.

"Oh, I love you Mom, everything will be okay, won't it? You can't get sick." My child, no matter what, loves me. Even though I can't.

"Hold me, just hold me, hon."

As she holds me I feel the love, the unconditional love, wash over me.

"Say it again, I need to hear it again." She began to cry.

"I love you Mom. Everything will be okay." I feel the deep love tearing inside, feel it wash away the pain and guilt. Words I'd never had the courage to utter before surge forth. "I love me too." Tears splatter over my daughter's hair as I cry uncontrollably. "And you. Mommy loves you too."

This will not happen to her. Not everything would be okay, but I have hope. There was a phone number a social worker had given me last month, which I'd just tucked into a drawer. It was for a home, a home for battered women who had no place to go.

"Come on, help me to the bedroom. I have to make a phone call."

I blink and stare up at the face of the lady in the picture. I glance at the Hathor as it shimmers into view beside me, then down at myself and back at the picture. There is something odd about the lady I didn't realize. I hadn't seen the glint in her eyes before.

"So, what did you learn?"

I turn towards the tall being. "That in all of that despair and abuse, this woman managed to find hope. Tell me, was that an exercise or was that real?"

"What is reality but the ultimate illusion?"

"Sherida keeps saying stuff like that. I don't get it."

"Then you still have much to learn."

I try to focus, my mind whirling. What had just happened? My body is useless, I stare through eyes that don't move. I try to scream, "get me out. I'm here." But can't, my mouth is beyond reach. My wife, Beth, sits reading a book, holding my hand. A wave of cold washes over me. The blackness is coming, lopping towards me, I must go. Concentrating with all of my might I channel my energy into my hand and clench hers. She jumps as I fall down into the black cavern again.

I closed my eyes and he was there. "So, I don't totally understand. I go to sleep at night and you arrive. In one reality I'm in a coma in another here with you. Are you just a figment of my imagination?

Something I created to deal with what I'm going through? I've read that the human mind uses dreams and sleep to sift through the day's events and store what it needs to remember."

"Hmm, that is logical and a justifiable position. A skeptic could rationalize away everything that is happening to them. Convince themselves that all of this is simply dreams. Rationalize until they sort order from chaos. Quiet the fear inside that exists when we confront that edge of the unknown. And in the end, the skeptic believes in nothing. How do you know that the coma state is not the fictional one?"

I hesitate, I don't know which is the real one, except why would I be here then. "I call myself a skeptic, and a strong one. But with everything that has begun to happen I find myself wondering about a lot of things."

"Wondering is good, believing is better, but believers can only work on trust and love of self and of life."

"And something else, I'm starting to realize."

"What?" it asked, and as it looked to me for an answer, I saw what I took to be curiosity cross its face. The first glimmer of any emotion from this being.

"Connection, I'm beginning to see connections."

"Good. That is important. You are doing well in this learning of the gateways and of journeying through the chakras."

"But, you never answered my questions."

"You will find your own answers. Right now, you are establishing will and purpose, the foundation of the third chakra. Understanding comes later."

Aggravating bastard. It was like being stuck in the swamp with Yoda. Only this Hathor talked in more riddles than he did.

It gestured toward another inset tile. Deep in a cavernous pyramid, tall columns disappeared into the darkness, preventing me from seeing where the roof was, or even if there was a roof. The tile was of petals surrounding a circle and inset was a crystal that began to glow as I stared at it. Below that a ram stood.

"The strong horns of will, power and internal purpose." The crystal grew even brighter until I was nearly blind, covering my eyes as the Hathor talked. "Manipura. The first two chakras are of flow downward. This one is of eruption, fire, determination and upwards flow. Internal will and purpose."

I reached out to cover the crystal and attempted to block out the blinding light. Instead of touching the glowing surface I encountered nothing. It slipped away and I fell into the tile and into darkness.

I stood up in the darkness, the crystal glow hovered behind me. I reached again for it. Glittering flashes sparkled everywhere. Blinded I chased the crystal as it weaved out of my grasp.

Every time I reached out and got close the light intensified, my fingers grew hot. Afraid, I withdrew, not wanting to burn myself. So I closed up and I sat until the sun broke over my shoulder and light filled the room.

I stood up, trinkets and rattles stirred. I looked down. Hair flowed long, dirty and coarse in my face. I was a female again, but not helpless this time. Leathers of animal hides covered my body and, around my neck, bits of dried flesh strung in a necklace.

A medicine pouch hung on my side. Outside seagulls squawked, air was heavy with humid salt smell of the ocean. Simple white painted buildings of the town yard glinted through the windows.

I knew what had to be done and shoved aside the two austere looking women staring at me in disgust from their black and white outfits. Nuns, they were called. It suited them, for they had 'none' connection to the Earth and even though they considered themselves pious and strongly spiritual, I knew they were missing a connection to this world and this land. But I wasn't here to save them, it was the one inside that needed my attentions.

"Begone, savage," one said as she made signs on her chest that I knew were of the cross bearing their god. "You'll harm her. She is in God's Good Hands now."

I stood over Crystal Running Water, or Mary as they called her. She had already been tainted by their ways and had denied all the teachings of our people, our ancestors. She would have been picked to be a shaman in training as she had great gifts of healing. I should not have come, but one never turns their back on their own people in need. "Not as much as the harm you've already done. She will not live the night and you have no means of saving her." I grunt in their foreign tongue.

"No, we are praying for God to come and save her soul. She will join St. Peter and live with Jesus in heaven."

"Your God will not have her yet. Her time is not yet. Leave this room." I growl and shake my raven's rattle at her. The head nun turns and runs from the room screaming to get the men to come. I pick up Crystal, her body is hot and easily mistaken for fever-ridden but it is not fever that resides in this one. Still, it will eat her alive just the same. I open the side window, no one is around. They are guarding the front entrance. I pull myself and Crystal through the window and carry her to a sacred grove in the woods.

I deposit her body on the ground I've covered in cedar boughs and pine needles ahead of time. I quickly light smudge to burn all around us. No spirits will dare enter past these boundaries while I begin my work.

Crystal's eyes flicker open. "Grandmother, what are you doing?"

"They would let you die. You are not meant to die, you will live a long life. Some of this you will remember, most you will not." I bark in our tongue, she nods and falls unconscious again. The evil spirit inside is eating her spirit with great haste. I have not much time. Cries of alarm ring out from the village, they have discovered my doing and I have less time now.

I close my eyes and begin a slow walk around the body, knowing it is not the eyes I need to see with. Instead I see the demon twisting around inside her, it is hungry, gnawing away at her spirit. I shake the raven's rattle and the ground shakes. The creature stops and turns to look at me.

Great red eyes of hunger glare out from the shaggy fur of the grizzly looking beast. It is strong, savage like the grizzly. Teeth glint in a snarl. They want to devour Crystal's essence and perhaps mine if it could.

I pull another rattle from my belt and shake it several times until her body is frozen solid. The beast looks down and snarls, it cannot enter her again easily. It turns to leap at me, enter me if it cannot have the girl. I shake the raven's rattle again and it staggers, dizzy. This battle is greater than it had hoped for.

"Begone, foul demon, there are others for you to devour, but she is not yours."

I hear people approaching and the voice of the mother nun yelling, as soon as it sees the face of the head nun projected from my mind's eye the beast nods and is gone. She is far easier prey. I shake the rattle again and I am back.

"I am so cold now. Thank you."

"That is a good sign. You'll be okay. Know this, your son will become a powerful minister among the whites. He will be half white and will lead the missionaries to destroy the last of the old ways, the native ways. There will be no more Ska-ga shamans after me. None will follow, the old ways will die."

"Why do you save me then?"

"Because you are one of my blood, and as a healer of my people, I could not let you die knowing I have the ability to save your life. I cannot judge those I save, that is not the way of our people, nor the Ska-ga. We do what we must."

"Thank you, grandmother."

Shouts burst from the woods as she stands up on shaky legs. I turn to leave and a crack from one of their thundersticks rings out. Searing pain bursts from my shoulder and I stagger backwards, blood pours into the sky. Several men burst into the glade.

The head nun points an accusing finger at me. "You should rot in hell for taking this child from us and trying to kill her with your heathen ways."

"No!" young Crystal screams. "Don't harm her, she has saved my life, I am cured."

The head nun feels Crystal's head. "Goodness the fever has left her. Get this girl some clothes."

They wrestle me to the ground, crushing me into the still burning smudge. It cannot protect me and keep these men from me, just as I cannot prevent what will happen in the future.

Young Crystal Running Water turns to me as they shackle my hands. "Howa, thank you, again. I shall never forget I was born native, no matter what they teach me."

Later I know she will help me escape. My time is not yet either. I am picked up and shoved forward to fall face first into the cedar boughs, with my hands bound behind me. My medicine bag is trampled and kicked aside. My blood flows back into the earth that created it.

"You should be punished for this. But she lives, so we will take you in to attend to your wound and teach you the kindness of Jesus and begin to teach you his ways, cleanse you of this heathenism. Someone make sure her hair is cut and she gets a bath." The head nun holds a hand over her face, as I watch a bead of sweat break her brow. "Let us hurry back, this accursed glade gives me shivers."

"We'll see just how strong your God is now." I lean in to her and whisper, "forgive them, for they fear the unknown and they know not what they do."

Beth is sobbing as the hospital staff pour all around me in a wave of medical diligence. "He gripped my hand. He did," she cries.

The head doctor looks at all the monitors. "Well, we did pick up a EEG spike a few minutes ago. But it's gone now. This could be a good thing, however don't get your hopes up yet. We may not get anything else or this could be the start of his return. Timewise could still be weeks or months. Sorry."

They leave and Beth leans over to her husband. "I ain't giving up. I know you're still there." She kisses him on the temple.

Mist, heavy and oppressive, hangs in the air. The stink of death permeates up through the soil. I stare at crumbling stone. An old graveyard. Edifices to forgotten lives lean at obscene angles. Moss, with its slow vociferous touch obliterates humanity's struggles with nature's relentlessly obscuring hands. It claims back entire generations, past loves, broken dreams, and fulfilled lives. Dew covers the grass in the dim sunlight, dawn or dusk, I can't tell which.

Gravel crunches behind me and I turn, my heart catching in my throat. The Hathor, sliding from behind one of the obelisks that bore a figure in its image, I step closer. But can't read the language on the marbled surface. Perhaps I'm not even on Earth. "This is you?"

"I left my body many lifetimes ago. This realm of the fourth chakra that you enter next is of the heart."

I smell the dankness, the must of earth, raw decaying earth. Fetid dampness with the decomposing remains of what once was alive and vibrant in anther age. "What heart is there in death?" And, I wonder, in this being that seems so drab and unassumingly boring.

The Hathor appears to ignore my question. "Breath is the connection between the lower body chakras and the mind or the higher chakras, and comes from the heart. The heart is where everything comes together and begins to form into the higher spiritual forms."

"There is only death, decay, and rotting memories here. I don't get it."

"Hm, you've worked hard and well to come this far. I'd hate to have to begin again."

I stare into the shifting mist. "I guess I'm not quite ready for this learning. I don't see the connection, I can only see finality and death."

"Ah, perhaps that is the problem, awareness?"

"Well I ..." My answer is crucial. I've come far, but not far enough. I blink, and in the flicker between the shutter of eyelids, the brush of mist, the cool of night air caresses me. "Wait. There is more here. I have let the eyes become my consciousness again."

The Hathor smiles. "They are the doorways of illusion."

"Like blinders, they show the easy road before me. I haven't truly tried to perceive what exists beyond vision. Just like there is much existence beyond death." As I speak blurred images shift by. Vague thoughts creep in.

"Then you have learned much more than you realize. So, close the doorways and be still, listen. Allow your other senses to enter and be heard for they are trying to speak."

Nearly the exact words that Charlie had said to me once. "Have you ever dealt with a native shaman from the west coast of my world?"

"Orca cane, sardonic humor, intuitive beyond his own good?"

"That sums him up."

"Can't say I have." It smiles, I laugh. Both sardonic bastards in their own right.

There is much heart, more than I realized in this austere being called the Hathor. I close my eyes and begin the hard process of washing away thoughts, blocking them as they enter, until only my heartbeat pounds in my ears. Another gift of learning from Charlie, I wondered if I'd ever get the chance to thank the man I've never met, yet.

"Breathe, listen only to your own breath as you go inside, but not your thoughts, to where the fourth chakra dwells."

Soon all I hear is the sound of air entering, air leaving, keeping me alive. Oxygen entering the bloodstream, rushing back and forth to a soothing rhythmic throb from the machines keeping me alive. Beating, no stress, a body at peace, in harmony with itself and its environment.

Then I hear another's beat, rapid and small, weak. I open my eyes and cry out. The voice of a newborn? A woman's tear streaked face. She smiles, the joy emanating from her eyes overwhelming. I want to cry, to hold her, only I can't. My arms are too weak, I can barely lift them. The constant burble of liquid and the steady thump of the heart that sustains my life is replaced by audible voices and the odd cooling sensation of moisture evaporating from my skin, air, drying me for the first time. This is what it is like to be born? From somewhere I hear a snip and her heartbeat is gone. My heartbeat accelerates. I'm on my own, my life has begun without the life-support of my mother. All that I know, my sustenance, my security is gone. Now it is up to me to begin the life she started. Somewhere on a blank stage my heart pounds and begins to memorize this new life.

I'm wrapped in bedding and snuggle up next to her. She hugs me, places a kiss on my forehead and places me next to her breast. Her familiar heartbeat, my old life returns, but it is so different now, in the background. I've experienced so much since I've heard it last. Air on my skin, roughness of blanket cuddling me, hands touching. Voices talking in the background, once mere reverberations and the smell of skin against me.

The compulsion to suckle is strong so I latch on and warm nourishment enters my body. I smile up at her, milk dribbling from my lips as her life essence enters me again. I close my eyes content.

I stare down at my child, my first. She is so helpless, so tiny. No one said they were so tiny. I want to cry, from jubilation and fear. So much I have to do for her now. How could I possibly look after her and raise ... my God! Life takes on a terrifying slant.

Still, this is my creation, my child, my charge. Happiness sings to my soul as I clasp her to my breast and close my eyes to tears of joy.

In the next breath I watch the young playing in my yard. "Come in my dears, I've a fresh batch of cookies for you," I call to my grandchildren. My hand shakes, withered and feeble.

They scream in delight and chase each other around, such energy to expend while I struggle just to get out of bed every morning. "You're the best, Granny," one yells, and the rest agree. They gobble down the cookies and juice, wiggle in their chairs, push each other, jiggle and go running off.

Not a word of thanks but the look on their faces is enough.

I breathe again and hear the sound of a very old heart, a struggle just to beat. My hands are unable to lift, and I have trouble focusing more than a few feet away.

"She hasn't much longer," someone says from the gray haze around me. Each inrush of oxygen a struggle, no longer counted as millions, but one of a handful, on fingers stiff and shriveled. Life has already ebbed from the extremities and I can no longer feel them. Heavy, so heavy, an effort to breathe, even to keep myself beating. Arteries sag as the time between surges diminish. I struggle to find the strength to take the next breath, knowing death's hand is near, fearing the touch.

At a moment's grace I stop fighting and let go. Only air rushing back and forth and soon that is gone and I am left with solitude. The physical pain of an old shell is no more. I am released from my confinement.

Silence. For the longest time, if time could be measured at all, only silence. I swirl in mists, sensing a pulling, a funneling, another beginning and another breath. Warmth flows around me and gurgles fill my ears. I listen to a heartbeat issuing life into my soul once again.

A thump and eyes open awaiting a smack to begin the process all over again. My hands are weak and I can barely make out anything around me.

But I am back in the graveyard staring at the words written in stone. "Gone from us. The gentlest mother, the kindest grandmother we have ever known. You, who brought so much joy to our hearts, leave a void."

A tear streaks my cheek as I understand a bit more and awake.

"*I'm sorry, but it's been months. No sign of any breakthrough.*" The doctor speaks to Beth. "*His brain activity is beginning to dimish.*"

"*As long as his mind is active, I know he's inside. You are not unplugging a damn thing.*"

A growl shakes the darkness, I see nothing. But it is familiar. I remember this from somewhere.

"So far you have been very quick to learn and understand, but the last three chakras are more challenging because they are not of things tangible."

"Not tangible and the last three were?"

"They are of things your science can't put a definition to. This is why it is important to be clearly defined in the lower chakras, as the higher we climb now the more nebulous we become. The last chakra was the link between the more substantial chakras and these higher ones. The fifth chakra is of sound and vibration. This is the chakra of ether and spirit. Spirit is often called the fifth element."

I stare up into the bright blue of the sky. "When will I begin to see how knowledge of the chakras can be of any use?"

"When you need to use it."

"Thanks." I thought it might say something useless like that.

"Sound is the basis of life. This you must understand before you can continue. Everything, life itself, begins with sound, as do all foundations of communication. Sound, vibration, and hence self-expression, and from there to creativity. Communication focuses consciousness along the pathways of the chakras. The breeding ground of true creativity is the place where abstracted thought and manifested idea meet. That locale is where the physical plane begins. Order from chaos, the gateway." It hissed the last two words.

I watched the fingers of mist reaching down to flow into the valley. "What a load of shit going in one ear and out the other." How am I ever going to learn with this double-talking bozo?

The Hathor sighed and continued. "Sound is not as fast as light, nor is light as fast as thought. Understand the secret of sound and uncover the key to the mysteries of the universe."

I turn and the Hathor is gone, only the bright blue of the sky remains. As I look down the ground too is gone. I am the mist and everything becomes a haze. I begin to panic, this is so disorientating. I feel my atoms dissipating, I'm dissolving, flowing.

Wait; flowing? There is flow here even in this vaporous arena? No wonder the Hathor had given such a stern talk on this state. It would be so easy to melt away into the mist. Instead I relished the freedom, the gentleness. Drifting effortlessly like water vapors rising up mountain slopes in the early morning.

Then from the mists a pulse of light appeared, and another. Drums began and, just as I was beginning to enjoy this state of ether, of non-being, I felt myself being pulled back to earth and a more corporeal shape.

The mist lifts and I am a dancer, one of many dancing wildly around a bonfire. I am in Africa, in some native village. The ebony of our skins shines with sweat and dirt encrusted from the stirred ground we are stamping on.

Drums, dozens of drums, pounding a beat that sends vibrations deep into me. Releasing all inhibitions I begin to gyrate like the others. I'd been here on nights like this many times before. Sparks of firelight crackle heavenward, flashes of spears, beads spinning away, headdresses of bird feathers and shells glitter. The sound of their clanging lost in the pounding of the drums and the voices of the people singing in some language I'd forgotten.

Each drumbeat now begins a resonance echoing inside. Pulsing, grinding.

Basic, earthy.

Booming.

Pulling at me.

I don't resist and become lost in the flashes of bonfire.

One flash I am here, in another I am on a dance floor. Techno beats pounding overhead. I am in some modern nightclub. Strobe lights begin and each flash puts me in another scene, on another dance floor, around ancient fires. People dancing to the throb of rhythm, of life. Becoming the player, the band. Sound and vibration, so basic.

Heavy bass thunders into me, allowing me to dissolve again, becoming the player, the singer and finally the music itself.

In another beat I open my eyes and stare at a canvas before me. It is blank. I have been staring at it for many days. Empty canvas, staring back.

Beside me an assortment of oils and colored pigments dabbled haphazardly on a palette board.

I pick up the brush, dabble in the colors and put a few swirls of paint on the canvas.

Not right. Try again. I wipe away the paint.

I stop, asking not what it is I want to paint, but instead what image is locked within the weave of the canvas. A true artist can only release that which is contained already on the object inside.

I close my eyes, quiet the voice inside and stare from inside my mind at the paper, at the blankness. Then the whiteness begins to move, murky lines begin to erupt all around me as peels of music, soft and operatic, condense into rain falling in the background, revealing more hazy lines and I begin to move.

My brush doesn't hesitate, it knows what has to be done. Slowly at first, like the beginning of a waltz, and then as confidence grows and the images on the canvas solidify I let go, allowing the paint to speak and the brush to be the ears.

Brush dips in paint, scratches sing over the canvas; caressing hair on Bristol board. Mist swirls all around me and I become the arm, the hand, the brush, the paper and, finally, the hardening paint. Seeping into the spaces between the weave. Into the space between, becoming the void and watching the swirls of paint forming all around me on the darkness, like Aurora Borealis on Northern skies.

Green, reds flaring the gap between dimensions. The gateway.

I am there like Van Gogh on a Starry Night.

I move to proceed and another voice calls.

The Hathor pulls me back, "You have done well, but not yet. There is more you need to know first."

I fall earthward into a deep sleep.

I walked along in the dark forest. I was being watched. The crunch of vegetation. Malevolent eyes studied me in the dark, I could sense it.

Again.

It was there! I followed the sound; entered a worn pathway and saw something slide back into the bushes. A dog. A large black dog. A Rottweiler.

As a child I'd been attacked by one very similar. It had barked at me, nipped at my heels. I'd been terrified. Was this some childhood fear manifesting itself? Or was it something darker, something more urgent. The dog disappeared into the undergrowth.

"Why did you stop me in that last dream?"

The Hathor stood calmly beside me as sparkles of stars slid by, flittering through the tiles of the dark hallway we stood in. "You were not ready. The threshold is a scary place to be, you reached it far more quickly than I thought you might. This is a good thing, but there are a few things to show you first. The next chakra is about light. Light travels faster than sound and thought faster than light. Light is the connecting thread to the universe, to the Creator."

As he talked the flicks of light below began to speed up. "As sound begins life, light connects and light spreads."

Beams of light began to lift from the tiles. Filling the corridor, until it seemed we walked only on a thin line of flooring amid the night sky of the galaxy. Paintings hung suspended from the stars as we walked. I stopped and stared at a painting of a sun simply shining above some mountains.

The sun sank behind the peaks capped with ice and snow. In an instant darkness swarmed over the sky and stars blinked into existence.

I lay awake, staring into the infinite night sky, or so it appears. The stars go on forever. I am only ten again. And beside me lies the Hathor pointing to various stars, telling me their names and which races live on the planets that orbit them. It has been going on for hours.

"The night sky isn't so dark after all. There's quadrillions of stars out there."

"Yes, quite right. One of the secrets of this dimension and the rest, I suppose, is that reality broken down is simply light. All matter is trapped light. Everything is light and light is."

"How is that possible?" We are suddenly in the hallway of pictures and standing before a painting of someone standing over a body. A healer, his hands are touching the still person on the table and his eyes are closed, concentrating on healing the one before him.

I step forward and not just I, but we, are in the body of the healer. Energy, a river of energy, is flowing from the space all around him into his hands, into the person he is touching. We shrink down and join the river, a swirling mass of light, of atoms bursting with energy, and of smaller particles. Like a biz-zillion fireflies, galaxies of brilliance awhirl. "These aren't atoms."

"You call them tachyons. Faster than the speed of light, they are tiny energy beings, like soldiers of light, they flow when called, to the healers that beckon."

Then the flow stops. "He is done." We return to stand by the body and I notice a dark spot that the healer missed. I inadvertently reach out and in a flash I'm standing in a field of heartbeats and blood racing. Veins are pulsing with life, flowing back and forth, in and out as the heart beats before me. Lungs throb with a heavy basic pulse as intestines move like snakes gurgling away, as they process food. There, clinging to an area just behind the stomach, but pressed tightly to it like a Plecostomus catfish, I see it. A dark area, from within emanates another pulse. A hungry pulse. It breathes with an intensity like the fires of an out of control sun and begins to feed off its host, growing with each moment. The voracious appetite of the entity called Cancer is terrifying to watch as it readies itself to multiply and resume its mission, its need like every other living being; to live. Only it lives in an insatiable state, like a vampiric cat set on a platter of simpering mice.

I reach out and showers of tachyons surround the area, with tens of thousands joining in. The battle is intense, swirls of lights exploding, colliding. Sparks of dying tachyons litter the area until finally the dark area begins to shrinks in on itself. Compressing, condensing, increasing in mass until ignition point is reached. Exploding into a spray of light.

We are back on the hillside. "I see you are beginning to understand, even darkness has light," it whispers, and vanishes.

I roll over and breathe the damp grass, wondering how one can understand anything when nothing makes sense.

"Son, it's your bedtime," my mom calls and I rise. The stars blink overhead, as they've been doing for longer than I've been born, for longer than this planet has been born. The screen door slams behind me leaving the nagging question wafting to the winds, trees, skies and heavens.

We sit in the hall with pictures again. I remember my summers as a child, spending many an evening staring up at the stars in the backyard of my grandparents' home. They lived in the country. Without the interference of city lights the stars were so bright and without end. I knew a couple of constellations; the Big Dipper and Orion, and would catch the odd satellite skimming by. But the nights when the moon was absent and no clouds interfered with the view I'd see other things. Movements of lights that couldn't be explained. Almost like a haphazard skitter of bugs, fireflies, beams of light that turned at ninety degree angles or sped up and slowed down. The comings and goings of vast armadas of alien ships, I'd dream. Myself riding out there, like Buck Rogers or Luke Skywalker, off on some incredible journey to battle the most insidious of menaces. But the one thing I remembered the most was the nagging question left inside as the screen door slammed behind me and I retired to bed. What was life like out there? Really like?

"Again," the Hathor simply said without emotion, knowing that lessons and learnings take sometimes more than once to grasp, longer to master. It has far more patience than I do.

We were standing on a sky of iridescent colors shimmering all around us while a erratic collage of energy patterns whizzed by. Over, around, below a crazy swirl of light with no set or measured rationality. Points of light stop, hover and explode into phantasms of fireworks.

"Energy is light, trapped in one form or another. All light, and conversely energy, is holographic in nature. Like a pebble dropped in a pond, each wave cascading outward contains all the knowledge of the event. Another pebble dropped contains all the knowledge of its event carried in each of the waves produced. When two or more lines intersect information can be exchanged inter-dimensionally producing a third dimensional image you call a hologram. Each bit of the image contains energy, each bit reproduces the whole.

"Since energy is light, all light is holographic." I struggle to understand.

"Depending on its coherency or wavelength," it responds, adding to the overloading stress on my brain. I know from my school days that incoherent light doesn't produce anything, that in the case of a laser beam all light is in one coherent direction producing a powerful beam.

I look around trying to adjust myself to the swirling madness. "Wait a minute, if all light is holographic then coherency is merely a viewpoint seen from the ability of the individual to comprehend, to organize."

The Hathor says nothing.

He does that when I'm on the right track. I begin after all of this time to finally understand. "Even in the depths of chaos and pandemonium, order and coherency are there." I focus on several specters of light flashing by. It, at least part of it, begins to make sense. "Everything, even in essence, must be connected. Holographically speaking. Order is a function of chaos."

The Hathor smiles. "The blue sparkles are fascinating to watch."

I study the shifting waves of light, watching the rising crescendos of fireworks flaring away. "I rather like the greens myself."

"You are learning well." It smiles and fades away as I awake in my room.

The musings of a child's mind, of my mind. Only now was I starting to know, to realize, as the child did, the changes unfolding out there and within. And in some ways the truth was more incredible than even I could have imagined as a child. That dream, or whatever is was. Astral traveling? That was the illusion, this was real. Or was it?

I lay there alone in the room and try to imagine myself floating out into the space. But can't. "Ah this is crap," I mutter and turn over, dragging covers over the warm bed. I close my eyes and try falling asleep, hoping to dream of my wife Beth, whom I missed and not of aliens, starships nor black dogs a-prowl.

Beth watched the monitor. It's steady thump kept Roger's heart going. But she clenched her teeth. The brain activity worried her. She didn't need a doctor to know, it was lessening.

The darkness hangs a cold blanket around me. I look behind, a large black dog has stepped out onto the trail and stares silently at me, eyes of cancerous red.

The look of hunger, and want inside its hatred. The want of his blood on its teeth.

I fight to waken, shake the dream's hold, only I can't. Sinking back into it.

"For a third dimensional being to enter the fourth dimension he must overcome his fears. The last chakra is about thought." The Hathor spoke as they walked into a temple complex. "All of these temples are part of the initiation. To train individuals to be ready for the experience of the fourth dimension."

Light streamed in from an opening in the roof of the complex, shining behind a wall that stood in a large pool of water.

"You must get to the other side of an identical wall and stand on a platform like this one."

I walked out to the platform that stood away from the water and looked around, "But there's no way around this wall. Except..."

"And what did this have to do with thought?" I asked. The being that called itself Hathor had vanished. I was alone. I stared at the wall. "No way over, it's twenty feet high. So the only way is to go under." I stripped off everything except my shorts, took several deep breaths saturating my lungs and dove under the water.

As I descended I noticed a dim light and swam towards it. The wall didn't connect to the floor of the pool. There was a gap of about two feet. As I swam under the wall the light increased from above, light and movement in the water. I swam up to the top, and gasped for breath. Dark objects that appeared to be logs floated in the water. I gulped in air and blinked, trying to get the water out of my eyes. In front of me another wall, an intense beam of light cast above it, and another identical platform to the one I started at.

This seems easier then I thought. A current of cooler water suddenly welled up as something moved below disturbing the stillness. I heard a splash behind me and flinched as a log to my right opened its eyes. They weren't logs. Another splash as something large entered the pool. Crocodiles! I was in the middle of a pool of live crocodiles. Something rough brushed against my feet and I watched a large shape move below me.

Panic seized me in its frigid arms. I had only one chance. Either stay here and die or make for the platform. I gulped, staying still would probably not give away my location. The second I moved I knew the crocs would be on me. I wanted to strike out and swim with everything I had. I knew I couldn't stay where I was. My heart raced, as I slowly filled my lungs with air and allowed myself to float on the top. With slow measured undulations I eased towards the platform. Trying to be as still as possible, sliding across the waters like the crocs did. Trying to become one of them. About ten feet away my hand slipped and made an audible splash. Instantly the crocs around me opened their eyes and some dove under the water.

Move your arms, I screamed at myself.

My heart threatened to explode as I swam with everything I had. My hand grasped the edge of the platform. I began to pull myself out of the water and stopped. Something wasn't right. The Hathor said I had to stand on another platform like the first one, on the other side of a second wall. Not before it.

I gulped, the wall was about twenty feet away.

No, I wracked my mind, this wasn't the right platform. Even if it was bathed in light. I turned and took a deep breath as the crocs moved through the water. None appeared to be really heading in his direction. They appeared to be aimlessly swimming about, nearly in contentment or idle laziness.

I swallowed, and gripping my fear like a knife dove under the water. Down into the darkness of the pool. Only there was no opening, no light and the wall did extend all the way to the pool's bottom. There was no way under it. Light shone above me. No, my intuition, called. There had to be an opening. I raced along the wall, frantic as my lungs began to ache.

Near the center of the wall I spied a darker area and swam closer. A large croc swam just above me. There was an opening into the wall, a dark opening. I stared into it. Blackness stared back at me. A square area barely larger than my shoulders.

What if I got stuck? What if I ran out of air? I couldn't turn around in that tunnel.

I swallowed. This had to be the way, it had to be. Trust the intuition. Blood pounded in my temples as I forced myself into the tunnel. Trust yourself.

I woke up.

We stood in a long unending corridor, full of books towering in shelves up into the darkness. "I ... I know this place."

"The last chakra is about thought."

"I know, you've told me this before. A long time ago."

"Yes, you failed last time."

"The fact that I remember this conversation tells me that."

"Then perhaps you have not failed after all."

I turn stunned, overwhelmed by what is before me. I don't want to breathe, the thought of everything contained here is mind blowing beyond the wildest dreams. It has been written that in our current history there were several events that forever changed our view on life and the past, that destroyed so much of what we knew once. The sacking and burning of the libraries of Alexandria, Egypt and Nalanda, India among others and the ordered burning of over 700,000 texts at Tenochtitlan and Texcoco.

Hundreds of thousands of books, some dating from as far back as the ancient realms of Atlantis, Lemuria, even ancient Mu. I turn in awe, utter awe.

"Does this place actually exist?"

"Yes, on Earth, below the ancient Seer of Sirius you call the Sphinx."

"On Earth?"

"Yes, your fellow being called Edgar Cayce was right, below the right paw is the entrance to this. The Akashic records, the hall of records."

"The sum total of mankind's knowledge. All here. Do I have time?"

"That is an irrelevant question. Time is irrelevant."

"Yes, right. So how do I?"

"Just think it."

"Jesus, where do I begin?"

"Ah, a good place."

Images of a woman being struck by light from a bright star overhead. Her son being born, growing up, long walks by himself and deep reflections. He begins his studies early, travels to all the holiest of places, India, Egypt, China and learns as much as possible. His understanding and perceptions immense, he walks on water, a dark Arabian man that radiated love and put his hands on people, gave life and hope to those suffering. His love of Mary, their children smuggled away to Massada by the Essenes. Trapped there by the Romans after his death, suicides. Mary dead, their son escaped to modern day France. He himself died a lonely, silent monk in the hills of Kashmir. "Shocking, this is wild."

"This is the real truth contained within these texts, not the versions you'd be lead to believe by certain authorities that are in power at the time and altered by men of power to suit their needs."

I let go of the book and touch another. Michelangelo, dabbling away on his back painting the Sistine chapel, year after painstaking year. Another, the sack of Peking by the Mongols. The fire bombing of Dresdan, human bodies igniting from the heat of the firestorm. The tens of thousands killed by the hands of despots, Adi Amin, Saddam Hussein, Pol Pot.

"So much violence." I shake my head trying to contain my tears.

"Then shift your thoughts to something else. The choice is yours."

"I don't understand."

Einstein plugging away on a chalk board. A young Indian named Gandhi staring up at the heavens. I blink and see myself as a child staring up at the stars.

"The pyramids. Tell me about the pyramids."

"Ah, for that we need to go to another room." We walk into a larger room.

"This is older, isn't it?"

"Yes. This is the entire history of the last cycle of Atlantis."

"Last cycle? I remember the Hopi and the Dogon stating that we were in a fifth cycle. Does that mean that there were four previous cycles of Atlantis?"

"Yes, as a matter of fact that is correct. The place you come from is the current reincarnation."

"America?" I sit stunned for a moment before staring at the date of the last cycle, it is nearly twenty-six thousand years ago. I watch as remnants of Atlantis mystics move them with the power of crystals.

"They were later rebuilt by your pharaoh, Khufu around 4,000 BC."

I see flying ships in the Indus Valley. "Explains the thousands of ancient text found in the oldest of Indian ruins regarding how to fly and maintain flying craft." I wonder why they'd need these?

Visions of mining activity on the moon, crystal structures towering over a mile high. The Face on Mars and entire cities there. "Wow."

Another room, even older. "From the time of Lemuria." The Hathor answers the question fermenting in my mind. I see the destruction of the fifth planet in our system, Maldek.

"Our asteroid belt now," I gasp.

Another room, so very old, "Mu," it whispers in reverence. "My ancestors lived here then."

"Why? I don't understand. Why do we save this? I've been studying my friend's notes, the Hopi talk about cycles as do the Mayans and many very old cultures."

"When all of this knowledge is stored, it empowers the pyramids, the ley lines of energy that emanate from here."

"Ley line energy from books?"

"Our knowledge encircles the globe, superconcious energy. Everything converts to energy. Different building blocks, for different kinds of energy. All of this for a reason."

We walked into the long endless corridor. "I know everything is energy and energy converts to light. But why? I still don't understand the why."

"You will at some point. But not yet. This Orion transmitter was built for several reasons, one of which is to withstand the photon belt we have recently entered."

"To survive what?"

"The photon belt, the energy source that culminates as we end this cycle and begin the next." The Hathor began to shimmer, preparing to leave I knew.

"If everything is trapped light, everything converts to light. I've been told that light is the Creator. This photon belt energy comes from the center of the galaxy doesn't it?"

"Light is the connection to God, the Creator. Perhaps you understand more than you know." With that it disappeared in a flash and I woke up.

Or had I?

"The last Chakra is about thought."

"I know you've told me this before. A long time ago."

"Yes, you failed last time as well."

Again I'm on the path again. A crack in the bushes, the pungent smell of wet canine. This time it takes a step forward and begins to follow him me. Fear screams at me in all of its myriad forms of electrifying panic. Run, run, now.

And I did. I ran through the forest, yet it was forever there, behind me, getting closer, lopping along. Branches slap at my face. The faster I ran, the closer it got. I knew I couldn't outrun this beast. It had me. The silence from its slavering jaws beseeching for my flesh down its throat. It exists for only one thing, to feel the crunch of my bones between its teeth and the pungent taste of my blood, wet on his tongue. It cared nothing of civilization or consciousness.

It only wanted to be fed and its thirst assuaged. It thirsted for me.

Eyes of blood red, filled with delight. It was gaining, it was winning.

From the place in his mind that held no room for forgiveness, the place where everything he kept hidden from everyone else dwelled. From the darkness of his soul came a loping figure he knew all too well. The creature that in his dreams had attacked and killed him several times. The black dog had returned, to finish him off. He could taste his own flesh tearing. Feel its teeth razoring, ripping into him like they had done so many times before.

It moved closer. Roger cringed and backed into a wall of thickening cold. Ice, groaning, fissuring across the dark, cutting off all escape. Coldness, flesh sticking to ice, he pulled away, frost's frigid bite stinging at his flesh. Shapes formed around him. Columns of ice. Pillars?

The teachings of the Mystery Schools, of Hathor. What good could that do now when he had only time to die? First water and a pit full of crocodiles. Now this, a wall of ice closing in.

The dog drew nearer, eyes of blood-fire, jaws slavering.

"Well, this'll be the last time, then, won't it?" To his own ears, his laugh sounded insane. Madness, it all ended here, but wasn't laughter the best medicine in the moment of his demise. He felt a twinge in his left hand.

He opened his palm and found the sliver of ice, like a toothpick compared to...

Illusion.

What had Charlie and the Hathor said? So hard to think in the cold. He coughed, seeing his breath. Illusion ... how many times had he heard that the eyes were the deceivers of illusion. This time he laughed louder. A shudder rang through the ice sheet that was rapidly engulfing everything around him. The cracking, thunder of ice straining. The dog, still loping towards him, growling. Everything repeating itself in slow motion. He'd done this before.

You are my greatest fear, one I've been running from since I was a child, when that black dog, a Rottweiler, nearly attacked me. The soul is eternal, the Hathor taught me that. And the light of life will always conquer darkness. So in essence I have nothing to fear except life itself and I am life, will always be life.

The growls grew angrier, louder. Roger leaned back. *It begins to make sense: my greatest fear, my subconscious, my demons all rolled into* one. *The me I keep denying, a higher self. I know now.* The beast was nearly on him. The Hathor had said that no one can fight anything until they become conscious of what isn't working. "You chasing me isn't working. Me, denying the truth isn't working. But this is!" He held up the sliver of ice. It burst into blue flame, engulfing his hand and expanding into the mercuric gleam of a silver blade. "Ah, the brilliance of Illusion."

The dog snapped at him, its eyes narrowing in the fear usually mirrored in Roger's own eyes. How he knew this Roger wasn't sure, he just knew fear had shifted from one place to another, like rats in an abandoned house when a cat sets up residence. He hefted the heavy handle of the sword and the canine's growl reduced to a whimper.

He held the blade in front of him. The Hathor had done this. Given him the sword of consciousness, of awareness. Had set him on the right path.

The dog stopped in front of him, barking. *Oh yes, you're just an illusion. Fear is merely an emotion, its flip side excitement.* Roger waved the sword of awareness before him. "Ah, the bitter throes of madness. There's a time for everything, isn't there Poochy? Including a time to die." The dog howled and leaped for his throat.

He ripped the sword upward, tearing into the canine's chest, staring into its eyes as the sword gutted the dog, spraying the crushing ice and Roger in a spray of red and intestines. The light faded from its dark sight. "I say begone with the likes of you." *I have no need of you, no room for fear now. The time for change is begun. He* knew this, it was the lesson the Hathor had tried to instill into his thick head, time and again.

Inside, walls collapsing, doors opening, others swinging shut. Everything he'd been shown and taught had finally begun to make sense. Gateways awaited to be walked.

He dragged the sword downwards, splattering himself and the ice with the ruby stains of blood and entrails. The dog fell to a heap by his feet, one cold eye staring at him from the congealing pile of once-great terror.

When you know this, you will have succeeded, the Hathor had said.

Roger turned. No escape. The ice had closed all around. He slashed at it; it exploded and a few shards fell away, only to regenerate. Groaning, it kept growing inward. His breath came shivering on icy currents. Thoughts slowing down. The dog's blood and entrails congealed into frozen iced parts.

"Illusion, this is all illusion." *No escape, not this way. Time for the greatest illusion of them all. Time to surrender all that this mortal body contains.* He stood over the remains of the dog. *If am to die here then I will stand over the corpse of my fears, anchor myself with this sword and wait for the wall of ice, of death to claim me. For I know it cannot. Beth, wherever you are, I love you.*

The ice surged forth to sear him with its final embrace. Congealing thoughts, solidifying memories. Roger thrust the sword, punching it straight through the corpse and dove into the remains. "I've become my greatest fear."

The ground collapsed, plunging him into an unending pit. Everything fading, going blank, tumbling into frozen nothingness.

Becoming nothing but infinitesimal substance dissipating into the ether until only one cell, one single speck of himself, remained.

No running, no fighting, only eternal peace. He should have feared what was now happening; instead he surrendered to the blackness.

The Hathor had said that the end of all illusion is the reality of illusion. There were no senses here. Only stillness. Was this death? Or was this truth, stripped of all his preconceptions, all his fears, the absolute reality. A single cell of life floating on the cosmic soup. So hard to think. His mind slowed down, evaporating into the void.

All he had to do was trust.

Simply trust.

And that faded,

until nothing remained,

not even a single cell of memory.

It's no use. He's gone, as of this morning his mind has stopped functioning. We have to unplug the machines. Beth sobbed loudly. "NO, not yet."

OM

OM

Tonal vibrations sweep the dark, beginning a rhythmic dance answering the call. A single cell fluttered. Tremblings. An egg thumped with its first heart beat.

OM

Life beginning. Darkness, floating in darkness. He was but one cell. How was it possible that he could think? Comprehend?

An urge came from within as the tones ringing through the shell he was encased in reverberated again. He shuddered through his being.

The need to pull. Overloading pressure, growing at a phenomenal rate, until it became too great. Intense constrictions, the need to pull out, away from pain. He felt himself twisting in two directions. He yelled as the time came, he split. Anchored together, himself, yet two.

He floated on the warmth of a black ether. How long had he lain asleep? Hadn't he read that some believe that all of your entire history, past experiences and lifetimes, resides in your DNA, in each cell? It was obviously true. Was this place the fourth dimension then or another?

Wind borne on cosmic currents began to moan by, dormant sparkles stirred, sprinkling the heavens with a glittering light. The awe of wind sighing like angels humming and fairies breathing. Surf, gentle surf moved through him and the drumbeats returned. Inside a compulsion formed again as the pressure grew.

The need, the time to split. And another surge, like birthing, now he was no longer two but four, again, now eight.

He shuddered, the joy within, love flowing through every part of his being. The drone of Buddhist monks on their long, low, bassy, and tonerous horns.

Again the surge, the need to pull and he divided again. It was quickening now. From within, warmth poured up from below, filling him with the white light of pure love, swelling the root chakra, filling the next as it rose, a bowl running over with water. Fishnets brimming over with fish.

Again he divided.

White light surged upward, igniting the next chakra, he shuddered in response. The surge began again, and again. A flow of erupting life, cells replicating and duplicating themselves.

Again and again. Unto the next, until it reached his brow, the crown chakra. Splitting, growing life beginning? The clutches of becoming alive, the merest chance that this was what it was like for the first conscious cells, so many millions of years ago?

Let me breathe, let me open my eyes and walk?

Warmth flooded him as the song of the interstellar currents rushed by. Music from somewhere. A soft hum of violins and mothers singing babies asleep. The dirge of Celtic monks. Drums, the measured rhythms of drums. Vedic verses on Indian lips, haunting melodies of Hindu holy men praying, while Indian sitars sang to the heavens.

The deep throb of Australian aborigines and their didgeridoos, calling. Calling him into dreamtime. Everything exploding in orchestrated uprisings as an urge to speak, to utter a single powerful word craves its way over his lips.

OM

He was told within the harmonics of that note resides the voice of God. Completing the circle started, releasing back to the darkness the essence of beginnings.

Celtic chants and the rambling patter of Welsh, gaelic mutters in time to beats of soul. He knows now that he could never die, not today, not ever. Druidic rituals flowed over ancient stone on henge. Chanting. Black gospel singers belting out heart and soul. African drums and natives dancing to keep away the hyenas lurking nearby. Chanting.

Vastness of space fills with a volume of awe. Scottish bagpipes playing Amazing Grace. Choirs of Christian and Catholic voices raised in great cathedrals. Millions of Muslims flowing in circular tempo during the pilgrimage of hajj. Around and around the sacred rock of Kaaba at Mecca. Praying in salat, one voice.

A rock band in front of tens of thousands, clapping and singing to them as guitars screamed electrically into the night. Drummer, pounding a relentless beat.

West coast natives in longhouses, smoke curling through cedar roofs, calling in ancestral beings in shrill wailings on deep bass drums. Pounding on sinew and hide stretched over cedar and pine.

Spirits being blessed on Hopi ceremonies. Incense burners carrying away the deep droning murmurs of Buddhist monks and in the sunlight reflection of their shaved heads are cast the prayers to Amaterasu of Shinto followers. Kami energies rise up through mountain slopes, mixing with the tread of footsteps traversing Mt. Fuji. Russian dervishes swirling as a Mayan priest slices down through bone and muscle until he holds a pulsing heart to the heavens.

A single child singing to itself as it plays

OM

Silence like Jews praying in reverence before the wailing wall while vibrations pull at him and like the horn of Jericho the very air collapses all around. Vacuum inhales and expels. No longer a prisoner, no longer separate, no longer one.

No longer...

And he knows.

Ascension, true ascension. Brilliant white light floods him from above, as above is defined from below in a void, funneling into a beam. Entering his head flooding the seventh chakra. And the light that has been there all this time flows downward in a spiraling flashflood, absorbing and spinning into alignment the other chakras one after another until...

Silence.

A long cry of a wolf on a full moon night cuts the void.

Enough, eyes grow heavy and he fades into a blissful sleep, cuddled in darkness. Floating on the nether of space. Curling into a ball, finding solace in sucking on his thumb.

Done, for now.

"It's been days, no brain function. I'm afraid we lost him. Only the machines are keeping his body going."

Tears flooded her cheeks as Beth sobbed. "Okay, disconnect him. But leave me alone with him for awhile so I can say goodbye."

The room turned silent for the first time in months. "Goodbye, my love, if you are anywhere close, return to me now." She leaned over and kissed his still warm lips.

Roger awoke in dark stillness. He turned and saw a thin blur in the distance denoting a horizon. Gentle swaying of waters or at least some viscous substance of similarity. The sense of a great ocean at night, resting, calm.

Moving he realized he was in a membrane thin capsule encircling him. He reached up, feeling the edges of his enclosure. Naked, trapped in a jelly-like cocoon. Drifting alone on a vast ocean. A serene calmness sung home to his senses, averting fears.

Was this what a baby felt like within its mother?

He turned carefully, fearing rupturing the thin protection that kept him from falling into the dark waters.

Warmth welled up from below, like the up welling of volcanic vents or the breath of a large creature. Something below stirred, shifting him in his light compartment. Sending him bobbing along like jetsam.

A spot of light, then several moving up from the abysmal depths. Luminous greens and blues, surging, flowing directly to him. Roger waited as something approached.

The lights grew until they reached nearly human sized proportions and hovered below him. They formed a circle around him. Lights surging changing in color, pulsing in a rhythmic pattern. Flowing as if they were talking to each other, using light and colors to communicate between themselves, studying him.

Rising they broke the surface of the water hovered over him. Gelatinous, indistinct shapes in the dark. With many long flowing finlike members, elegant angels with lion fish appendages. Fluttering in the air, they watched him until a surge of white light burst suddenly from all of them.

As if panicked they flowed upwards to disappear into the heavens becoming pinpricks of lights, like stars winking overhead, then gone.

What had scared them?

It began, an upwelling from the depths again. Only far larger. Water swirled.

Something very large, from a great distance below was coming. Heated water from the deep pumped upwards, the surface heaved in tsunami like undulations, tossing Roger on the waters. Clinging to his sac of fluid praying to his luck that it hadn't ruptured yet or would.

Lights approaching. Huge pools of brightness from each side of him, illuminating everything above and below him. Massive, on a scale beyond comprehension, crossing the gulfs of dark oceans, moving up and him directly in its path.

So large he realized there was just two groupings of lights approaching. He wanted to swim out of the way, but was afraid of wrecking the safety of his capsule. Only to realize there was no escape as whatever was coming continued to grow in size until the two lights filled the entire ocean and he knew that whatever this was coming, it was still very far away.

Galaxies away.

The sensation of being a gnat on the back of a flea on a dog, was how he felt as it slowly advanced. From the center of both lights, atoms swirled like pulsars and whole solar systems turned on their axis. Merging in the center of the two lights forming a heavier area, darker, like … he hesitated … like two iris. Whirlpools of black holes lost in their depths.

He was in awe, total awe.

This entity, the matter of all creation.

The all that is.

Moments of eternity, spent focusing on him.

A being of timelessness, who'd seen the beginning of the universe, for it was the cause.

It was the universe and it …

STARED

AT

HIM.

At the far end of his vision he caught the subtle flicker of movement, like the lifting of an eyelash. Galaxies swirled away. Approval and love, overwhelming love flooded him. The true essence of this being.

Pure, unadulterated love.

Then it pulled itself back to where it came from, the center of the universe. Creations roost. Dark waters of space swirled in quieting eddies cast by its retreat.

Roger trembled. To be the focus of something so overwhelmingly massive. So inspiring. So, the thought clung to him, denying comprehension, so godlike. He wept, his tears filling the capsule. It was time.

He screamed exploding upward rupturing the embryonic sac.

I surge upward, yelling in utter agony.

"Oh god, you're back." Beth jumps in shock and hugs me as I kiss her back. My arms feeble from lack of use try to raise to hold her.

"I love you."

"I love you too. But first there is something I must finish." I slump back into my mind and collapse back into my bed. My heart thumping life back into my extremities. She hits the alarm for the doctors.

At certain times in our lives a rare wind blows across the fields of our minds that like others before it, stirs leaves and rustles grasses. Only this breeze disturbs dust covering dormant memories thought buried beneath the weight of time's passage. Stricken chords begin vibrations, opening barbs of echoes nagging at the consciousness. Singing to voices thought gone from previous incarnations, former lives and sequestered dreams.

As dust settles and the wind diminishes, illusions present themselves that everything appears the same as before. Except the eyes and their four accompanying cohorts are in a sense easily deceived fools, allowing self-absorbed egos to bask in their own vanities. Oblivious to the fact that evolution is an aching compulsion beckoning with greater urgency at every passing breath to let change occur naturally. While within, the subconscious relentlessly hammers away at logic's walls with persistent scratches of intuition's voice.

Calling out to the settling dust, that as the wind quiets, something has inexplicably changed.

And as the stirred leaf is returned to its former position, awakenings take root in the realization, beneath knowing's furtive glances, that it can never be put back into the same state of cognizance as before.

Expelling the old self and inhaling the new is all part of the process, the rhythmicity of life, like the waves of the ocean stealing at the shore's foundation of imposed truths.

In the Akashic Hall of Records I look up from the Tome, my mind inscribing astral light thoughts onto the blank pages set before me. "Why am I here?" I ask.

The Hathor guide moves behind me. "Sundering one's self from the whole and from All That Is brings not truly understanding, not knowing Thyself." He glances at my words. "You begin to understand this final Chakra lesson well. It is time for this teacher to leave, for there is no more I can show you."

So much I have learned from the Hathor, so much still to learn in time. While time itself becomes lost and meaningless in the scheme of universal matters.

The Hathor vanishes in a haze of violet light as I finish:

Yet enlightenment cannot be won without darkness and from that void comes the sacred knowledge that there is no going back, no retreating from awareness, for that surely leads on the path to madness. We have both inside, light and dark, awareness and ignorance. To deny one means to surrender to the other and that is one of the secrets in transcending this realm and in comprehending the existence of the others.

Still, somewhere on awareness' wind comes the tongues of chaos humming an endless incantation, as surely as old people whisper and children laugh freely, that nothing, absolutely nothing, is as we remembered it.

Nor can it ever be as it once was.

That wind blew today.

Dedicated to Michael Schumacher and all the others in coma.
May they return from their journeys.

Through all the days that eat away
at every breath that I take.
Through all the nights I've lain alone
in someone else's dream.
Awake.
The Crossing (OSIYEZA), Johnny Clegg

Stillwaters Runs Deep Series,

BOOK THREE:

The Awakening

Prelude

Water lapping at his feet, Charlie awoke alone on the beach, cold, shuddering and naked. Mist rolled in waves, clinging to everything with its clammy, smothering embrace.

He caught shadows shifting. The mist circled around a figure emerging from the sodden grip of trees lining the shore. Thunder shook overhead and lightning danced like snakes frying.

He closed his eyes and it began again.

* * *

An eye opens after eons of sleep.
It breathes deep.
At last.
I smell him.

Chapter One

"What makes you think you qualify for this job?" asked the stern-looking white man heading the hiring committee.

"Well, I'm native aren't I?" Charlie responded, smiling at him and the six other Caucasian members of the review board. He figured they felt protected behind their heavy desks, wanting him to feel exposed in the one chair centred in the large stark, empty office. He tapped his cane on the floor. "Nice."

One raised a head and stared at him.

"Real wood, pine, probably eighty years old. Nice stuff." He smiled back.

The five-man, two-woman board flipped through the pages on their clipboards desperately hoping to find other applications. There weren't any, and his didn't take much reading.

"And being a man of deep spiritual connections, I reckoned this was up my alley. If you look under 'Hobbies' you'll see I love to watch baseball."

"Yes," the same man said dryly. "Montreal Expos in particular. I do believe they no longer exist."

"Yeah, go those Blue Jays." Charlie beamed at the man. "Been meaning to get a new cap, rather attached to this old friend though, we've been through a lot. Although I guess for special occasions like this I should've splurged, look a little more respectable. If I get a spending budget on this job, could afford a new cap."

"Ah, yes." The man reading the resume cleared his throat. The scowl on his face showed he wasn't much of a baseball fan or any kind of sports fan for that matter. "You also cite 'watching documentaries' as well as baseball. These aren't really hobbies, Mr. ah, Stillwater."

"Charlie."

"What?"

"It's not Ah Stillwater. It's Charlie Stillwater-S." He smiled and leaned on his cane. "I guess you could be right. Watching the Expos was more like my passion. Got hooked on them after they were top of the standings in eighty-four and probably would have taken the World Series if it wasn't for the strike. Eighty-four. Man, that's been awhile. I guess it is time for a new cap, or at least get this one cleaned. As for the documentaries, I think Dr. Suzuki has for the most part got it right. Bit slow to figure things out, but the man's on the right path. I think he's Chinese. Oops, I mean Oriental. Don't want to be politically incorrect these days. But I reckon he's got some native blood in him. I like the guy, looks a lot like my uncle Ralph."

The committee flipped through their blank pages again, wishing at least one other application would materialize. They were disappointed.

"It's hard finding anyone willing to relocate to Prince Rupert to fill any position, but especially in the psychological fields," one rather well-nourished woman whispered to the cookie-cutter figure next to her. "I remind you that the head warden has warned that if a candidate isn't found by the end of this week, one of us will have to go in and deal with them and I for one am not walking in there with the vile creatures. The way their dirty eyes linger, undressing me." She shivered and flushed a deep red, either embarrassed or aroused by the thought. "I wouldn't be caught alone with any of them in a cell, probably get raped. I'll quit if we don't get someone."

The head interviewer looked at his papers again and back at the others. "I agree. The natives are starting to get out of hand. We'll take on Mr. Shaman man, let him try to deal with them. Better he gets assaulted than one of us. We have our Elder, the jail keeps its licence and after the Federal inspector leaves next week, we either fire him or find another to fill in. I request we send out a new listing for the position." The suits all nodded their agreement.

He cleared his throat. "Okay, Mr. Ah, Charlie Stillwater, we'll give you a two week trial."

"Oh good. Ends on a night of the full moon." Charlie smiled. "I'll be feeling a mite hairy then. Should bring my silver razor for protection."

They glared at him. "Won't last a day," one stern woman whispered to the colleague next to her. "Arrogant bastard, but feed him to the wolves instead of one of us. I agree."

"I'll be surprised if he lasts two hours. But we have no choice. It's him or one of us. We file the paperwork, get our federal funding. If he quits, well, we'll have to hope we get a better response next time. Everyone agreed?" he whispered to the others. They nodded back.

"Ahem! Be reminded Mr. Charlie Stillwater, that you've few credentials. No psychiatric training of any kind, not even tribal endorsements to prove that you are the shaman you claim to be.

However, if you are a shaman, even self-taught, it does help you qualify for the position of Native Elder that we are seeking. You'll really need to prove yourself though. This is no place for amateurs. We're dealing with dangerous persons in here, killers, sociopaths, psychopaths and rapists."

"Well, I didn't think this would be a kindergarten picnic. These folks aren't here just because they tripped up grandma at the bus stop. I've got me trusty bag and this...', he tapped the side of his head with his orca headed cane. "A full deck of marbles, that don't rattle. Oh, I didn't mention that I've watched the original Karate Kid eighteen times, got the crane kick down pat. Try me."

The overweight woman choked down her disgust. "I think some discussion should be made regarding certain standards of uniform ethics later. However you're the best candidate so far. So, before we change our minds, we are offering you the position. Sign this agreement so we can pass our findings to the warden." He shoved a paper towards him. Charlie leaned forward and scrawled his John Hancock.

"Well, you can count on me to get the job done. I've always had my trusty cane and my wits. Never failed me yet. Although come to think of it I'm pretty good at outside animal management. Should have put that on my resume."

"Outside... Animal ...Management..." one of the team slowly muttered aloud, like he couldn't believe what his ears had just received.

"I've handled some irate squirrels in my backyard. They'll never figure out where I've hidden those nuts. And a rather troublesome raccoon I named Rocky, although he tells me he likes Raymond better, raccoons are like that you know. Dealt with a pesky Raven too and he was more difficult to deal with than you could imagine but that's a whole 'nother story. Everything I needed to know I learned from my elders and from out there in the wilderness. Does this job include lunch and my own office?" He looked about tapping his cane on the floor.

"There is a canteen here. Meals are included."

"Well, this could be an interesting two weeks and at least I'll get some free grub. Should have brought my other jacket, it's got bigger pocket for leftovers. Oh, and no name plaque."

"Name plaque?"

"Yeah, on the door to my office. I don't care for titles. Besides after a few days I think I should remember which office was mine."

"If you last that long Mr. Stillwater."

He retreated to the back of the room and reached for the doorknob. "And we'll talk about a raise in two weeks. This should be my kind of job, dealing with natives, riffraff and awful canteen food. Man, I should have applied for this earlier." He laughed. "Don't reckon the food will be up to the organic stuff I usually eat when I'm out in the woods, but hey, its food. And free. Now that's a bonus plan." He tilted his button-festooned Expos cap. "So I'm off to check on the rabble. How long before I begin to build towards a pension?"

The main interviewer, now almost regretting his decision, closed his eyes. "You've a client to deal with later this afternoon. The pension you'll be building towards from your first paycheque. Now get to work, Mr. Stillwater. We'll file the contract with the warden this afternoon. All the details regarding benefits, pay and holidays will be in it."

"Yes boss. And you can call me Charlie. Boss. Hmm. Never had a boss before, this could be fun. Holidays! You mean I can get time off and fly to exotic locations, like LA? Never been to Leduc, Alberta. Some distant cousins out there." He turned and wandered off into the corridor.

"One hour! I give him one hour."

"Yeah, but at least none of us have to go in there to deal with THEM." The overweight woman grunted. "And I for one, hope he gets what he deserves."

*   *   *

Charlie limped down the hall, leaning on his orca-headed cane, whistling. "Oh, I forgot to tell them I don't do suits and ties. Although a new plaid shirt would be nice, I think I got this one in ninety-three."

He winked at one of the guards as he led a prisoner down the hall. "Great day, lovely day. Nice uniform."

The guard scowled back as the prisoner glared at Charlie. "Oh, I must admit that pin stripe does make you look rather thin." He said to the guard as they passed.

"Who the fuck is that?" the prisoner grumbled.

"Don't know and none of your damn business anyways. Get a move on." He pushed him forward.

"Charlie Stillwaters, your new Native Elder." He whistled, again tapping the walls and floor with his cane. "Could use a bit of more cheery paint colour. Will have to suggest that to the warden. Okay, time for some lunch and then off to work. Off to work, man can't say I've ever said that before."

*　　*　　*

In the darkness I wait.

Humming songs, like I always did, ever since it could remember.

Waiting.

Knowing they would come.

I smile and hum another song.

Waiting.

*　　*　　*

Charlie grabbed his meal tray and sat down at the only empty table in the canteen. The inmates stared and snickered to each other. "Must be the hat. Obviously jealous," he muttered as he began to dig into his soup.

A large shadow blocked out the glow of florescent. "You're at my table," barked a heavy gruff voice.

Charlie looked up and gulped. A virtual mountain of a man stood before him. Native, with greasy dark hair, deep set eyes, face contorted into a nasty grimace. Standing well over six foot, bordering on seven, and nearly four hundred pounds. Not much of which was fat, but mostly anger buried in several large chips on his shoulder. The tables held at least six, nearly every table full, except for the one that only Charlie sat at. "There's plenty of room for two of us."

The babble of conversation ceased, spoons hung in the air. A dollop of soup echoed with a plop as everyone stopped to watch the unfolding massacre. This, Charlie knew could go well or totally sideways, like a hockey player getting slammed into the boards head down, not looking.

"You . . . are . . . sitting . . . at . . . my . . . fucking . . . table," growled the mass that made Rocky Mountains look small. Great meaty fists grated on the lunch tray.

Charlie didn't really think getting thumped on his first day would make a good impression on the others. "You've a licence for that hotdog stand?" Charlie waved his hand.

"What?"

A single fly buzzing reverberated through the canteen. Several breaths inhaled.

"A hotdog stand."

The behemoth stood gritting his teeth. "What the hell you going on about?" Charlie could tell the giant's puzzlement was winning over the rage to crush the annoying insect before him. Which he could in one swat, like a grizzly tagging a poodle. "Your fly is undone."

The man lifted his tray, looked down and blushed.

A sneer cracked one side of his mouth, intimidation at its best, backed by three hundred plus pounds of muscle. He looked at

Charlie and laughed. "Move the fuck over. For an old bastard, you're alright."

He thumped the tray down, slopping some of the soup, and sat next to the suddenly relieved shaman who'd just seen his next three lifetimes sail before his eyes. After zipping his fly, he thumped Charlie on the back. Charlie gagged, nearly swallowing his back and front teeth at the same time. "Hey, you're okay. Most people are usually scared of me."

The other inmates blinked in disbelief, looking from each other to the no longer impeding demise of the newest member of staff, thinking they'd just seen the Titanic miss the iceberg and land at New York, before returning disappointedly to their meals.

"Well of course they would be. Yours are the size of a pair of grizzly bears stacked on top of each other in a totem, wearing the grimace of the bottom one suffering from fighting off the butt of the other after he ate a load of Tacos." Charlie stuck out his tongue and squinted his eyes like he'd just smelled fresh cow patty.

The big man laughed again. Puzzlement showed on the other inmates' faces, not understanding what was going on and rather disappointed that today's massacre had turned into a Laurel and Hardy love-in. Most had never even seen him smile let alone heard him laugh out loud, nor say more than three words in any one sitting. "Who are you?"

Charlie knew humour was rare on this one's face by the well-ingrained frown lines. "Charlie Stillwaters. Your new Prison Elder." He stuck his hand forward after wiping it on his jean jacket.

"I'm Thomas Johnson." He shook the shaman's hand, somewhat gently, although Charlie's eyes opened as far as they could as the natural muscle crumpled three of his fingers into his elbow.

"Wow, bet the Man of Steel would have a bitch of a time winning against you in an arm wrestle. Your real name?"

"That is my real name."

"Raised in a residential school?"

"Yeah! How'd you know?"

"It's my job to know," he lied, thinking he should sound like he knew something about being a legal Prison Elder, even though he was only a half day into the job. "No, I meant the real name your parents gave you."

He frowned. "My parents died when I was very young. Don't know my real name, or if I have one."

"Well I'm naming you with your native name. Now then, I'm thinking its T'aalgii Tilldagaaw Xuuajii, Big Mountain Grizzly."

The man ladled soup into his mouth, pausing for thought. "Big Mountain. I like that." Charlie breathed deeply, realizing he'd just befriended undoubtedly the best, or perhaps worst, guy in the place. The one everyone else feared.

"Charles Stillwater report to the warden's office." Spoke the disembodied voice over the PA.

"Duty calls." Charlie rose. "Didn't like the soup anyways, too salty. I'll have to talk to the cook about that and give them heck. I told them it's Charlie Stillwater-S. Government never can get things right. Probably have to redo all six hundred and forty pages of the contract. Did know you they only allow me two urine breaks and nine ounces of coffee? A day? Man, might have to buy diapers to make it through."

Big Mountain laughed and wiped the back of his hand across his mouth and slid Charlie's tray towards himself. "I'll eat the rest of your soup then, and you're welcome at my table anytime. But don't any of you other bastards get any ideas," he grumbled loudly to the others. "And if you need someone to back you up in here..." he said more softly, and winked at Charlie.

"Tell you what, if you want I could dig into your files and see if I could find out some background history."

"I'd like that. Told I had a sister, but never met her."

"I'll see what I can do and no cracking any heads while I'm on shift. You wouldn't want to make me mad, I crack a mean face." Charlie cracked several ridiculous faces as he got up. Big Mountain snorted a load of soup out of his nose, gagging.

"Quick! He's choking! Someone get Arnold Schgartabugger to perform mouth to mouth, cause no one else is going to press lips to the Griz here and walk away without missing limbs."

The big man laughed even harder, turning puce. Charlie slapped him on the back several times until the big man spit a chunk of food out.

"Hey, funny place to hide a Colt .45," he said looking up at the approaching guards. They reached for their guns. "Oh just kidding, it's just a chunk of hot dog, shaped like a gun." The two guards looked at him like he was mad. Griz just wiped at the tears of laughter running down his cheeks.

Walking away, Charlie realized he'd just found his first client as an Elder and his first prison friend.

*   *   *

I am a being, alone, entirely alone. Except there are others. I want to meet the others. I want to be me. Only who am I?

I had others in my life. Older, parents. Then why am I here? Alone?

And who? The question remains. Of who?

Am I?

*   *   *

"So this is where the last Elder expired. Don't disturb anything. They're still not sure whether it's a crime or an accident. Wish they'd make their minds up so we don't have to spend shifts guarding a damn tent." The guard indicated his work-mate whose duty today was to babysit the scene so it couldn't be tampered with. "My turn tomorrow." The yellow Police Line Do Not Cross tape surrounding the sweat lodge in the grounds behind the penitentiary sagged and swayed in the breeze.

"Boy, you guys aren't very sociable around here. No wonder you can't get any help. Darn it though," he tut-tutted as he walked around the sweat lodge, "I wanted to arrange a really swanky soiree tonight. You know, tux, champagne and horses douvres."

"It's hors d'oeuvres, I believe," the man grumbled, "and those are big words for a native."

"I watch a lot of educational TV. Gives you a large vocabulary. You know, documentaries, educational programs and the like. Pick up the odd phrase. I bet you like to watch tripe like all of those insipid reality shows."

"Yeah, how'd you know that?"

"Just a wild guess. Rots your mind that stuff." Charlie continued pacing around the sweat lodge trying to get a sense of what may have happened here. This was the reason he'd received some weird calls from the spirits in his dreams recently. Only why, he wasn't sure. A death didn't usually raise such unrest from the spirit world. He knew that no one inside would leave until the sweat was done, although on the usual sessions they often took three breaks to cool down, one for each of the four directions. Once inside, there would be very little light to see by, only the glow of the rocks, which had been burning for hours. The person leading, usually but not always the Elder himself would be moving about, flapping eagles' feathers and other objects for effect, but how a murder could be committed with not one of the inhabitants noticing was a mystery. The guard scowled as he followed the still-pacing Charlie. "Do you have a list of the people in the group?"

"I don't, but the office does, and the police and WCB. Why are you asking? Figure one of your relatives was in on it or you decided to become the next Dick Tracy?" the guard, Jenkins grumbled, obviously put off by having to hang around while Charlie checked out the scene.

"Just curious as to how someone could have died without anyone noticing. I'll have to lead a sweat sooner or later. WCB?"

"All accidents or deaths at work are treated as just 'work related incidents', unless foul play can be determined. If I was you, I'd hope they'd find any killer damn quick before they had to start asking for applications for my replacement." He snickered at what he thought was a great joke.

Charlie sniffed the air ignoring the guard's threats. Death never left a pleasant aroma but a murder created a foul stench. He sniffed again, loudly. Odd, no lingering after tones. Almost as if... he sniffed again.

"Hey, you got allergies, short of coke or something? There's plenty of drugs around this place, no matter how hard we try to police the inmates." His walkie-talkie went off. "Time to go. I've got duties besides babysitting you, old man."

"Some of us can sense and smell things better than most animals. Any chance you were on duty that day?" Charlie inhaled again, overly loudly.

"Yeah. What's it to ya?"

"Oh, just asking." He knew one thing, this guard was not only belligerent, but possibly capable of murder. He'd keep an eye on him. Charlie inhaled again. The wood-smoke of the sweat had covered the subtle floating aromas, but there was something underlying everything here. Something worse than menacing. The spirits were right. There was something very unnatural here.

"The only animal I want to smell is frying cow, as in a burger. Now time to beat it."

"There!" he yelled.

The guard jumped, "What the fuck..."

Charlie stopped and moved his head side to side, sniffing loudly. It was gone. Out of the corner of his eye he caught the shadow of something moving on the edge of the forest, by the fences.

"You, old man, are the freakiest bastard I ever met and I'll tell you I've met quite the collection of freaks here. Now get moving. Sniffing time is over, or go join the hound dog society if that's your bag."

Charlie moved to the doorway, careful not to disturb the tape or scene. He'd have to come back alone. There was something lurking there alright, something masking everything else under the smell of sweat and wood-smoke. Something fouler than death. The spirits usually weren't wrong about getting him here. He glanced past the grounds to the dark edge of the forest.

A branch shifted.

And he'd been watched. Yup most curious. And since I can't get into the lodge or the adjacent women's prison, I think I need to contact someone who can. Going to need some help on this one and I know just the person that owes me a favour.

*   *   *

The floor bed shook. From a dark cave one eye opened, then another. It looked around in the darkness before stretching slowly from the cramped form it had endured all this time. Poking its head up into the ocean's waters, the creature took one deep sniff. The salty waters told it all it needed to know.

It is time. We need to act again.

It let out a high pitched squeal to the others, also long buried. The ground shook in response.

But first a feeding. It has been a very long time since we've awoken and I'm sure the others are, like me, famished.

And it knew who would do.

*   *   *

Charlie strode down the hall towards his office. There was something out there watching him, he knew it. As he left the washroom he turned the corner and ran into two men dressed in suits. Charlie glanced at the name tag on the one that said Warden.

"Oh, the big guy, the big Cheese, el capitan, the dude who signs my paycheque."

"Who the hell are you, Sir?"

"Charlie Stillwaters"

"Not on any payroll I know of around here."

"We hired him this morning, sir. Remember the 'I need an Elder pronto or we lose our Federal funding for the next six months,' speech?"

"Yes, what was that got to do with this, I might say, disheveled looking, fellow?"

"Your new Elder counsellor, Boss Man." He grabbed the warden's hand and shook it hard three times before wiping his hand on his shirt. "Crap, forgot to dry my hands after that last trip to the pisser. Actually didn't notice any paper dispensers in the cans. But you should have someone look into those vacuum cleaner ducts they've installed in the washroom. Makes lots of noise, but didn't pick much off the floor. Oh and no ties. I don't do ties. Yours I'll have to admit is rather smart. Solid one colour, denotes lack of character, bland in tastes and preferences, but very dapper, as they say in England. Goes well with the fancy cufflinks. Gotta run, don't want the boss to think I'm loitering about on my first day. Need to make a good first impression and all."

With that Charlie sauntered off, limping on his cane. Still wiping his hands as he muttered more to himself than anyone else. "Glad that wasn't a number two."

"Sorry sir, there weren't any other applications."

The warden stood there blinking, calmly pulled a hanky from his vest pocket and wiped his damp hand. "Henricks, in my fucking office now." Red rushing in to replace the white sheen of mortification.

*   *   *

In the darkness deep breathing echoed. A flipper broke the centuries old sand. We are called, the others must awake before it is too late.

*   *   *

Charlie limped up behind Carol as she lay sun-tanning on Agate Beach on Haida Gwaii. "Nice tan. Heard you were here on holidays."

Carol jumped. "Hate it when you do that." Squinting, she yanked herself upright in her deckchair and peered over her dark sunglasses. "I didn't expect to see you on the islands. Although with your woo-woo stuff I might have figured I'd run into you sooner or later."

"Good to see you too, Carol. What drags you out here?" He hadn't seen her since they worked on solving the death of Vancouver's mayor last year.

"You hooked me. Decided I gotta see more of this place. And let me guess, I'm presuming this is probably a business call, since you're a bit over dressed for the beach." She looked him up and down over her sunglasses realizing it was the same getup he wore then, probably was like Einstein who kept ten same outfits of everything in his closet. No, with Charlie, probably just the same one.

"Yeah, this is my office suit now." Charlie referred to his usual get up of seen-better-days denim. "I got hired by the Federal Government to be a paid Elder for the Prince Rupert Penitentiary."

"What? Were they mad?"

"No, I was the only one that applied. It seemed the other applications got lost."

Carol shook her head. "I've heard this story before. Lost by, let me guess, cousins of yours."

"Big family. We don't see each other much, but we're tight. Man, it's hot out here. Their last Elder died, more aptly was murdered, although I think the pen don't like that idea and are trying everything they know to get it signed off as what the WCB call 'a work related incident'. Covers all sorts of wrongdoing that title."

"Which, unless someone finds three knives in his back or several bullet holes, it is, and the police involvement ceases."

"Got that from the no-humour jail guard and a little bird that whispered it in my ear."

"A little bird whispered in your ear? That someone was murdered? Man, you hang out with a strange crowd. But then I already know that."

"Yeah, little bird, not you-know-who-giant-raven-type-bird, built like a triple-stacked burger, but sparrow sized. One of those woo-woo things of mine that you talk about was disturbed by something that happened at the supposed accident. Whatever is happening is sending physic shockwaves through the unknown world, as you'd probably call it, and the authorities won't let me near the scene. The disturbance happened in a native sweat lodge out on the back grounds, only some of the suspects involved are female. While I've got access to the men I can't enter the women's prison."

"They won't let you near the scene until it is ruled either a WCB incident or the coroner warrants there's enough evidence to open a homicide investigation." Carol knew where this was going. "So let me guess. You want me to cut my holiday short because a sparrow whispered in your ear and go to a penitentiary full of women to investigate a murder? Many of whom would just as soon blink and either kill me for being a cop, make goggle eyes at me or just out-and-out rape me?"

"Well, you're good at summing things up. Sharp cookie, Ms. Ainsworth. You did say you owe me a favour as I did save your, what do the gangstas on TV call it? Oh yeah, your white skinny ho ass. Which by the way is starting to burn. You need some higher SPF or some of my herbal cream."

Carol reached for her pack of smokes. "I've tried your herbal remedies. Bear-sweat, weasel pee and oak-tree pumice. Thanks, but I'll stick to the drugstore products. At least they have a money back guarantee." Carol remembered the large burl along Rawlings Trail in Stanley Park that, if you caught it just right, looked like the face of an old woman. Or at least to everyone else it was a burl with an old woman's face in it. She knew it was the living witch called the Lure trapped inside. It still gave her the creeps to think how close to death she came. She would have died if it wasn't for Charlie, in their last and, she thought at the time, only adventure together. *I'm not really thinking what I'm thinking, am I? Why didn't I bring a flask of wine with me or at least a mickey of whiskey?*

"Ah what the heck. I was getting bored anyway, already hung out up at Rosespit. Wanted to chat with my mom's spirit up there, but couldn't hook up with her. Need to work on that woo-woo stuff of yours some more." She paused and shook her head. "I know I'm going to regret what I'm about to say, but okay. And after this we're even. I can't be seen to be constantly talking to an old native man dressed forever in the same clothes. People will begin to think we're a team, or, heaven forbid, an item."

Charlie waited for Carol as she collected her things together. A couple with kids in tow walked by, all were staring at Charlie sweating away in his jeans and jean jacket. One of the children, a rotund girl of about twelve, was eating an ice cream cone. She frowned at the older man and stuck her tongue out. "Smelly Indian."

"Rude little girl." Charlie waved his cane and a stick that was lying in the sand lifted between the girl's shins and sent her flying. She tripped and fell face first, mashing ice cream and sand all over her face.

"Deal. We're even after this." Carol giggled as the girl screamed, spitting sand.

"Oh dear." Charlie walked on and said as he passed the couple, "You know its bad luck to take any agates and sand away from here, even ingested. Native legend, just like the ones in Hawaii regarding Pele', their fire goddess. She brings bad luck to anyone that takes away her sand and agates. I'd make sure you wash her mouth out, with soap preferably. Sand isn't good for the digestion anyways. Good day." He smiled as he passed.

The girl kept spitting sand and ice cream from her mouth. "He did it! He made me trip. Stinky old ..."

Charlie gave her a nasty glare. The girl decided to shut up.

"Now, you were just clumsy. I've told you before to watch where you're going. He wasn't even near you at the time," her mother scolded.

"But I know he ..."

"Enough! Get in the car now!" her dad yelled, "serves you right for being rude to your elders."

"See, my work precedes me." He walked with a swagger.

Carol looked quizzically at Charlie as they walked towards her car. "Did you do something to that girl back there?"

"My dad always told me to never piss off certain people in your life; your doctor, lawyer, a police officer or your shaman."

"Don't think he said shaman, probably minister."

"You didn't know my dad."

Carol laughed. "And now I know why you don't cheese off shamans."

Charlie laughed back. "Come to think of it, he might have said minister."

Seeds Of Ascension,

BOOK ONE:

Spirits

Awakening

Prelude

Stars hung in eternity threaten to fall into each other winking in disbelief. My breath wafts its cooling warmth into the darkness as I turn to answer the call from inside.

That beckoning voice that brought me here.

Only there are no tomorrows, no yesterdays, and one time eternal. The now.

A cry rents the stillness, it is not possible, is it?

The pad of feet issues from somewhere. No reassurance that I will leave here alive or whole or even if my spirit will be cleansed from my bones. Nicely or rendered horribly apart like from some Grade B horror movie.

So coming here was not at all wise.

Still my breath issues forth joining the clouds that skirt soundlessly by as mist curls among trees, like angelic spirits melted into smoke tendrils by this place.

Chill surges upwards as fog thickens, cooling and undulating like a snake on a river of calling.

Whatever this is drawing me here, asking of those that will answer and speak before it.

Denying touch, taste, sound, smell and clamping numbness to my ears, I remain open to its only way of being.

The here. The now.

Dew drips from grass, leaves, everywhere. The soft plodding of water coming home to earth. A cycle born again, returning.

Padding sounds end as I take another step forward, answering the call that beckons.

While silence answers me with its own questions.

Once again.

Roger woke in a lurch from his dreams.

He got up and walked slowly to the bathroom making sure Beth, his wife, wouldn't wake. Outside the full moon hung in abeyance, calling to him to sleep some more and continue this insane journey he began, or at least was called to perform.

Bugger that, I have to urinate first before my bladder bursts.

He closed his eyes and let his waters flow into the toilet before him.

Yeah, I know, Words from the song echoed in him, *the Orinoco Flow.*

What a Bag.

John Lennon's song added to the echoes descending away into dribbles. 'Let it be'. Let it be, let it be, let it be. Whispering words of wisdom. Let it be.

And that was where it began.

Only it won't, will it?

Let anything be, anymore?

Chapter One

"The End is near! Repent sinners! Set your spirit free, join Jehovah at the right hand of God!" The man dressed in a black suit bellowed to the crowd of people, most of whom were simply trying to get either into the airport before they missed their flight, or were waiting for their rides out of this chaos.

Unfortunately, Roger had picked a spot to get out of his taxicab right next to the Jehovah's Witness and two newly-bald Hare Krishna dressed in their flowing robes, chanting in time to the rhythm of their tambourines. "Join the pure love of God. Set your spirit free." The two chanted brazenly trying to overcome the Jehovah's Witness man thumping his bible loudly exclaimed in a baritone voice, "Ignore false prophets."

The two being ex-WFC converts didn't take well to the rude preacher stealing the show beside them with his boisterous Sunday-morning-at-the-pulpit voice and began to thump their tambourines even louder.

The Jehovah man glared and raised his voice.

Roger Harrison and his new wife Beth waited while the taxi driver unloaded their luggage as all Hell broke loose. The man in black started thumping one of the Hare Krishna over the head with his bible as the other put him in a headlock shouting, "Find the love of God and yourself." Prayer beads went flying in all directions as the Jehovah man grabbed one of the tambourines and slammed one of the Hare Krishna's in the head.

Roger glanced at his watch; they didn't have much time to make their plane, let alone watch the bizarre spectacle unfolding in front of him. Already security guards were running in from all directions adding to the ensuing melee.

"Wow, don't see that every day," Beth spurted.

An older man, obviously a former love-child of the sixties according to his long hard and faded, well-worn peace-emblem tee-shirt, shoved by Roger. "Peace Bro."

He gave Roger the two-fingered sign once common in the sixties. Roger caught the line 'If I could turn myself inside out and set my spirit free' playing from the man's headset. U2, he thought, as he managed to squeeze into the terminal building. "I've got to help my brethren fight the fascist pigs in power, the times they are a-changing." He smiled and grabbed a fallen tambourine and belted one of the guards over the head.

"Oh, that they will be if we miss our flight. They'll be changing me into the ranks of the newly divorced." He hurried his new bride inside. "Yup," he said, "you don't get to see that every day."

Set my spirit free.

Lyrics echoed in his head.

My spirit free?

The question fluttered away. *As somewhere in the mists of his mind angels fluttered wings and rain fell on delicate ferns, uncurling into the light generated by the sun overhead.*

What?

February 4th, 1971,
The Moon; Fra Mauro Crater

"One small step for man... one giant leap for mankind."

The words of Neil Armstrong echoed through Edwin Mitchell's mind as he stared up at the Earth rising over the horizon, the music of 2001: A Space Odyssey playing in his head.

Earth: continents, surrounded by the deep blue of the oceans cradled in billowy arms of clouds. He tried to spot the USA and, more importantly, the location of his hometown, where his wife and kids were probably staring back up at the moon. No markings existed to distinguish one country from another, nor to distinguish democracies from communistic societies or dictatorships. Land and mountains, ocean and clouds. Just one world spinning. Odd, he'd not really expected it to be like this.

Spinning, like so many of the other dots of light shining by the untold billions amid all this magnificence and the darkness of space, without the filter of sky and atmosphere. One spec, a mote revolving in a sea of infinity, all part of the cosmos. At peace with the universe. At one with itself.

At one with the Universe; connected.

Edwin smiled. He'd never imagined it would be like this. No lines, no boundaries out here. Nothing like he'd been told, had read about in the books: light years of frozen emptiness separated by mere molecules and photons floating in vastness. This was different. Something no books, no professors could describe, and none could experience. He was only the sixth man to walk on the moon, blessed to have left Earth and view it from the outside in. Whole, suspended in the firmament of the heavens.

Tones of awe, like angels humming in reverence, filled his head. As the light of Earth flooded the plain he stood on, Ed gasped. Lights dancing, reflecting. Lights touching him as he grasped the rocks around him. Lights dancing? On the Moon?

He turned and stared into the heavens. Flashes of flares or rocket-fire, too small to be anything propelled, streaked off the moon's surface into space. Heading in the direction of Earth.

Beep.

"Ed, your vital signs are going offline. Ed, you've stopped breathing. CO levels are rising. Ed, you okay?"

"Yes, Mission Control, I'm fine. Did you register any unusual activity?"

"Nothing other than some of the seismic sensors indicating several tremors in the area."

"How many?"

He counted the streaks heading away from the moon.

"Looks like about twelve peaks in activity, just beyond the Fra Mauro crater. Are you over the top yet?"

He counted the same number of lights ascending into the dark universal sky heading towards earth. "Another couple of steps." *They aren't going to believe this back home are they?*

He took a long breath and sighed, lost in crystalline reflections as he crested the crater.

"Ed? Everything okay? Your monitors are going nuts again."

"Jeez." *No one, absolutely no one would believe this.* He didn't believe it himself. "Just admiring old Mother Earth," he lied. "It's not every day you get to see an Earthrise."

No, nothing was as he'd been taught. Oh, it was all there, the stars, the sun, the blackness of space, everything where it should be. Only it was different, as different as the plateau before him. A whole lifetime of teachings and beliefs blown aside by invisible winds, like dust before reality's vision. He shook his head, scrambled back down the way he'd come and returned to his work of digging up moon rocks to take home. Was it possible? *Did I just see that?*

Home, he thought, how funny. In some ways as he stared up into the heavens, he was home.

Sea Tac Airport

"If I could turn myself inside out and break my spirit free."

The U2 song line stuck, stewing away in his head, too many times to be coincidence. Spinning at the unconscious like a dog digging aimlessly in the dirt at something tantalizing it smelled. Compelling him on and on.

Compelling him on and on.

The near riot outside began to die down, with the security guards resorting to Tasering and handcuffing the troublemakers. The Jehovah man yelling obscenities at the bleeding Hari Krishna's as they cursed back in some Indian dialect that only Buddha would know.

Words, all words pulling at him, like spirit things. Echoing, so strange. His whole day had begun to have a feeling of surrealism.

The scene outside didn't help. He was supposed to be on his honeymoon. Buddha, incense and mystical music echoed in his head.

Echoing winds, words.

Spirit.

Drifting, pulling him away.

Intangible presences.

Pooling like dew on grass, drip, dripping, flowing into a burbling stream.

Consciousness.

Spirit flowing.

To places, dimensions unknown.

Inevitable things.

His subconscious nagging at him, it's sublime finger jabbing into his head, Roger shuffled forward joining the long queue in the ticket line.

Why? Why here? Why now?

"What are you so nervous about?" Beth prodded him.

"Who says I'm nervous?" She broke him away from his musing as fairies folded their arms and tapped their slippered feet, waiting for an answer only they knew would come.

"Because you always turn pale and squeeze your hands together, or mine."

He yanked himself back to earth and realized he'd been gripping her hand so tight her wedding band had marked her finger. "Sorry." All day he'd felt odd, like something wasn't right. That commotion outside hadn't helped ease his fears. The repeated chanting of voices? Haunting his memory like niggling tendrils of spirit things. *Fuck, get out of my head,* he swore to himself. *And where the eff did this come from? It was like what I just saw or heard twigged some memory of myself, or at least of what I once was?*

Roger simply looked blanked at his new wife, not sure what to say to mollify her, when his heart was beginning to race on a journey he'd never taken, but knew he was on. Once before.

"I don't get it. You've flown dozens of times on business. Or are you afraid of me? Don't worry I don't bite; although I do nibble rather fine. Remember the first time we kissed? I thought you were going to crush my fingers."

"And the second and the third. You know I get nervous around women." *Yes, talk to Beth, it helped to get the visions of angels out of my head. Only why are they there in the first place?* He aimlessly scratched at an itchy part of his stomach that had begun to throb. Heat spread as he scratched at it.

"Hey, I'm your wife now. It's okay."

"I know. I think lunch didn't agree with me, damn Burritos." He hugged her. A strange day threatened, that's what it was. Be prepared for the most unexpected on those days, a colleague once told him. *Easier said than done.* It reminded him of a poster from his younger days, 'It's hard to remember your objective is to drain the swamp, when you're up to your armpits in alligators.'

Roger frowned, the soft cry of a child caught his ears from somewhere in the distance or from inside his heart. "Do you hear that?" He cranked his head around, scanning the crowd.

"No, I don't. Hear what?"

"Young girl, crying." Roger spotted the young black girl standing by the candy counter about thirty feet away. No one seemed to be paying any attention to her. Everyone too busy rushing around trying to catch planes. He muttered. She was clutching a doll, tears streaming down her ebony face. "Keep our place, I'll be right back."

"You okay young lady," he bent over and held out a Kleenex as he approached.

"Can't find my mommy." She started to cry harder.

"It's okay, we'll find her. Let's go over here to security and I'll buy you a candy bar while we page her." He was careful not to touch her as they walked over to the counter. Even acts of kindness he knew could be wrongly construed. Best to be careful, didn't want to be thrown in the clink on child molestation charges on his honeymoon.

A minute later, after the pager called out the lady's name and the young girl had nearly finished the Mars bar he bought, a rather frightened large black lady came running from across the crowded terminal. "My baby! One second she was by my side and the next she was gone." She sobbed as she clutched the young girl. "Thank you, kind sir, and you young lady are going to get a good scolding."

"No problem, but be kind, she was only a child, doing what kids do, exploring strange environs."

She looked weirdly at him and crushed her kid closer to him, like he was someone suddenly not to be trusted.

He walked back to join Beth in their lineup, which had moved only about three people closer to the front. He scratched at the throb in his stomach. The heat pulsating.

"You're always helping kids. Why is that?"

"Don't know. Something to do with having no dad as I grew up. Perhaps." In his head the words, *teachers call out to those that need attention and protection before their time is ready to begin their teachings. Protectors insure the lives of the innocent so that they can one day replace them.* Echoed like an opera in the void. *Why do I get the feeling this trip is nowhere where I think it will take me?* He smiled to her as the vision of some Buddhaistic being winked back at him.

"Only your mom to raise you. Must have brought out your feminine, sensitive side. Another reason why I love you. I've never met a man with such a spiritual deepness." She winked. "Just wait until I get you alone."

"Is that a promise?" *Spiritual deepness? Never had anyone say that to me before. Doesn't everyone listen to Enya in their car or Delirium?* He thought a moment as the throb in his stomach increased.

Promises, promises of inevitable things. Inevitable things unfolding. Fuck.

They were on their honeymoon, full of excitement for the new journey together as man and wife. But inside Roger sensed another journey unfolding, one he had dreamt about for days now in his dreams. Unsettling dreams, that at first he'd put it down to his anticipation of getting married, his nervousness regarding the honeymoon trip, but feared it was much more. The incident earlier with U2 and the chanting Hare Krishna's had unleashed something buried in his mind. He began to drift away again, some forgotten thread inside nagging at him. Pulling him on some pathway he'd never recall going down ever before.

An awakening.

Journeys on paths unbidden, a soul's course, and destiny denied like the flashflood down desert canyons, every breath, every step sweeping him away. Thrust to the embrace of fate and futures scrawled into sacred rock. Knowing, the ache of knowing that things were unfolding in the universe all around him and there was nothing he could do. Roger sighed. *This wasn't going to be an ordinary honeymoon was it? I hope whatever happens at least let me get laid tonight first then I'd be open to learning the spiritual pathways of turtles swimming under full moons while fairies caressed their bellies.*

Man, I gotta write this stuff down. Don't know where it is coming from?

He scratched at the hardness forming in his stomach.

They'd made love many times, but he wanted to do it on a Hawaiian beach in the moonlight. Naked, with sand stuck in his cheeks, Blue Hawaiian drinks beside them. Although, intuitively he knew there was little he could do now, except watch it crash into him, into his orderly existence, wiping rationality aside like dust from bookshelves. But the bookshelf didn't exist, and each dust speck was a world unto itself. Nor was the dusting rag just a rag but a curtain of time sweeping all before it, while only chaos talked, reeling in its own hosts. Inevitable things. *Damn, it was like watching the wall approach as your car veers out of control towards it. Again the hymn of angels.*

"We're next, honey."

Hardness in my stomach? What the? Roger tensed, gripping her hand as he rubbed against something in his stomach that shouldn't be there, nor was yesterday.

Yesterday, a Beatles song echoed in the background. *When time was gone away.*

"Ow, you're crushing my hand again. What is wrong?"

"Don't know." *I've done this dozens of times, this is my honeymoon.* He reminded himself he was setting off on his honeymoon with Beth. They were heading for Hawaii and then on a free Grand Canyon whitewater rafting trip he'd won in a company contest last year. He'd promised Bill, his buddy, that he'd also visit Sedona, Arizona. Land of the red rock, canyons and Hopi Indians as part of the package. He shook his head, still not sure why he'd let Bill talk him into going to Sedona, yet something about that name intrigued him, called him. Like this moment, haunted him. What if he said no, *I can't do this. Won't.*

Maybe he should turn around. If he was smart, he would and run before everything he knew up til now in his life melted into a slagheap before his feet.

But destiny was a capricious child at best. Unruly and without definition, no boundaries. No knowing when it would call or where it would surface. Major moments that changed lifetimes and entire nations in the blink of an eye, when a shift of one single belief or thought pattern came without deliberation and totally unexpectedly. Roger held his ground, one foot demanding resolutely to go back and the other? *Into nowhere land.*

"You okay?"

"Yeah, just keep thinking I've forgotten something," he lied. Trying to release her hand, his grip to the now. **Damn it. Run.**

He stared into her sweet, concerned face. The brown eyes he'd fallen instantly in love with. The petite nose, half-hidden by the cascade of brunette hair, and the twin dimples that erupted with each smile, framing the luscious lips he wanted more than anything to be kissing on a Hawaiian beach.

He shook his head, clearing it, grounding himself with deep breaths, back into his life. His dreams the last few nights had been filled with insights and the dull ache of knowing inevitable things were taking place. Hadn't he read that the big events in one's life are all preordained and in those moments, time slows to a crawl and eternity grips each syllable until half lights shutter away in strobe-lamp fashion? Or was it simply the fact that he was worried about flying, especially after the ISIS and all the constant hysteria induced by the government regarding retaliation or all the conspiracy theories over Covid-19 and government control.

As he stepped through the metal detector he knew.

Everything in his orderly, ordinary, run of the mill, two point five kids, a mortgage, good paying job, benefits, would change.

Fuck, why didn't I run?

Forever.

And ever.

Amen.

Beep. Beep.

Angels snickered and fairies spat magic into the earth before them. Causing new fairies to be born.

Double fuck.

"Sorry, sir. Please go back and remove any coins and other metal objects."

"Oh. Thought I already did that." *The Inevitability of too late to turn back. One path set, the others discarded.* His heart pounded. *Angels were laughing behind my back right now as devilish beings played in the band and others joined in a jig.*

Beth went through while he did as the attendant instructed him, a thorough check of his pockets confirmed that he didn't have any metal on him. The lineup behind him was lengthening, other travelers as eager as he was to set off for their destination waiting patiently. He stepped back through the metal detector's frame again.

Beep. Beep.

The bastards were rolling in the aisles of heaven, howling and whoever held the wild card was gleaming like a jackdaw in heat.

"Over here, sir. Spread your legs and raise your arms. Do you have any metal on your body?" The attendant scanned him with his wand.

"Not that I know of." He wanted to add, *except for the metal plate in my skull,* but he figured anyone who had to stand there doing this job day after day wouldn't have much of a sense of humor. The scene from the movie <u>Spinal Tap</u> came to mind, where the hip rock star with the spray-on leather pants and hefty package bulging from his crotch area is stopped at an airport scanner. Much to the macho dude's chagrin, security discovers a concealed Bierwurst sausage wrapped in tinfoil.

Beep. Beep.

The detector went off around his midsection. "Must be my high-iron diet," he joked weakly, the attendant didn't smile.

"This is no laughing matter sir. Have you had any operations?"

"No, **sir**." Roger leaned heavily on the "sir". Sweat was breaking out on his forehead. "Never had an operation in my life."

"Proceed to that room over there." *It was now too late to run.*

"Ah, but ... will I miss my flight?"

"Proceed to that room. You have not been cleared for boarding."

"Roger, what's going on here?" Beth stared, frowning, an eye twitching. She hated being singled out in a crowd and he knew he was to blame.

"Don't worry, babe. Something seems to be setting off the metal detectors. I can't board until they check it out." Crap, years later he was still antsy enough after the bombing of the World Trade Towers, and now this. The smirk of chaos commencing its numbing jumbled dance, taking control ... the lines between his dream-world and reality blurred. Had he already set something in place that would lead to change? The trouble with inevitable things and chaos is that there's no secretary keeping notes, no Dictaphone to replay the events or a cellphone to take images. Only hands-on experience and he'd never experienced anything deep or religious or wildly spiritual in his life, until now. *Well other than listening to the Orinoco flow by Enya, I knew that listening to that irish bag would get me into trouble. Yet something in her cadence called.*

So where was all this coming from? And why couldn't I shut up that voice in my head?

Three guards lounged in the small room, the two males casually snapped their gum. A rotund female guard sat in the corner reading the National Enquirer, scowl pinching her ruddy face. Dealing with her, he sensed, would be like taking sirloin from a pit-bull. It could be done but chances were you'd lose more blood and flesh than you'd gain.

"Hands up. Gotta run another scanner over you," the first male ordered.

It beeped in the same area as before. "Ever have an operation, sir?" The second stared him in the eyes.

"Nope. And I'm a frequent flyer. Never had a problem with security."

"Yeah, got it. Open your shirt, please." The guard was still staring him down. He'd read that police and security personnel were trained to detect if a person was lying just by the way their eyes moved when he was asked a question. Roger stared straight back at the guard as he unbuttoned his shirt.

There, outlined just below his right ribcage, barely visible, was an irregular bulge. The throb he'd scratched at several times, earlier. He turned white; *I should have run, fucking inevitable things. Fucking haloed thy bloody angels.*

"What's that?" The guard poked at him.

Roger winced as he ran his fingers over the area. It wasn't hot to the touch, like he expected a tumor or blood clot to be, nor discolored, in fact it felt smooth, almost metallic. What was it? How'd it get there? Was he going to die? The visions of a woman he'd just seen on TV dying from some sort of viral infection, her body covered in massive sores. The doctors puzzled by this unknown affliction. "I ... ah ... can only say I've never seen this before." *And that was the bloody truth, how is this possible?*

What the hell was going on here? He'd recently had a physical and his doctor hadn't said anything about this. Surely he would have noticed it himself, in the shower this morning? Wouldn't he?

"So you're standing here trying to tell me you've never seen this before?"

"Yes."

"One more time, sir. Explain to me what that is." The guard raised his voice.

"I ... ah ... can't. I didn't even know it was there." *Christ, what was this?* Some kind of nightmare? The kind of things that happen only in Sci-Fi movies. The guard held the scanner directly over the lump. It began beeping madly.

"Well, I think you're full of shit myself. I've seen some pretty inventive ways to smuggle things in and out of this country. Ever seen puppies with sown up stomachs, hiding coke? What do you think, Ernie? Dope?" He nodded to the other male.

"Hey, just relax, Burt. We can't assume our mister ready to go on holidays here and relax on a Hawaiian beach sipping Mai Tais is up to something. Maybe he's got some cancerous growth or worse..."

"Oh like the scene from the movie, which one?" He snapped his fingers.

"Alien! Where the baby bursts out from the guys chest."

"Yeah, that's the one." He laughed ignoring the almost shivering Roger, as he kept glancing at the clock on the wall. Ernie turned back to him, all sign of joviality gone. "Nah, you know what I'm thinking? Dope." He eyed him directly again.

The only dopes here were the Dumb and Dumber rejects from security guard school. These were people used to being in control, who enjoyed watching others squirm. This was too surreal, not really happening, like the sensations that had assaulted him as he waited in line, like the hallucinations of marijuana. Like he was floating over all of this and watching, like this was meant to happen, only he didn't know why.

"Dope? How can that be dope, up there?"

"You tell us, sir. But we need to get you checked out. Maybe you've got some kind of explosives taped up inside you, behind some sort of fake skin graft. Never know what these whack job extremist Moslems come up with. Stand behind the screen, remove all your clothing and put on the robe. Over reacting? Remember nine-eleven. I lost an uncle in that pile of rubble and it ain't happening here again on my shift."

"Do I look like a Muslim suicidal type of dude?"

"Don't care, my job is to ensure the national security of this great nation of the US of A. If Trump wants to keep all the Taco breaths out by building a wall, then no wacko is getting in or out past my shift. Prepare the lube Burt and if you give us any more static I'll let Helga over there check you out."

"Or maybe he'd like that," the other laughed.

Roger's ears turned hot. They were baiting him, trying to force him to lose his cool. They were not good people, they liked baiting, torturing others. His intuition was going off, just like at the lineup. He clenched his fists, had to stay calm or goodbye honeymoon, welcome jail cell.

He glanced down at the headlines on the paper Helga was reading, *Man claims aliens impregnated him. Has seven-pound baby girl and two others of unknown DNA.* He finished robing himself in the paper gown and stepped away from the screen. The snap of latex over fingers echoed. The next few minutes weren't going to be quite the honeymoon experience he had planned.

Why in hell didn't I run, when my guts told me to?

If you really enjoyed this Book,
Please, feel free to leave a review

The author will highly appreciate it
And will help my rankings on Amazon
Thank You!

Afterword

Other Novels by Frank Talaber

STILLWATER RUNS DEEP SERIES

Book One: Raven's Lament
(based on a true incident)

A madman cuts down a rare tree in protest of logging, releasing something he didn't intend to. Reporter Brooke Grant investigates the story, finds the love of his life, only to lose her to said being. Enlisting the aid of a deranged shaman he has to save his love and stop the world from being changed forever.

REVIEWS

This novel has the ring of an epic "Lord of the Rings" journey -this is one journey that I'll always remember!

Stephanie A. Bridgeman/ The Glow Faeries

This is one of these books that you don't want to lay down until it's finished. Great stuff!

Tara Swanson

"After being stranded twenty kilometers from the nearest road at the tip of Rose Spit, Haida Gwaii, and having to push Frank's spanking new SUV a few kilometers along the beach before the tide came in and we ran out of booze, my first reaction on being asked to write a back cover blurb was, "over my dead body." Some people will do anything to get an endorsement."

Susan Musgrave/Cargo of Orchids/Given

On The west Coast, a journalist investigates a killing linked to destruction of old growth forest on First Nations land, and finds a spirit war as well as a real-work environmental struggle. He also finds love and meaning. It's a lovely, timely story line, and the outcome is arrived at in a surprising confluence of plot and subplot which makes the book ultimately charming and moving.

Candas Jane Dorsey

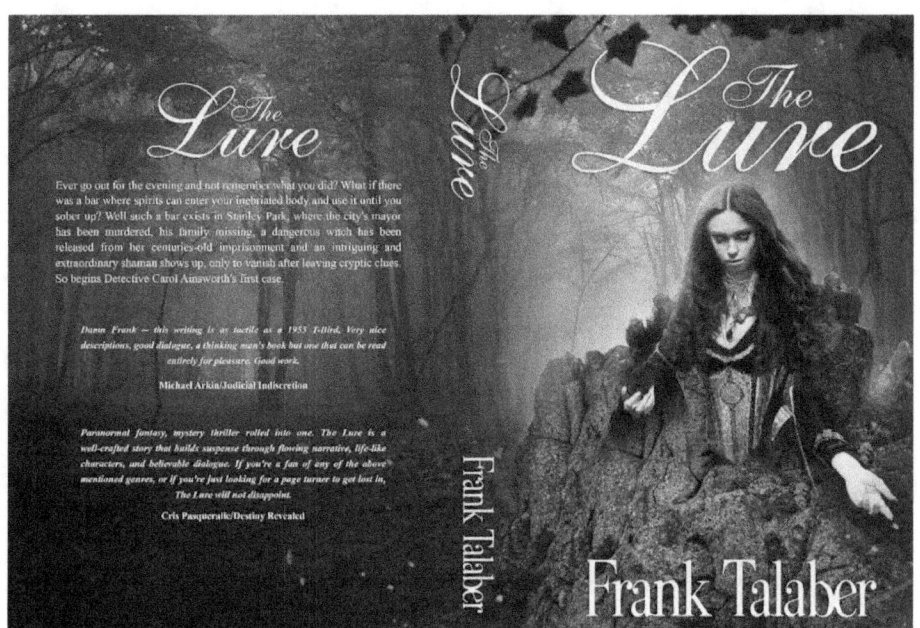

Book Two: The Lure

Ever go out drinking and don't remember what you did? What if there was a bar where spirits use your body for whatever they want until you sober up? What if the city's mayor has been murdered, his family missing, no clues and a witch has been released from her centuries old imprisonment? A deranged shaman shows up leaving clues and vanishes. So begins police detective, Carol Ainsworth's first big case.

REVIEWS

Your book kept my attention riveted from beginning to end. I liked the way you presented the female character being in control of the outcome and the fact the story was based on local settings. i.e. Victoria, B.C. Canada Riveting Work ...

Linda Low

A refreshing change from the usual and all too familiar cast of deities and spirits. Talaber pulls his characters from the vast and untapped riches of aboriginal myth and legend, bringing to life their intricate stories largely unfamiliar to wider audiences. He intertwines their ancient tales with the dark, gritty and dangerous under belly of contemporary urban life. The whole makes for an interesting and compelling read with an ending that's impossible to predict.

Robert Winslow

Damn Frank — this writing is as tactile as a 1955 T-Bird. Very nice descriptions, good dialogue, a thinking man's book but one that can be read entirely for pleasure. Good work.

Michael Arkin/Judicial Indiscretion

Paranormal fantasy, mystery thriller rolled into one. The Lure is a well-crafted story that builds suspense through flowing narrative, life-like characters, and believable dialogue. If you're a fan of any of the above mentioned genres, or if you're just looking for a page turner to get lost in, The Lure will not disappoint.

Cris Pasqueralle/Destiny Revealed

A gritty book flavored with primitive urges and mysticism. As I followed Carol's foray into the realm of shamanism, I realized that it took a special touch to pull off a complicated plot the way you did. Your prose was concise, powerfully descriptive, the dialogue lively, and your photographic mastery of the fixtures and streets in Vancouver's hub, in clear evidence.

Kenneth Edward Lim/The North Korean

Carol, the head detective, has to solve several murder cases: with many twists and turns. There's Shamans, Animal Spirits, and "The Lure" thrown in for good measure. No wonder, Carol wanted to resign! Yes, this novel is a roller-coaster ride, with the author cleverly hinting along the way, ending with a roller coaster ride! Read this book. It is different. It's as if Elmore Leonard has risen as a shaman, to guide others to write about Indian lore.

Nancy Bridgeman

Your book was a rollercoaster ride thorough my emotions which, when I got off, left me stunned and breathless.

Your portrayal of sociopaths and the criminal mind in the pursuit of the sexually willing was so disturbing I had nightmares and had to set the novel aside for days. But the writing was so compelling I had to finish it, and I'm glad I persevered.

I literally cheered "go get them!" when Charlie used his protectors to deal rather uniquely with the antagonists.

I was enlightened to the Native spiritual culture which pleased me for which I now have a greater understanding and respect.

Carol G.

Book Three: The Awakening

Its Ghostbusters teamed up with a female Mickey Spillane who has a Native Shaman sidekick nuttier than a squirrels winter stash as a side kick.

Agatha Christie, roll over in your grave, new sleuths on the prowl. A deranged shaman breaks his way into jail to stop all hell from breaking free while police detective Carol Ainsworth has to bring justice to a forest being's murdered mother.

How angry would a mythical god be if he found himself beginning to awake inside a mortal after centuries? The duo are determined to find out who killed the previous native elder before all lightning and thunder breaks loose. They encounter deranged inmates, mystical beings, ancient serpents, wood sprites and someone who should have been dead long ago.

Not your usual crime/mystery!
Not your usual criminal investigators!
You thought Jack Nicholson was mad in The Shining...
Wait until you meet Charlie Stillwaters in the Sweat lodge.

REVIEWS

There are many aspects true to First Nation's beliefs. For example the transformation of animals and anomalies within our realm. Frank Talaber's writing is clear and concise, leaving no grey areas. But his true talent as a writer is not only a sense of time, history and capturing First Nation's humor, but going from the real to the surreal and the supernatural. A gift he plies very well.

Tom Patterson Nuu-Cha-Nulth Artist and Master Carver

I've read and reread his previous series, Stillwaters Run Deep, several times. Frank's writing is original and compelling. You run into characters and situations totally unexpected. Keeps you on the edge of your seat and your heart.

Greta Olsson

Just when I was beginning to wonder where the next great Canadian story teller would emerge from, Frank Talaber has written a modern crime mystery with a twist. In "The Awakening" Talaber weaves the richness of Canada's west coast aboriginal spirituality into the science of modern forensics. CSI comes to Haida Gwaii as the shaman and the detective conduct an investigation that will take them and the reader on a journey to a place where murder, redemption and ancient mysticism intersect.

Michael G. de Jong, QC, Minister of Finance,
Government House Leader, Province of British Columbia

The Ainsworth Chronicles, Book One: The Joining

Welcome to Victoria in Beautiful British Columbia, the most haunted city in North America, and to Detective Carol Ainsworth's first day undercover at the very grand old lady, The Fairmont Empress Hotel. Ready to deal with the two Italian families flying in for a wedding to unite them, she did not bargain for the ghosts, the FBI agent or the ancient curses that come along too. Add to that the very wonderful and mysterious psychic lady claiming you've invited her, the young boys disappearing, and the weird things happening to the unfortunates looking for their next fix trapped alongside spirits in the sewers, Carol found her first undercover assignment way more challenging than she could have imagined.

The one saving grace was the great Empress High Tea that Agnes introduced her to and the fabulous scones that are to die for. Literally.

REVIEWS

I hate you! My wife, who is off on medical leave, won't get out of the bathroom. Can't put your book down. LOL.

Bruce W.

The ghosts of Victoria, BC are restless. The Joining is a riveting read for crime fiction lovers and those fascinated by tales of hauntings. Talaber expertly draws you into a multi-leveled world of local history, crime, and the supernatural, where a blue fairy, comprised of two sorrowful creatures, is more powerful than it knows. A perfect read for those foggy West Coast nights.

Melanie Cossey, A Peculiar Curiosity

I bought four of his novels, all right up my alley, urban Fantasy and Paranormal thrillers. But as we were leaving my girlfriend opened up the copy of The Joining, I had purchased and said, "Stop! You gotta go back I have to buy this book." Frank had hooked her in the first three pages. Well Done.

Joyce Nicholls

I've read and reread his previous series, Stillwaters Run Deep, several times. Frank's writing is original and compelling. You run into characters and situations totally unexpected. Keeps you on the edge of your seat and your heart.

Greta Olsson

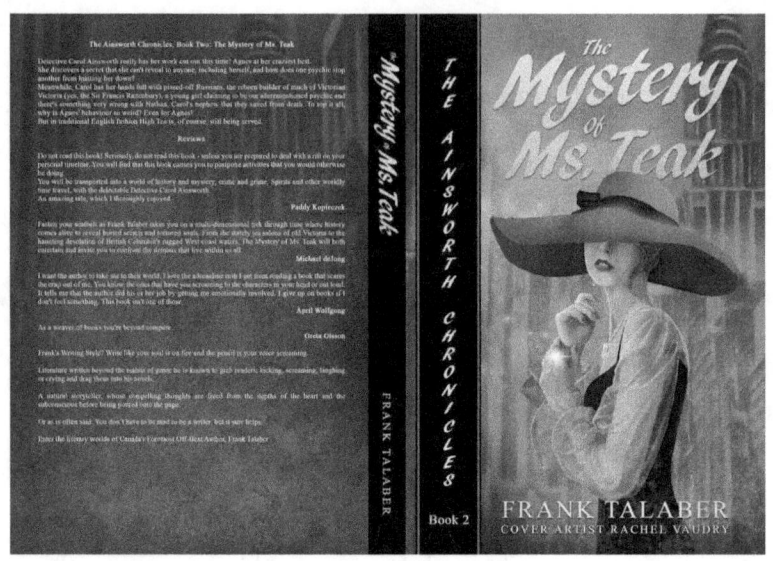

The Ainsworth Chronicles, Book Two: The Mystery of Ms. Teak

Agnes at her craziest best. Only what secret does she have to hide from herself and the one she thought dead? How does one psychic stop another from hunting her down, especially when the other hires the services of a mystical being long thought perished! As for Carol, she has her hands full with pissed-off Russians, the reborn builder of much of Victorian Victoria (yes, *the* Sir Francis Rattenbury), a young girl claiming to be our aforementioned psychic, and, to top it all off, there's something very wrong with Nathan, her nephew that they saved from death. But in traditional English fashion High Tea is *of course* still being served.

If you are into Videos, check out my newest Youtube video.
Trying To De Mystify The Mystery of Ms. Teak
https://youtu.be/TQKXOrJlpgw

On my YouTube Channel
Let's Be Frank, Canada's Foremost Off-Beat Author

REVIEWS

Do not read this book! Seriously, do not read this book - unless you are prepared to deal with a rift on your personal timeline. You will find that this book causes you to postpone activities that you would otherwise be doing.

You will be transported into a world of history and mystery, crime and grime, Spirits and other worldly time travel, with the delectable Detective Carol Ainsworth.

An amazing tale, which I thoroughly enjoyed.

Paddy Kopieczek

Fasten your seatbelt as Frank Talaber takes you on a multi-dimensional trek through time where history comes alive to reveal buried secrets and tortured souls. From the stately tea salons of old Victoria to the haunting desolation of British Columbia's rugged West coast waters, The Mystery of Ms. Teak will both entertain and invite you to confront the demons that live within us all.

Michael de Jong

I want the author to take me to their world. I love the adrenaline rush I get from reading a book that scares the crap out of me. You know, the ones that have you screaming to the characters in your head or out loud. It tells me that the author did his or her job by getting me emotionally involved. I give up on books if I don't feel something. This book isn't one of those.

April Wolfgong

As a weaver of books you're beyond compare.

Greta Olsson

Seeds Of Ascension Book One:
Spirits Awakening

In a normal relationship a man gets married and has the time of his life on a memorable honeymoon in Hawaii. A small dilemma begins for Roger Harrison when normality ceases existing with the discovery of metallic alien metal planted in his body.

Roger is thrust onto a path he never dreamed his life would ever take as one of the chosen few to start something that philosophers and spiritualists have discussed for centuries; the Ascension of humanity.

Only this isn't how the human race's next level of evolution was supposed to happen, and nor did Roger think he was the guy that would pull it off.

Toss in a guardian angel, alien hunters and Roger soon begins to realize his life's perfection ends with the understanding that memories are the illusion to which reality is draped and all is rarely as it seems in the journeys of a soul's growth. Especially when he doesn't even know how to spell chakra, let alone deal with having to master the seven levels in order to attain ascension.

Nor can time, as he knows it, be measured in heartbeats or lifespans and a heavy price must be exacted in order to stand in the gateway between memory and knowing, reality and illusion.

Especially when that effort means stopping those who would doom humanity's next phase of evolution.

Short Story Anthology Volume One:

What I'd Say To Buddha
If I Met Him In The Pub

(Includes Sylvia's Suncatchers, voted #1 out of 300 entries, by
the readers in Rejected Manuscripts Anthology)

Enter the literary world of Frank Talaber, Canada's
Foremost Off-Beat Author

A natural storyteller, whose compelling thoughts are
freed from the depths of the heart and the subconscious
before being poured onto the page.

Literature written beyond the realms of genre he is
known to grab readers; kicking, screaming, laughing or
crying, and drag them into his novels.

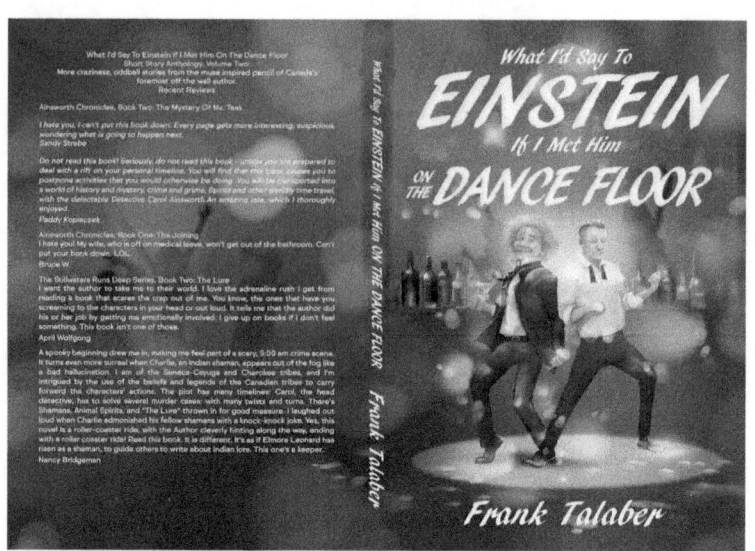

Short Story Anthology Volume Two:

What I'd Say To Einstein If I met Him
On The Dance Floor

Frank's Bio

Frank Talaber was born in Beaverlodge, Alberta, where the claim to fame is a fox with flashing eyes in the only pub. Yeah, big place, that's why his family left when he was knee high to a grasshopper and moved to Edmonton, Alberta. Eventually he got tired of ten months of winter and two of bad slush and moved to Chilliwack, BC. Great place, Cedar trees, can cut the grass nine months of the year and, oh, it does snow here once or twice. Just enough to have to find out what happened to the bloody snow shovel and have to use it. GRRR.

He's spent most of his life either fixing cars or managing automotive shops and is a licensed automotive technician. However, it's the little muses that keep twigging on his pencil won't let his writing pad stay blank.

He has several novels published, which include the genres of urban fantasy, thriller, crime and romance. He also has written in science fiction, spiritual, erotica and comedy genres.

When asked once, "where does this creativity spring from?" he answered, "It's the Gypsy blood from my mother's Hungarian ancestry."

Literary madness that drives his wife crazy when he leaves their bed in the middle of the night to pound out some sort of prosaic induced brilliance. "Here we go again, the next War and Peace, Aka 21st century," she moans, only to realize it's either gibberish or there's no lead in his pencil and he's scribbled on sixteen blank pages in the dark.

When asked about Frank Talaber's Writing Style? He usually responds with: Mix Dan Millman (Way of The Peaceful Warrior) with Charles De Lint (Moonheart) and throw in a mad scattering of Tom Robbins (Even Cowgirls Get The Blues).

PS: He's better looking than Stephen King (Carrie, The Stand, It, The Shining) and his romantic stuff will have you gasping quicker than Robert James Waller (Bridges Of Madison County).

Or as he has often said: Write like your soul is on fire and the pencil is your voice screaming.

You don't have to be mad to be a writer, but it sure helps.

Visit Frank Talaber's Published Author page on Facebook at:
https://www.facebook.com/FrankTalaber/

(If you want to join his fans' newsletter to hear about his latest ventures, go to the above page and scroll down on the column on the left).

Website:
https://franktalaberpublishedauthor.wordpress.com/

Facebook Short Stories Page:
https://www.facebook.com/franktalaberpublishedauthor/

Twitter:
@FrankTalaber https://about.me/ftalaber

Linkedin:
https://www.linkedin.com/feed/

www.ingramcontent.com/pod-product-compliance
Lightning Source LLC
Chambersburg PA
CBHW052015020726
47501CB00004B/1081